# Bridal Favors

## *Also by Connie Brockway*

**THE McCLAIREN'S ISLE TRILOGY**

McClairen's Isle:
*the ravishing one*

McClairen's Isle:
*the reckless one*

McClairen's Isle:
*the passionate one*

**AND . . .**

*a dangerous man*

*as you desire*

*all through the night*

*my dearest enemy*

*the bridal season*

# *Bridal Favors*

CONNIE
BROCKWAY

A DELL BOOK

Published by
Dell Publishing
a division of
Random House, Inc.
1540 Broadway
New York, New York 10036



ISBN: 0-7394-2824-1

Printed in the United States of America

September 2002

For my daughter, Rachel.
You are wonderful.
Mom

# ACKNOWLEDGMENTS

How do I stay this lucky? So many people kindly put their talents and knowledge at my disposal. In the BRIDAL series, Bill Paustis of Paustis Wine Company stepped up to the plate with information about nineteenth-century wines (but shouldn't we have drunk an actual bottle of that Rothschild, Bill? For verisimilitude?); Dr. Rick Sheely supplied me with all the croquet terminology, plus looked inspiringly dapper in whites: plot-maven Susan Sizemore, as always, leapt into the lurch with pithy (and sometimes pointed) suggestions. And of course, my gratitude goes to Merry for being such a good sport about her myriad appearances ("I go by many names"); all the MFWers who showed up to keep me company in the produce department; Terri, Susie, Christina, Geralyn for listening; David and Rachel for loving me rather than disowning me during crunch time; and finally to Grace Pedalino—again, for who knows what.

# Bridal Favors

# *Prologue*

*Chelsea, England*
*The last quarter of Victoria's reign*

YOUNG EVELYN CUMMINGS WHYTE'S STOMach growled loudly, and she shot a glance at the other side of the bed where her sister slept blissfully on. If this kept up, she'd have to do something to quell the sounds lest they wake Verity. It was unfortunate that they had to share a room, but the number of guests their parents had invited to the house for Verity's unofficial launch into Society had exceeded the number of bedrooms. Still, it was imperative that Verity be in good looks on the morrow. For herself... well, dark circles under her eyes really made no difference.

Evelyn tipped the pad of paper she held into the gaslight and squinted, idly wondering whether she ought to get spectacles. She wrote "Move Verity to Mama's room," beneath a column entitled "Things To Do," then regarded the other items as one would a familiar and irritating adversary one has met and bested countless times before.

Many a girl—let alone an adult—would find such a long inventory of duties and responsibilities intimidating, but not young Lady Evelyn. Her stomach growled again and Verity flopped over, muttering, her golden curls spilling across her plump, pink cheek.

Evelyn put the pad of paper down and flicked back the coverlet, resigning herself to a trip to the kitchen for a stomach-settling glass of milk. She snagged the first dressing gown her hand encountered, Verity's frilly peignoir, and shrugged into it. In doing so, she caught a glimpse of movement in the bedroom's large, beveled mirror. She hesitated before crossing to it, drawn by curiosity and trepidation—trepidation because Evelyn Cummings Whyte had only recently discovered she was ugly.

Somberly, she regarded her reflection.

She saw a small, childishly narrow figure drowning in an avalanche of lace. As the only light was behind her, her features were cast in deep shadows. Still, she could make out an angular face amidst a mass of black hair held atop a stalk of a neck so thin it seemed the weight of her head must snap it. Deep pools indicated where her eyes were located and a dark, wide line betrayed her mouth.

Impossible to tell anything of the figure beneath all that satin, but peeping from beneath the fabric cascading to the ground were narrow white feet. Curiously, she pulled the sleeves of the peignoir up and noted that her wrists were not appreciably smaller than her forearms.

She pulled the neck of her nightgown down. Morbidly thin, that woman had said, and seeing her chest, Evelyn had to agree. Even in the dim light she could make out her sternum; where the manubrium attached to the clavicle, the bones jutted out with knifelike acuity.

She recalled the overheard conversation: "A little stick person," kind-faced Mrs. Bernhardt had whispered to her friend. "A *golem*, the child is, dark and twiggy."

Evelyn hadn't realized they'd been speaking of her. Indeed, she'd been in the midst of turning around to see this "*golem*" herself when she'd heard Mrs. Bernhardt's friend reply, "It amazes me that sisters can be so dissimilar. Verity so pretty and the younger one—*tch!*"

Since then, she'd heard whispered charges of ugliness enough times to realize it must be true. The problem was she didn't *feel* ugly! And if Gregor Mendel's suggested method of foretelling the traits of inheritance were correct, she ought to be just as lovely as her mother and sister.

Unfortunately, apparently people were not beans.

Because Evelyn's mother Francesca was not only beautiful but ethereally so. And kind. And sweet-natured. Her father Charles, the Duke of Lally's heir, was certainly decent looking. He'd once been considered "a catch" who'd eluded the matrimonial for years before marrying Francesca.

In due course, she'd presented her husband with a beautiful girl. Charles was charmed, and prepared to be similarly dazzled three years later when Francesca gave birth to another daughter, as yellow and insistent as Verity was pink and sweet.

Francesca, who'd never spent much time considering her own beauty, certainly didn't spend any thinking about Evelyn's lack of it. And Charles, coming late to love, had love to spare. Looks, or lack thereof, were not much thought of in the Whyte household.

It wasn't that Evelyn was unaware of Verity's beauty—it just never occurred to her to measure her own looks against her sister's. Or anyone else's, for that matter. She'd too many other things to do and think about. For almost as soon as it became apparent that Evelyn was not going to be "a beauty," it became just as apparent that Evelyn was "an interesting and capable young person."

She became her father's favorite companion. Her curiosity aroused his, her dauntlessness provoked his pride, and her intelligent, homely little face touched his heart. Added to which, she was damned good company.

Not that she didn't work at maintaining her place in his affections. Since Charles was an indifferent planner, she became an expert planner, and since neither her parents nor her sister had the vaguest notion of what the word "economy" meant, Evelyn became a first-rate economizer.

Thus Evelyn, loved by her mother, cosseted by a tenderhearted sister, and adored by her father, had reached the ripe age of fifteen uniquely unaffected by the deficits the mirror reflected. But—a shiver of hurt flashed across her face—she'd never thought of herself as *ugly*.

She looked around, uncertain how to handle these new, unpleasant feelings, and her glance fell on the Bible open on the bedside table. Didn't the Bible advise "If thy right eye offend thee, pluck it out"? Well, she certainly wasn't going to perform self-mutilation, but she could keep with the spirit of the thing. She would simply have this and every other mirror in her room removed and by avoiding looking in them avoid being tempted to compare her looks to others'. She would not succumb to feelings of jealousy and self-consciousness. They were destructive. Besides, there was no use in wasting time or effort on that which could not be remedied.

With such a practical resolve already heartening her, Evelyn headed out of the bedroom toward the kitchen. She was halfway down the dark hall when she heard the click of a door opening ahead of her. She stopped. A tall, masculine figure in evening dress emerged from Mrs. Underhill's room.

Apparently Mr. Underhill had taken time out from his busy diplomatic schedule to attend the party after all. She waited politely for him to finish closing the door before speaking. But he turned so abruptly that he bumped into her before she could speak.

"Uff!"

Strong hands reached out and roughly clasped her upper arms.

"Please," she said, "if you are concerned that you are keeping me from falling, let me assure you, you are not. You may unhand me."

A soft, sharp inhalation came from somewhere above her head. "Who the devil are you?" a deep masculine voice demanded.

"I am Evelyn Cummings Whyte. Would you kindly let go of me?"

"Evelyn?" he murmured, loosening his grip. She waited. Adults, especially aristocratic adults, could be so thick. "The little sister?"

She peered up at him. "Yes, Mr.—" Her voice trailed off as her eyes adjusted to the darkness. It hadn't been Mr. Underhill who'd crept out of Mrs. Underhill's room. It was Mr. Justin Powell!

She tensed, realizing what she'd stumbled upon or, rather, what had stumbled upon her. A tryst. An assignation. A clandestine rendezvous! She gulped. "Mr. Powell!"

"Blast. Where were you going?" he whispered tautly.

"To the kitchen."

He'd released one of her arms, but his grip on the other tightened. He turned and pulled her after him toward the stairs. He must want to talk. Which should be very interesting, she thought grimly.

He certainly didn't fit her idea of a . . . a *masher*. During his days here, he'd been far more likely to be poring over the maps in her father's study than playing badminton with the other young people. Oh, he was pleasant and all, but he always seemed a bit . . . vague. Lackadaisical.

He wore no signs of nonchalance now. And she knew why.

Fortunately, Evelyn was not easily shocked, but poor Verity— "Verity," she said grimly, "will be horrified."

"Hush!" Mr. Powell grated out over his shoulder.

He hastened her down the stairs and to the back of the house, where he nudged the kitchen's green baize door open. He thrust her inside, following and fumbling for the gas jet beside the door. In a second, his aquiline features leapt to life in the harsh, sulfur glare.

Evelyn studied him. She'd thought him rather handsome, though she imagined the more particular young ladies would find his rumpled suit jacket and brown, overlong hair too raffish to invite admiration. And his manner too distracted to be nice. She did not think *any* woman would think him distracted now.

His lips were taut, and the amiable vacuity that was characteristic of him had been replaced with intensity. She'd assumed from his repeated polite refusal to join in any physical activity that he was lazy and unathletic. Now, she was not so sure. Certainly he'd dragged her after him easily enough.

He stood staring down at her a second before raking his hand through his hair. "What the devil am I— Damnation!"

"Probably," Evelyn agreed.

He glanced down, clearly startled.

"Oh," she said caustically, "your comment was rhetorical rather than prophetic."

A surprised smile danced momentarily on his lean face. "Impudent," he said.

"Imprudent," she rejoined.

"Gads! Quite a mouth you have for a... what? Twelve-year-old?"

"Fifteen," she stated, heat pouring into her cheeks. She knew she looked young for her years. She must also look bizarre, bundled in her sister's most feminine wrapper, her *golem* feet splayed out on the cold kitchen tiles. She lifted one foot and pressed it on top of the other.

He saw the involuntary movement and made an exasperated sound. Before she knew it, he'd placed his hands on either side of her waist and hoisted her up, depositing her on the edge of the kitchen worktable.

"What were you coming here for?" he asked.

"A glass of milk."

Calmly, he opened the icebox and withdrew a pitcher. Then he hunted through the cupboards until he found a mug. He poured milk into it and placed it in her hands. She sipped it politely as he watched like a determined nursemaid for a full minute before ducking into the larder.

He rooted about, returning with a loaf of bread and a slice of cold turkey breast from last night's menu. He tore the bread into two roughly equal-sized pieces and sandwiched the meat between them.

"Here," he said, holding it out.

"No, thank you," she said primly, feeling at a distinct disadvantage, what with her feet dangling thirty inches above the floor.

"Go on," he urged. "Eat. You need it."

She started to protest but then noticed that

he'd crossed his arms over his chest in what Evelyn was beginning to suspect was a universal sign of male intractability. With a shrug, she accepted the sandwich and bit into it. It tasted better than she'd anticipated.

When she finished she looked up. "Well?"

"Precisely," he said. "Now, Lady Evelyn, about what you saw..." He trailed off, frowning, and abruptly swiped her upper lip with his forefinger. At her shocked expression, he smiled. "Milk mustache. Are you *sure* you're fifteen?"

Again, she blushed. She refused to be flustered by a common masher. Or even an uncommon one. "Quite sure. Now, you were saying?"

"Blast if I know." He cocked his head.

"Why are you looking at me like that?" she asked.

"I am trying to decide how much you saw, what you suspect, and if I can convince you not only to be discreet but to be absolutely mum on the subject of my whereabouts this evening," he answered with amazing ingenuousness.

"I should imagine that depends on how glib you are over the next few minutes," she replied with equal candor.

He laughed. It was a deep, honest sound that nearly made her smile. But then she remembered that, in all probability, all mashers had rich, enticing laughs.

"Did you say fifteen or fifty?" he asked, the amusement still... *What a spectacular color!* How had she failed to notice his eyes before? They were pale blue-green, a sort of viridian, the silkier nephrite sort, like the little copper-flecked Ming dynasty horse in her father's library—

"Lady Evelyn?"

"Hm?" she replied, trying to drag her gaze away from the fascinating color of his eyes.

"Do you know who I am?"

The question was so absurd it managed to interrupt her even more absurd fascination with his eyes. "Of course I do. You are Mr. Justin Powell, until recently a military officer of some junior rank in Her Majesty's army—forgive me, but I have failed to remember which.

"Your father is Colonel Marcus Powell, Viscount Sumner, lately of Her Majesty's army. He owns a woolen mill in Hampshire and the majority share of a coal mine in the north of Canada. You are his only son and heir.

"Your maternal grandfather is retired Brigadier General John Harden, a rather famous career soldier who served with Wolseley in South Africa. Though he spends the greater part of the year in town, he also owns North Cross Abbey, a renovated abbey built in the mid–sixteenth century." Having finished her recital, she folded her hands in her lap and waited expectantly.

He stared at her, bemused. "My God, you are well versed."

"I went to great trouble to see that no unacceptable person was invited to Verity's party."

He ignored her pointed stare. "*You* went to trouble?"

"Yes. I made up the guest list."

"You're jesting."

"Not at all. You see, Father takes a dim view of *any* potential suitor for Verity's hand. The guest list would have been cut down to nothing if left up to him. And Mother is far too trusting." Evelyn shifted under his astonished gaze and added defensively, "Verity helped make the list."

"Kind of you to consult her."

"Well," Evelyn allowed, "it is *her* husband we're endeavoring to find." The mention of husbands brought Mr. Underhill back to mind. She narrowed her eyes on Mr. Powell as he leaned negligently against the wall. "You, of course, will be retired from the running."

"Running? Oh. Yes." He nodded morosely. "Of course."

She felt a grudging smidgen of respect for him. He'd taken that gracefully enough. Since there was nothing left to discuss, she prepared to slide off the table. He quickly pushed away from the wall.

"As interesting as your compendium of knowledge about me is, that wasn't what I meant when I asked if you knew who I was," he said.

"Oh?" she asked.

"I should have said, 'Do you know *what* I am?' "

She eyed him sourly. "I am afraid I do."

He went very still. "Yes?"

"Yes," she said severely. "You are what Verity's friends call 'a wolf.' "

He blinked. Straightened. Blinked again. And burst into delighted laughter. "That's not what I meant."

"Then what *do* you mean?" she asked, miffed he'd laughed at her cold, disapproving pronouncement.

"I am the Mr. Justin Powell you described, but I am also, in my own right, the very rich, the very influential Mr. Justin Powell."

Influential? Not that she'd ever heard, but she allowed that there might be things about him she hadn't uncovered. She regarded him doubtfully.

"I really am."

She remained mute.

He threw up his hands. "I cannot believe I am standing in a kitchen at two in the morning trying to persuade a skinny fifteen-year-old girl of my worth!" he muttered in exasperation. "Look, Lady Evelyn, I have friends. Important people listen to me."

Gads, Evelyn thought, this was verging on being pathetic.

"Bloody damn, I sound like a boasting schoolboy!" He must have read her mind. Then his sense of humor abruptly returned and he grinned.

"You can ask around later, if you like, but the bottom line, my scrawny little owlet, is this: Wouldn't you like to have a man of some consequence, no small wealth, and not a little influence *in your debt*?"

She eyed him thoughtfully. "What do you mean?"

"I mean that I am willing to trust you. You seem a levelheaded sort of girl. The sort of girl who would immediately realize that nothing good can come out of revealing whose room you saw me exit this evening, but indeed, only a great deal of harm."

"I should say," Evelyn agreed.

He tapped her lightly on the lips, quieting her as one would a pert child. "As well as besmirching Mrs. Underhill's name, it would cast a pall over Lady

Verity's coming-out. On the other hand, you would be doing everyone a kindness by staying quiet.

"And what harm could it do? As I am no longer a candidate for your lovely sister's hand, I am hardly a threat to your family's honor, am I?"

He had a point. Still . . .

"You're not one of those frightful creatures who actually *enjoys* bearing sordid tales, are you?" he asked.

"No!" she squawked. She absolutely *loathed* tell-tales.

He smiled. "And you are obviously mature enough to realize that not everything we see is exactly as it seems. You would not judge another, would you?"

She shook her head, albeit more slowly this time. In truth, she judged people all the time. But the way *he* said it made it seem a shallow, spiteful sort of thing.

"I didn't think so," he said kindly. "Now, if you keep this absolutely secret, not breathing a single word to a soul, not even your sister," he leaned down until he was eye to eye with her, "I promise you, you will have no cause to regret your great charity, and perhaps someday reason to be glad of it."

"I will?" she said suspiciously. "And why is that?"

"Because I will then be beholden to you, Lady Evelyn, and I always," he fixed her with an intent gaze, "*always* pay my debts."

He straightened and moved to Cook's small, battered desk. He picked up one of the cards Cook wrote out the daily menus on and scribbled something on it. He returned with it. "Can I rely on you?"

She studied him, thinking. Everything he'd said

was true. He'd already agreed he would not be paying court to Verity anymore. There was little to gain from exposing him. And if she let him "off the hook," someday his gratitude might actually prove useful.

"All right, Mr. Powell. I promise I will say nothing—unless you should decide to pursue Verity."

"I swear I won't."

"Then I swear, too." She stuck out her hand to seal the bargain and at once his own much larger one enveloped hers, pressing the card into her palm.

"Bless you, child. Now, can you find your way to your room?" he asked diffidently.

For the first time that evening, Evelyn smiled. "I've been doing so since I could walk."

He'd been in the process of turning away, but now he stopped. His brows lifted as if in surprise. "Why, you . . ." He stopped whatever he'd been about to say. "Then I will say good night, Lady Evelyn."

He inclined his head and a minute later vanished through the kitchen door, leaving her alone. Curiously, she turned over the card and read what he'd written.

*I O U*
*Justin Falloden Powell, the 9th of March, 1885*

# Chapter 1

*London, England*
*Ten years later*

"IF YOU DO NOT WANT BLOOD ALL OVER your carpet, I suggest you call a physician," Evelyn called out from where she lay flat on her back. She pushed her spectacles back into place and turned her head to look at the unbroken window.

The reflected image of the tall man who'd walked into the library abruptly stopped, caught in a pool of bright mid-morning sunlight. He wore shirtsleeves, the white cuffs rolled halfway up sinewy, tanned forearms, the collar open at the throat.

"Which carpet?" he asked, looking about for her.

Ten years had passed, but it might have been yesterday that she'd last seen him. The easy, imperturbable voice was the same, as was his loose-limbed build and disheveled good looks.

"Here," Evelyn called. "On the floor by the window. The broken one."

Justin Powell closed the book he'd been carrying and came round the side of the desk. Looking up past his expensive shoes, she could see the subtle changes a decade had wrought. Thin lines radiated from the corners of his eyes and little comma-shapes bracketed his wide mouth. A dusting of gray threaded through dark brown hair in dire need of a good clip.

Mutely, he gazed down at her. Just as mute, she returned his regard.

What was wrong with a man when even the sight of a woman bleeding on his floor couldn't excite him to action?

"I understand how the sight of a woman lying in a pool of her own blood might be off-putting, Mr. Powell," she said. "But can I do anything to dispel the paralysis that seems to have gripped you and encourage you to act?"

"Woman, eh?" he murmured, calmly setting his book on the desk. He hunkered down, his elbows on his knees and his hands hanging between his legs. Gingerly, he lifted the torn flap in the knickers she'd borrowed from her nephew Stanley.

She dared a glance at her leg, saw the red blood, and averted her face. She looked up at him in order to read in his expression the severity of her injury, but instead found herself staring in fascination at his eyes. They were just as she remembered, too, a fascinating, glinty-soft bluish-green. Forest pond beneath brilliant autumn sky. Gold leaf swirling through liquid jade—

"You aren't bleeding to death," Justin said matter-of-factly. He released the flap of twill. "And that spot isn't a pool." He frowned at his fingertips, looked around, and ended up wiping them on her pant leg. "Though the cut is long, it's not very deep."

"Thank heavens!" She released the breath she'd been holding. She was, admittedly, a bit of a sissy where blood was concerned.

"Not much more than a scratch," he said calmly. "A tad messy, but nothing any English schoolboy hasn't suffered a dozen times over."

His lack of sympathy made her bristle. "I am *not* an English schoolboy."

"Since Mrs. Boyle's Finishing School opened in the neighborhood, I have learned that the difference between the average English schoolgirl and the average English schoolboy isn't all that great." His gaze drifted in a purely impersonal manner over poor Stanley's blouse, knotted kerchief, and ruined knickers.

She frowned. "I dressed this way only because I expected I would need to crawl up the trellis outside your library window in order to get in."

"Now that you explain, it makes perfect sense."

She was wounded and he was being sarcastic. She lifted herself to her elbows, preparing to deliver him a stinging set-down, but as soon as her head rose above her chest and she saw the sticky red flap of cloth, her head swam. She dropped back with a moan.

"Are you hurt elsewhere?" Justin asked quickly.

"No. It's just that . . . Blood." She shuddered. "I'll be fine as long as I don't look at it."

"Then by all means, don't look. You're as white as

Devon sand." He uncoiled. "Just lie there quietly while I nip off and raid the old medicine cabinet. I'll be back in a trice."

Only after he'd left did it occur to Evelyn that he hadn't asked *why* she was lying in such a condition on his library floor. Most men would have demanded to know. At the very least, they would have been unnerved by her appearance. But then, she recalled, Justin Powell had no nerves.

She twisted her head, looking about the library. A small, untidy working library, just the sort she'd have loved to explore—and put in order. A pair of deep leather club chairs faced a ceiling-high bookshelf outfitted with a rolling brass ladder. Across the room, a library desk basked in the light pouring in through a now permanently open east-facing window.

She was squinting through her glasses, trying to read some of the titles on the bookshelves, when she heard returning footsteps. A second later Justin came in with a tray filled with medical paraphernalia: a bowl of water, scissors, a brown bottle, a roll of bandages, and a cloth.

Without wasting time fussing about proprieties, he simply knelt beside her and proceeded to cut off the right leg of her nephew's knickers five inches above the knee. He wadded the ruined material and tossed it into the wastebasket, then dipped the towel into the water. "I'm going to clean you up a bit, all right?"

Before she could answer, he started dabbing at the wound. She took a deep breath and stared bravely at the coffered ceiling.

"Nice wood, that," she said in a high, thin voice.

"Cherry," he muttered distractedly.

She winced as the warm water seeped into the cut. "You're sure it's not deep?"

"Very sure."

She sucked in as his dabbing became more pronounced—very like scrubbing, in fact. "It *feels* as though it's been cut to the bone. Tell me. I can take it."

"True, you're slender, but it's nowhere near the bone," he replied, sitting back on his heels and tossing the washcloth after the pant leg. "There. All nice and clean. Have a look for yourself."

"Thank you, no. If you'd be so kind as to put a bandage over it, I'm sure I can finish tying it up." She began struggling to a seated position but he stopped her, his big hand enveloping her shoulder and gently pushing her back down.

"Not a bit of it, m'dear," he said cheerfully. "Besides, always finish what you begin. Or so me old granny used to say."

She breathed a heartfelt "thank you." She hated being brave about blood. She'd never seen any real value in it, except that it made everyone else feel better just when you were feeling your worst, which was generally the time a girl needed a bit of sympathy.

"You just rest easy and think of something else. I know," he said, as if a novel idea had only just occurred to him. "Why don't you tell me *why* you broke into my house?"

"Broke . . . ? Oh. That. The insufferable person who answers your door kept insisting that you were not at home. As I had to see you, I had no choice but to find an alternative entry."

"Beverly told you I wasn't in? How reprehensible!" Justin said and then, "I suppose there was some good reason you didn't believe him?"

"Of course," she answered. "I saw you."

"Saw me?" Justin repeated mildly. He opened the little amber bottle and withdrew a small glass wand from it. Carefully, he guided it along the cut.

"Ow!" Evelyn squealed, pulling away and glowering at him with the air of one grossly betrayed. "You *hurt* me!"

He grimaced apologetically. "Sorry. Carbolic acid. Should have warned you it would sting a bit."

"I should say," Evelyn muttered bad-temperedly.

"Almost done. Just a bit of bandaging and you'll be right as rain. Now, then," he began unrolling a linen bandage, "you were saying how you spied me in the house and thus deduced Beverly to be the lying knave he undoubtedly is. Where did you see me?"

"Through the back window here."

"Ah." Justin nodded. "So, having been told I was not at home, you at once became suspicious of Beverly's villainous mien and decided to walk around to the back of the house, climb the alley wall, and look through the windows. Most enterprising."

Evelyn frowned. "Put that way, it sounds rather... intrusive."

"No, no," Justin said affably. "I'd say the actual *intrusive* spot came when you broke into the house. Up to that point I'd call you merely..." He looked at her hopefully, as though she would supply the word that eluded him.

"Prying."

"Ah, *prying,*" he said happily. "Yes. That might do."

She couldn't detect the least bit of sarcasm in his tone, but it was there, as was his amusement. She thought over all the reports she'd heard of him through the years, which were few enough.

*Eccentric. Reclusive,* or was it *exclusive*? *Clever. Unflappable.* Some people had deemed him inattentive, others preferred oblivious. Obviously none of them had ever spent any time with him, for clearly a razor-sharp intellect lurked beneath his pleasant, obliging manner.

"And exactly why were you prying?" he asked.

"Because," she replied, "it was absolutely essential that I speak to you."

"Me? How flattering! Young girls are so seldom so resourceful. Or persistent." He clipped off a length of linen and deftly wound it around her thigh, securing it with a piece of sticking plaster. He admired his work. "The medical field will ever feel my loss, I'm afraid."

She grinned at his nonsense. He definitely had a way of getting around a girl.

He uncoiled with feline grace and she was reminded of another adjective that had on occasion been associated with him. He seemed so gentlemanly, without being the least stiff, that for a moment she'd forgotten the circumstances under which they'd originally met. But being the recipient of his indisputable charm and seeing him move with such fluid ease, it all came rushing back. A dark hall long past midnight, another man's wife, another man's room.

He was a Lothario.

Not that for one second she feared *she* was in danger of exciting any romantic efforts on his part. Heavens, no! But that didn't mean she couldn't see why other women found him hard to resist.

Though, now that she thought of it, it was odd that since that night she hadn't heard any sordid stories about him. Perhaps it was because one only heard stories about the incompetent Lotharios, the ones that got caught—

She gasped as he suddenly stooped down and scooped her up in his arms. She blushed, warmed by the notion that he'd read her thoughts.

"You can put me down. I can easily walk."

"Of course you can, if you want," he replied in the tone one would use on a recalcitrant child. He didn't stop, however. He strode into the narrow, carpeted hall, heading for the back of the town house. "But why should you? A lift is the least I can offer you by way of making reparation for owning such shoddy, easily broken windows, as well as for employing such a scoundrel for a butler."

She searched his face. "You're mocking me."

"Never!" he denied. "I'm perfectly serious. I'm just thankful you aren't this very minute sending for your parents' lawyer in order to press suit, and I wish to express my gratitude by offering you a nice glass of lemonade. Which is in the kitchen. Which is where I am taking you."

Gads! Listening to him she could almost believe she *was* in the moral right and he *ought* to be making amends, when she knew very well that she should be offering him every apology she could think of to keep him from ringing up the local constable and having her carted away to the jail for breaking into his home.

"Besides," he was saying, "I should dearly love to hear why it was 'essential' that you speak to me."

She hesitated, knowing she should protest further. But he didn't seem to mind carrying her and she didn't seem to mind being carried, not in the least, so she relaxed in his arms and sank comfortably against his chest.

It was a nice broad chest. And warm under the starched, white shirt. He smelled fascinating, too: sharp astringent soap, earthy warmth, and something else, something unique.

She closed her eyes, trying to pinpoint the aroma and finding instead a whole new vista of sensations opening before her. The easy, rhythmical motion of his stride carrying her, the gentle swing of her legs in counterpoint, the soft feathering of his breath on her face. She held herself still, soaking up impressions. Lovely.

She smiled and opened her eyes just as he looked down and knocked her glasses askew with his chin. She shoved them back into place, the movement causing her to shift in his embrace. He jounced her up, settling her more comfortably and in doing so his hand slipped up her rib cage and his fingers brushed the curve of her breast. His hand jerked back. His brows suddenly dipped in a scowl.

"You're not from Mrs. Boyle's school, are you?" he asked in a voice tinged with accusation. He looked down into her upturned face, peering past the faintly smoked lenses, touching on her mouth and moving to the dark tumble of hair that had come undone during her escapade and now swirled like a gorgon's tresses around her shoulders. "Why you're not a *girl*, at all!"

"I beg your pardon." Evelyn stiffened.

"You are a *woman*."

By God! He'd thought she was . . . a *child*! That's why he hadn't castigated her, or sent for the authorities, or treated her as a real person at all. He'd thought she was from this girls' school he'd been babbling about, and that this was some girlish prank!

Evelyn, who had spent the last decade fighting the prejudices roused by her youthful appearance, who was always, in spite of her best efforts, a *little* too aware of her lack of female curves and thus a *tad* defensive about her womanliness, spoke before she thought. "Heavens, you're perceptive! I bet that you might even be able to find your way to the front door!"

# Chapter 2

JUSTIN WINCED. "I SUSPECT I DESERVED THAT."

He backed his way into a small kitchen, looked around, and deposited her on a kitchen chair.

"Yes, you did," Evelyn replied, chancing a glance at the bandage around her thigh. It was utterly unstained, she noted with an eccentric mix of disappointment and relief. She felt every sort of fool. Had she really claimed she'd been lying in a "pool of blood"?

"Do you have the odd sensation that this has happened before?" he asked as he opened the icebox and withdrew a pitcher. He didn't wait for an answer but poured two glasses of lemonade and handed her one. "Cheers," he said, clicking his rim to hers.

She took a sip, furtively watching him studying her, his frown back in place. Any minute now, he'd remember the unfortunate circumstances of their initial meeting, and who knew how he'd react then? Men, in her admittedly limited experience, dearly hated being reminded of having been caught in some misdeed. He might throw her out before she had a chance to explain why she was here.

"You asked why I was here. I would like to tell you." She set her glass down. "Five months ago my aunt, Lady Agatha Whyte, eloped to France with a Frenchman." She waited to see if the information struck a chord. It would for most people.

"Then it's fortunate they are in France," Justin finally said. "At least the bloke should know some decent restaurants." He paused. "But then, that isn't always the case. Once, when I was traveling in Austria, I had for a guide a fellow who had the most underdeveloped palate it has ever been my misfortune to—"

She cleared her throat.

"Excuse me. You were saying?"

"My aunt eloped. That the fellow she eloped with is French is of no consequence." Evelyn hesitated as the lack of veracity struck her. She disliked dishonesty above all things. Particularly dishonesty with oneself. "Well, actually, it is. He managed to undermine my aunt's sound judgment and her sense of duty to her clients to a spectacular degree."

Seeing Justin's brow lift inquiringly, she explained. "Frankly, I can't see any Englishman achieving a level of fascination that could so overwhelm a lady that she would forget everything, in her desire—"

She broke off. Judging from his odd expression she

had misstepped, either in her use of the word "desire" or her charge that an Englishman couldn't engender much of it.

Maybe Lotharios took pride in their—what would one call it? Conquests? Perhaps she should reassure him that she was quite certain he could give any Frenchman a run for his money? Or was he offended by her choice of the word "desire"? Though it would seem peculiar for a masher to take exception to such a simple word.

But then she'd done it before, offended people because of her unfortunate predilection for choosing an appropriate word for an inappropriate thing. Happily, Justin only looked a little dazed. That look, too, was unfortunately not an entirely unfamiliar experience for her.

"Well, the French *are* renowned for their, er, beguiling ways, are they not?" she asked defensively.

"Are they?"

His query sounded sincere, and as Evelyn was always happy to dispense information, she replied. "Yes."

"Who's have thought it? But we digress. Now," he raised his forefinger, "let me see if I have this right. Auntie's off having a high old time with her new beguiling French husband, and you . . . ?" he trailed off invitingly.

"And I am left in charge of her business. She seems to have gone off on her honeymoon without having made any arrangements for the tending of her business while she was away. I, of course, took action at once."

"I say, well done. Kudos to the loving niece for jumping into the lurch when family duty calls," he declared.

She eyed him closely but, try as she might, she couldn't tell if he was twitting her. If he was, he did it so disarmingly she couldn't help but smile.

"Yes, at least, kudos for the loving niece's good intentions," she said. "But there won't be any medals for a job well done."

"No? Why is that?"

"Because—" She stopped. This was the hardest part. The part she'd never admitted aloud and resisted doing so now, particularly as she still didn't quite believe it herself. She took a deep breath. "Because I am . . ." She took another breath. "I am . . ."

"You are . . . ?" he prodded.

She closed her eyes and forced the words out. "*I am no good at it.*"

There. She'd said it. And because confession was good for the soul, and even more importantly because Evelyn never did anything by half-measures, she went on.

"I am not only no good at it, Mr. Powell, I am *horrible* at it." The confession did nothing to ameliorate her bruised ego; she still felt like a failure.

"Damn shame, that," he replied in properly sympathetic tones. "Might I be so bold as to ask exactly what 'it' is?"

"Whyte's Wedding," she said. "You know, Whyte's Nuptial Celebrations?" He continued looking at her in unblinking incomprehension.

"Aunt Agatha is a wedding planner. *The* wedding

planner. Her services are used by the most distinguished families in society. In fact, there are some who claim that the *only* way to properly celebrate a marriage is to have Whyte's do it."

Or, she thought wincing inwardly, that's what they *had* said.

"So," he said, "as I understand it, you've taken over this wedding planning business, but are afraid that you're not performing your duties to your aunt's former standards. Is that more or less right?"

"More or less," she said forlornly.

"Come, now." He reached out and patted her awkwardly atop her head, rather as one would a dispirited spaniel. "I'm sure you aren't all that bad."

"Ha!" He hadn't seen the Nortons' ice swan, the centerpiece of a wedding theme built around the Tchaikovsky ballet. It had been shipped to the Nortons' house hours too early, and on an unseasonably hot day. The delivery men had set it out on a huge glass platter surrounded by painstakingly made pâté *choux* baby swans.

By the time the wedding party arrived, it had melted. Instead of a gallant swan sliding across a silver pool surrounded by diminutive cygnets, a headless barnyard duck listed sideways in a puddle amongst the soggy, bloated pastry bodies of its progeny.

Nor had he witnessed the debacle with the five hundred white doves she'd ordered released at the Reynolds' wedding. She'd been so proud of herself for buying their feed at a cut rate. She should have asked why it was so cheap. It was cheap because it had gotten damp and started to ferment.

By the day of the wedding, the doves, cunningly concealed in rafters of the outdoor pavilion, were thoroughly pickled. Instead of releasing them to fly gracefully away, opening the trapdoor had simply dumped them en masse on the banquet tables, where they waddled in drunken ecstasy amongst the dessert plates, gorging themselves on wedding cake as the guests fled shrieking.

There had been other "wrinkles," too. Small things but, when added up, condemning. She lifted her gaze to his, the remembered evidence of her own ineptitude stripping away every shred of her self-protective veneer. "Mr. Powell," she said, "I am a *disaster*!"

He looked at her stricken face and made no further attempt to argue. His hand rose toward her cheek and stopped. He frowned at it, as if he wasn't exactly sure how it had moved, and let it drop. "I'm sorry. But what has that got to do with me?"

Ashamed of such weakness, she dashed away the tear that had slipped down her cheek and readjusted her glasses. She folded her hands primly in her lap.

"First," she said, "I want you to understand that my desire to do well by my aunt isn't motivated by pride and self-conceit. At least," she added honestly, "not *primarily* by pride and self-conceit. If it was only my vanity that was at stake, I would just go quietly away."

He looked doubtful.

"I am a mature woman. I can accept that there are things of which I am not capable. Though," she continued, pleased with how reasonable she sounded, "I confess I wouldn't have suspected something which, at its core, is nothing more than a matter of simple logistics and management to prove so formidable. Would you?"

She didn't wait for an answer. "I mean, though I dislike boasting, I *have* managed my parents' estate during their absences, traveled extensively by myself, and only last year founded a school for itinerant farm laborers in our parish."

She tried to relax but her jaw seemed to have seized up. She continued through her teeth, "I also opened a housemaid training service for the local girls, and have sat on our district's council for three years running. Now, Mr. Powell, given these facts, don't you find it amusing," she tried to laugh to prove just *how* amusing it was and failed, "how silly and aggravating and out-and-out *stupid* it is that something as simple as planning a wedding reception should be the one thing I *cannot seem to get right*?"

She looked up at him for concurrence and found him staring at her. Had she shouted that last bit? She forced herself to smile brightly.

"Of course you do," she answered. She picked up her abandoned glass and took a ladylike sip of lemonade. "Do you have any questions?"

"Well, yes."

"And that is . . . ?"

"I suspect I missed something—happens to me all the time, so wouldn't be surprising—but did you ever tell me how your current, er, difficulty involves me?"

"Oh, didn't I say?" she answered, happy that her voice had regained it usual calm. "You are involved because I need you in order to once again establish Whyte's Nuptial Celebrations as the uncontested leader in wedding planner services."

"And how am I to do that?"

"By renting me North Cross Abbey for six weeks."

"The Granddad General's old place?" he said, clearly surprised. "It's just a tumbled-down rubble heap in the middle of sheep country. Can't imagine why you'd want to rent it."

"I don't. My client does. I explained to her that it likely has none of the modern conveniences. It doesn't matter. She insists she wants to have her wedding celebration there."

"Great sheep fancier, is she?" Justin asked, and Evelyn felt a smile slip out.

"Not that I know," she said. "She is Mrs. Edith Vandervoort of the New York City Vandervoorts."

"Never heard of her," Justin said. He picked up her glass and carried it to the sink.

"She's a very, very wealthy American widow," Evelyn called after him. "*Very* high society. Her first husband was a Knickerbocker."

The term, adopted by the ancestors of the Dutch settlers who considered themselves the aristocrats of New York society, didn't appear to mean anything to Justin. He turned around and regarded her blankly.

She tried a different tack. "She is marrying Lord Boniface Cuthbert, one of the most celebrated economists of our day."

This got a response. "She's marrying old Bunny Cuthbert?" Justin exclaimed, grinning broadly. "Well, well."

"Bunny?"

"He was one of my professors at Oxford. First-rate chap, though timid as a blind tortoise. She must be quite the effervescent creature to have lured Bunny out of his shell."

Evelyn thought of the cool, blond American woman. Mrs. Vandervoort had more hauteur in her little finger than any European crown princess but, as for effervescence, Evelyn had seen mud more bubbly. "She's certainly unique."

"Why does she want to have her wedding at North Cross Abbey?"

Evelyn wasn't sure she had the right to reveal the information Mrs. Vandervoort had given her. On the other hand, it might persuade Justin to grant her request.

"It's a personal matter that I divulge in the strictest confidence. You see, though her first husband was a Knickerbocker, Mrs. Vandervoort herself comes from less illustrious stock. In fact, before emigrating to America, her grandmother served as the cook at North Cross Abbey."

Justin gave a low whistle and leaned back against the sink. "I can't say which is more surprising, that the old skinflint actually paid to keep a cook, or that Mrs. Van-whatever's granny liked him well enough to have fond memories of the place."

Evelyn shifted uncomfortably. "They're not exactly 'fond.' Mrs. Vandervoort grew up on her grandmother's stories about North Cross and its inhabitants, but they weren't very nice stories, I'm afraid. She—the grandmother, that is—" Evelyn cleared her throat, "felt ill-treated."

"Aha," Justin said. "What happened? Was one of the footmen fresh?"

"No, no. Nothing like that. Actually, she felt a grievance against your grandfather. Thought he looked down on her and treated her contemptuously. I'm sure he didn't," she hastened to reassure him. "Most likely it was all in the poor woman's mind. When some people find themselves in positions inferior to others they get to imagining all sorts of things that never—"

"Oh, no. I 'spect he did," Justin interjected calmly. "He was frightfully bigoted, loud, and critical," Justin went on. "Recall the first words he said to me—well, not actually to me, but to my father. Suspect he didn't think I was worth addressing. 'Good God, Marcus!'—that's my father's name—'Good God, Marcus, I do hope you produce a soldier to carry on the family tradition before I die, something other than this *dilettante*.' 'Dilettante' being not the worst but, I like to think, one of the more accurate terms my dear grandfather applied to me."

Evelyn's eyes grew wide. "How terrible for you."

Justin gave her a wicked smile. "Not anywhere near as terrible as it was for him; I never was blessed with a little brother. But, as you can imagine, I am in full sympathy with anyone who suffered under the old tyrant's domestic rule."

"Then you'll rent the abbey to me?" Evelyn asked eagerly.

He shook his head. "I didn't say that. I only said I was in sympathy. It would take a good deal more than sympathy to incite me into allowing a bunch of Yanks to invade the familial sanctuary."

"That's terrible! I bet you sound just like your grandfather," Evelyn declared hotly, drawing a startled, if appreciative, glance from Justin. "Besides, you yourself said it was a ghastly old place. Well, I will transform it."

"I don't want it transformed. I like ghastly old places."

"Now you're being arbitrary. Come, I won't hurt your old abbey. I'll ship in my boxes of trims and trappings and such and when we're done, I'll ship it all out again leaving the place cleaner, neater, and probably in a good deal better repair. All at Mrs. Vandervoort's expense."

An unreadable expression stole across Justin's face. He crossed his arms over his chest. He had very nice arms, the muscles moved smoothly beneath his skin. "When would you want to be renting the place?"

"Next month." She held her breath.

He threw up his hands in an exaggerated gesture of defeat. "Now, that *is* too bad. I really am sorry. Any other time and I might have been able to accommodate you."

She stared at him. She'd almost had the abbey. Instead, what she saw was her aunt's reputation slipping into infamy. "What's wrong with next month?"

"Next month is April," Justin said patiently. "*I* always spend April at North Cross Abbey."

She couldn't believe this. "And it would be too much trouble to go, say, in June? Which is a much more convivial month to spend in the country, I might point out."

"No," he said. "The migrations will be over by June."

"Migrations? As in birds? You have to be teasing me!" She'd been so close to redeeming herself. "You're not going to refuse me because of a bunch of birds?"

"I'm sure you understand."

"No! *You* don't understand. I'll pay you. Enough so that you could spend April in some nice, cozy little cottage anywhere in England. One *with* porcelain facilities."

"Sorry," he said. "Love to oblige. Can't."

He *had* to oblige. This was her only chance to restore Whyte's good name. After the last two debacles, she couldn't *give* her services away. But if she pulled this off and impressed the international set that constantly moved with and around Mrs. Vandervoort, English society would once again be pounding down the mahogany door of Whyte's Nuptial Celebrations.

She steeled her resolve. She was sorry it had come to this. But a woman had to do what a woman had to do.

"You *have* to let me rent the place." She dug into the pocket of her knickers and produced a yellowing note card.

"I do?" His dark brows climbed again. "And why is that?"

She handed him the card. "Because I'm turning in your marker."

# *Chapter 3*

JUSTIN ACCEPTED THE NOTE CARD AND READ the elegant scrawl of his own hand. "Why, of course! You're the owlet!"

"Excuse me?"

"The owlet!" he repeated exuberantly. "Broughton's unexpected progeny. The little girl with the dowager's manner. Ellie? Ivy?"

"Evelyn."

He snapped his fingers. "That's right. Evie."

"Evelyn," she corrected him. No one called her Evie, not even her family. She was the least Evie-like person in the world. Evies were demure, pretty, and shapely. She was . . . well, she wasn't an Evie.

"Will you honor your note, Mr. Powell?" she asked, ignoring his nonsense.

He leaned back, his hands curling around the

edge of the counter, and smiled cheerfully. "I say, has it occurred to you that your 'request' is remarkably like extortion?"

"A bit," she admitted. "I'd hoped to be spared this—"

"*You'd* hoped to be spared?"

She contrived to look wounded. "You gave me no choice. You should have been gallant when you had the opportunity."

"Forgive me."

"Besides," she said, "if I were you, I'd have expected something like this. I mean, a woman who would break into your house is likely at the end of her options, isn't she?" She shook her head woefully. "Just look at what I've been forced to because of you."

He laughed, surprising a grin out of her. She peeked over the top rim of her glasses in amused exasperation. Couldn't he at least *pretend* to give her words credence?

"I take it you're not filled with remorse?" she asked without much hope. "*Will* you help me, anyway? Please?"

For a long moment, he considered.

"All right, Evie, I'll tell you what," he finally said. "I'll let your American have her party at my abbey. I'll even allow you to transform the old place into whatever set piece you want—provided you cart away the props once the happy couple is united. But," he added severely, pushing away from the counter and coming to stand directly over her, "there is one condition."

"Anything! What?"

"I'll be at the abbey."

Evelyn face fell. "I can't ask Mrs. Vandervoort to invite a stranger to her wedding!"

"Cheer up, Evie." He chucked her under the chin, amazing her. No one chucked young ladies under their chins. And *most* certainly not her chin.

"I shouldn't care to be invited," he said. "Exceptionally dull affairs, weddings. Can't see why anyone who can possibly avoid them doesn't. No. I'm simply going to *be* at the abbey. Watching the migration of the," he glanced at her, "the *Bubo Formosa Plurimus*." He hesitated and added, "*Minor*."

"*Bubo* what?" Evelyn asked. It sounded like Latin and the most Latin she knew was *amo, amas, amat*.

He pulled a professorial face. "You don't know the *Bubo Formosa Plurimus, Minor*? Well, I can't say that I'm surprised. It's a very rare, exceptional little bird that I had the honor and great privilege of discovering when it flew into my window."

"You're an ornithologist?" Evelyn blurted out.

"An ardent enthusiast," he said modestly. "Though I do claim some small expertise and in some circles might be regarded as an authority." He turned his hand over and examined his nails.

Evelyn studied him suspiciously. It never occurred to her that a masher might have other activities besides, well, *mashing*. But, of course, there was nothing to say they couldn't have outside interests. Well, well, one learned something every day.

"So you see," he met her eye, "I'm afraid I must insist."

Evelyn wavered. If nothing else, he was discreet—as

proved by the absolute silence surrounding his affair with Mrs. Underhill. And having him on the premises might prove a spot of good luck, say, if some problem with the plumbing should arise. On the other hand, there would be a score of lovely, sophisticated women at the party, and a bunch of birds couldn't hold his attention indefinitely.

"Mr. Powell. Can you promise not to—" She paused. How did one put this delicately?

"I assure you, I won't be the least bit underfoot."

She fidgeted. "That's not exactly what I meant. You mustn't . . ."

"Mustn't what?"

She took a deep breath. "You mustn't embark on any relationships during my tenancy."

He regarded her blankly. She'd been too subtle.

"I mean you mustn't use the abbey for any untoward purposes during the tenure of our contract."

He looked completely mystified. "Pardon me?"

*Gads!* She stared at him in embarrassment, utterly flustered. "Tryst, rendezvous, criminal converse, liaison! Whatever you call it—don't have one while I'm at North Cross Abbey!" she blurted out. "I mean while *Mrs. Vandervoort* is there. I mean either of us!"

She'd startled him. His eyes widened and his body stiffened. Then, amazingly, he flushed. But that didn't stop the lupine smile from curving his sensuous mouth, or the glint of unholy amusement that brightened his blue-green eyes.

"Well, that rather takes the fun out of things, doesn't it?" he asked.

She felt an answering blush sweep up her throat. "You must promise."

He regarded her with mock solemnity. "I swear. Besides, I am quite reformed. The only female I find fascinating these days is my little *Bubo*."

She couldn't explain why his words should give her any pleasure, but they did. If he really had reformed... She snatched her wayward thoughts from their present course. If he'd reformed that only meant one less possible thing about which to worry.

"Then we have a deal?"

"We do."

She quite liked Justin Powell at that moment. Very much, in fact. Which surprised her. She normally didn't care for rakish sorts. But then, he didn't seem all that rakish. He smiled too often, for one thing, and he didn't seem to smolder with anger or cynicism or any other dark, subterranean passions that the penny dreadfuls assured her women found irresistible.

In fact, he seemed arrestingly open. He reminded her more of Verity's artless, self-assured son, Stanley, than of Lord Byron.

But, she thought, her mood darkening, maybe he simply didn't want to waste a perfectly good smolder on her. Maybe he saved his smoldering for sophisticated ladies. Married ladies. Beautiful ladies.

She found the thought unaccountably disheartening, and was therefore surprised when his hand engulfed hers. Immediately, she became attuned to every aspect of him: the crisp brilliance of his rolled-up starched shirtsleeves in contrast to the tanned skin of his forearms; the place where his razor had rasped the side of his throat; the noble dimensions of his nose; the firm curve of his lip; the slight cleft in his chin.

And he was large. Much larger than she. In a more forceful man, such height might even be daunting.

"Partners, then," he said. She could not read his expression. His hand tightened, and she felt the tentative stirrings of—

"Mr. Powell! Sir!" A thin, dapper, middle-aged man in pinstriped trousers and a black cutaway coat burst through the swinging kitchen door. "Someone has smashed—"

The man pulled up short. Stared. Hissed. "You!" He took a step forward. Evelyn shrank back in her chair. Justin released her hand and turned to face the furious butler.

"Beverly," Justin greeted him somberly. "Miss Whyte says you've been putting about the rumor that I'm not here. Is this true?"

Beverly's skin turned magenta; even his scalp beneath his formidable comb-over looked purple. *"Thz mung yadee hazben mos perthitint."*

"Are those supposed to be words you're spitting between your teeth, Beverly, you troublemaker?" Justin asked casually. "Because if they are, I'm afraid you'll have to go a sight better at pronunciation. I swear I didn't make out one single clear syllable. Did you, Evie?" He looked at her inquiringly.

Evie, wide-eyed at the spectacle of Beverly trying to regain his composure, shook her head mutely.

Justin turned his hand in her direction and smiled

triumphantly at the butler. "See, Beverly? It isn't just me who finds your mumblings incomprehensible. Now, have you or have you not been telling folks that I'm not here?"

Beverly shut his eyes. Took a deep breath through pinched, narrow nostrils. Released his breath in one long exhalation. Opened his eyes.

"Yes, sir. I am afraid I have. Sir."

"Ah!" Justin said happily, rubbing his palms together and looking at Evelyn. "Now we're getting somewhere. And why is that, Beverly?"

Beverly looked determinedly at a point above Evelyn's head. "Whim, sir," he clipped out.

One side of Justin's mouth twitched irrepressibly before he looked back at Evelyn. "Told you he was a malicious dog, didn't I?"

He returned his attention to the butler. "Well, you must stop these pranks, Beverly. It just won't do, having people turned away from the front door and forced to break in through rear windows. Why, poor Evie here suffered a nasty gash because of your bit of tomfoolery—"

"It really isn't all that bad," Eve cut in timidly. "I can't even feel the sting anymore."

Justin smiled at her kindly before turning a scowl on Beverly. Evelyn almost felt sorry for the poor man, and had it not been for the metaphorical daggers he was hurling at her, she would have.

"You are very lucky Miss Evie is kindhearted, Beverly," Justin said. "We shall let it pass this time. But no more of your loathsome pranks in the future. Do we understand each other?"

"Quite well, sir."

"Good. Then you may go about your usual business. Oh! Drat. Nearly forgot. You may *not* go about your usual business—which is undoubtedly a good thing, you hooligan—you must make ready for us to go to North Cross Abbey."

This won a startled glance from the butler. "North Cross Abbey, sir?"

Justin sighed. "Yes, yes. And why should you be regarding me as though I'd sprouted horns and a tail? Don't we go to North Cross Abbey every year?"

"Yes, sir. I forgot. Sir."

"We'll be going a bit earlier is all. And, Beverly, make sure I have sufficient white shirts and evening attire. We'll be having Knickerbockers at dinners. As well as Miss Evie."

By now, the butler had completely regained his aplomb. He replied in perfectly neutral tones, "Knickerbockers. Very well, sir. Will that be all?"

"Yes. I think so."

"Very good, sir." Beverly bowed and took his leave. Justin and Evelyn watched him depart.

"It's rather like having Puck as one's butler," Justin mused. "I never know what bit of mischief he'll get up to."

"He doesn't look like an irrepressible prankster. He doesn't look like he has any sense of humor at all," Evelyn replied. "He looks like the quintessential butler. Or a particularly severe church deacon."

"I know. That's the devil of it. But you heard him. Brash as brass and twice as bold," Justin said. "Honestly,

I don't know why I put up with him. Sentiment, I suppose. Beverly's a legacy from my grandparent."

"The one that didn't like you?"

"Oh, no," Justin said in surprise. "The one that did."

"Ah," Evelyn murmured, confounded.

Justin turned to her. "Now that you've accomplished your mission, I suspect you'd like to get home and out of those pants."

Evelyn looked down. She'd forgotten about the ruined knickers. "Yes. I suppose."

"Have you transportation, or should I have the carriage brought round?"

"No, thank you. I have already made arrangements. A hansom cab is waiting for me around the corner."

"Foolish of me to ask. I should have realized you'd have all contingencies accounted for. Now, then . . ."

Before she realized what he was about, he'd plucked her from the chair and was heading out the kitchen door toward the front door. He couldn't . . . He wouldn't . . . Hadn't she just been thinking she could trust his discretion?

"You can't carry me out your front door in the middle of the day and drop me on the sidewalk!"

"I wasn't going to." He sounded offended. "I was going to carry you to your cab."

"That's worse!" she exclaimed, drawing a confused look from him. Good heavens, one would think he'd no idea how one got rid of a female visitor without being seen!

"I can't be seen in public looking like this, Mr.

Powell. One leg of my pants is missing—and heaven knows, no respectable woman wears pants to begin with—"

"You look very nice in them," he said.

She perked up at that. She didn't think they looked so awfully bad, either. "Thank you. They're ever so comfortable, too, and—" *What was she thinking?* They were drawing perilously near the front door and he still showed no signs of releasing her. "That's beside the point! I shouldn't be wearing them and you know it. Just as you know you can't be seen carrying me out of your house, and *no,*" she answered his expression as clearly as if he'd spoken out loud, "it would not be better if you waited and carried me out tonight."

"But you're injured," Justin retorted, his arms tightening as though someone were about to snatch her from him. Which was a completely thrilling and unrealistic conjecture. "Surely allowances can be made?"

How was she going to make him understand? Lord, one would mistake his manner for naïveté, if it weren't so ludicrous. "No, no allowances can be made."

His jaw, just level with her eyes, bunched with irritation. "Stupid."

Her heart softened. "Please, don't castigate yourself. I am sure you meant well."

"Not *me,*" he replied with some heat. "Society."

She should have known. Casual and relaxed he might be, but there was no lack of pride in Mr. Justin Powell.

"Be that as it may, 'rules is rules,' as *my* grandfather used to say. Kindly meant as your impulses undoubtedly are, you will be doing me a great disservice if you refuse to allow me to sneak out the back of your house and up the alley. Alone."

He frowned. "But—"

"Please put me down," she cut him off severely.

Reluctantly, he lowered her to her feet. She stood looking up at him. Should she offer to shake his hand again? Yes, that seemed right. She thrust out her hand.

"Well," she said bracingly, though whom she meant to be braced was somewhat in question. "Until next month, then. Thank you."

He looked down at her outstretched hand and smiled. He took hold of it but instead of shaking it, he turned it over, lifted it to his mouth, and pressed his lips to her palm. A little shiver raced down her spine, turning into a shudder by the time it found its way to her legs.

He released her hand. It hung for a full three seconds between them before she realized it and thrust it behind her. His expression was creamy with self-satisfaction. "Sorry about that. Reformed though I am, old habits die hard."

He reached out again and she jumped back. He grinned, stretching his arm past her, and pushed open the door. He stepped back. "Until later."

Beverly was already on his hands and knees, cleaning up the broken glass, when Justin returned to the library.

"The girl ought to be doing this," he pronounced gloomily. As a confirmed misogynist, he considered it his special calling to point out the myriad unpleasantnesses supplied by the fairer sex, and he did so at length and in great detail. The only woman he had ever liked—and "like" did not seem an appropriate term for the regard with which he exalted her memory—was Justin's maternal grandmother.

"It wasn't a girl," Justin said. "It was a woman."

"Ah, no wonder she was able to cause so much mischief in such short order. She's had practice." Beverly paused in collecting shards from the Oriental carpet. "But why, might one ask, does it appear to please you that she's been wreaking havoc on the population for a longer rather than shorter period?"

Justin's usually candid gaze slipped away with a degree too much nonchalance. Beverly, who, nearly fifteen years ago, had been charged by Justin's grandmother—who loved her grandson as much as her husband despised him—with seeing to his well-being, felt his interest quicken.

For all those years he had taken that charge most seriously. It had led him to a brief stint in the army as Justin's batman, and then into his current interesting profession.

"Sir?"

Justin fidgeted, and now Beverly's interest scaled quickly to all-out concern.

"Well, blast it all, Beverly, one doesn't like to think one is stirred by a young girl in one's arms. It's perverse! So, you can imagine my relief when I discovered that my, er, senses were reacting perfectly naturally to a perfectly standard—no, no, there was nothing *standard* about her. Acceptable? Yes, *acceptable*—set of stimuli." He smiled.

Beverly's faced blanched with horror. "Sir, you're not . . . ?"

He had no idea how Justin knew what he'd been about to say, but Justin waved his hand airily. "Now, Beverly, don't go haring after some ridiculous notion. There's a great deal of difference between wanting and winning. Added to which, I haven't the time, the inclination, or a hope in hell of courting such a prickly creature. So, there it is."

He smiled. "I shall be out for the rest of the day. And, ah, thank you, Beverly. This little chat has quite cleared my thoughts," he said and was gone.

Beverly stared after him. For fifteen years, he'd watched various women from various social, economic, and chronological classes angle for Justin's attention. Not one of them had succeeded. Oh, the boy wasn't a saint by any means, but he'd never been truly smitten, which had been fine with Beverly.

But lately, Beverly had begun to wonder if perhaps his promise to see to Justin's well-being might not extend beyond simple physical consideration. As easy as Justin was with his own company, as seemingly cavalier and cheerful in society, more and more often of late Beverly was aware of Justin's isolation.

There was only one cure for the sort of loneliness a man feels: a son.

Unfortunately, producing one necessitated a

certain close association with the manufacturing element.

Whatever else Justin Powell's kiss did, it banished any doubts Evelyn had as to whether or not Justin Powell was a bona fide wolf. Dazed, she limped to the end of the alley. The hansom was waiting just as they'd arranged, Merry's fluffed red hair filling the small side window as she pressed her nose to the pane.

As soon as Evelyn reached the door, it swung open, and a hand reached out and seized her and hauled her into the carriage. Once inside, Merry stared at her shredded knickers and undone hair. Before Evelyn realized what was happening, the Frenchwoman had pulled Evelyn into a fierce embrace, and was smothering her face in her ample bosom.

"*Mon Dieu!* My poor little bird! You have been defiled! The filth. The bastard! I kill him!" she moaned, rocking back and forth. It took a minute, but Evelyn finally managed to escape. Merry was so . . . *French.*

"Stop this at once, Merry," she said severely, trying to straighten the wire bow of her glasses, which Merry, in her enthusiastic portrayal of Outraged Womanhood, had bent. "You've entirely misread the situation. Everything went perfectly."

# Chapter 4

BY LATE AFTERNOON, THE SUN BEGAN TO dissolve as a murky coolness replaced the day's bracing clarity. Families picnicking by the Thames gathered up their blankets and baskets and hailed cabs to take them home, leaving behind only a few of the cheerful crowd that had taken advantage of the rare March weather.

A rising fog coalesced above the river, little filigrees threading up along the embankments. Justin, strolling along the nearly deserted promenade, stopped at a bench near Tower Bridge and took a seat. Above him cartwheeled seabirds, disappearing and appearing into the mist.

He stretched his arm along the back of the bench and watched a reedy young man in a seersucker coat stroll by with his lady friend, a rosy-cheeked shop girl who'd forgotten to snip the tag off of her readymade coat. On the river below, a punt glided by. And then, as a church clock struck the seventh hour, a hale, middle-aged man in a dark frock coat and top hat appeared, ambling along, swinging a silver-headed cane. He came even with Justin and paused, turning to look out over the river.

"I know there's those who find the fog noxious and depressing, but what would London be without one of her famous pea-soupers?" he asked.

"A good sight drier, I should imagine," Justin replied.

The man smiled without turning. "Ah, Justin, ever the maudlin sentimentalist, I see."

"Cursed with a soft heart," Justin agreed.

"Soft as steel," the gentleman murmured. He shook his head and turned around. "Your day will come, m'boy. I only hope I live to see it."

"Me, too," Justin answered with a cheeky grin. "Have a seat, Bernard, you're putting a crick in my neck, forcing me to look up this way."

"Only way I will get you to look up to me, I suspect. And thus well worth the trouble," Bernard replied but nonetheless lowered himself down beside Justin. "Well, Jus, here I am. Now, why did you ask for this meeting?"

"I've a plan that might solve some of the problems you presented regarding that little matter of yours."

"Oh?"

"A simple plan," Justin leaned sideways and whispered, "but very, very cunning."

"Very dramatic." Bernard applauded with the tips of his fingers. "I know there's scant hope of your listening to me, but could you kindly refrain from treating our work as if it were some schoolboys' game?"

"As you say," Justin replied, "scant hope. Oh, come, Bernard, don't look so disapproving. It *is* a game. And I'm serious enough when the situation warrants—which this most decidedly does not. It's a simple drop-and-catch on home turf. What could be less perilous?"

When Bernard only frowned, Justin continued. "The gravest danger anyone faces is exposure. And, by the by, that 'anyone' is me. But what of it?"

"Hm." Bernard removed his top hat and set it carefully beside him.

"My sentiments exactly," Justin responded pleasantly. "I've been asking myself why you chose me for this assignment. It's not exactly what I've done in the past. One would think anyone would do. Which makes me rather uncomfortable."

Bernard heaved a heartfelt sigh. "My dear boy, you've begun to suspect *everyone* of nefarious purposes. Including your superiors."

"Not everyone," Justin replied.

"Good," Bernard said. "As for your question, the reasons we chose you for this job ought to be perfectly clear. First, it is precisely because you *don't* do this sort of thing. No one will suspect you. Second, this invention is important. Far too important to entrust to anyone less able than you. You're the ace up our sleeve, m'boy."

Justin's smile was acrid. "So lovely to be needed."

Bernard ignored the sarcasm. "Tell me about this plan of yours."

Justin relaxed and crossed an ankle over his knee. "I have been asked—no, that's not quite correct—I have been *coerced* into renting out North Cross Abbey for a society wedding."

"I take it you are not the lucky groom?"

"Gads, no," Justin said. "What woman in her right mind would have me? I have no ostensible career other than flittering about the world drawing pictures of birds and annoying the natives with impertinent questions about local habitat. Since I am constantly pressing my friends abroad for free room and board, the family coffers are viewed with the direst speculation. Added to which, I'm never home.

"No, I'm not the groom. Never will be. I'm simply the unfortunate owner of the house to which the bride feels she must return triumphant in order to expiate the grim ghosts of her working-class antecedents."

"I am sure you are making sense, Justin, but I must beg you to be tolerant of my advanced years," Bernard said. "What *are* you talking about?"

Justin didn't look in the least penitent. "There is an American widow who has cartloads of money and a grudge against my grandfather. Seems her granny worked for the old bastard and considered him punctilious, condescending, contemptuous, and unfair. Which he was, of course, only the old girl—the granny, that is—took it personally. She raised her granddaughter—our blushing bride—like some Yankee Miss Haversham."

Justin shook a finger in the air and intoned, " 'Return, child of my child, return to that cursed house richer, haughtier, and of more consequence than the old crock who paid me wages!' "

"Americans," Bernard sighed.

"Indeed." Justin lowered his hand and tucked it into his waistcoat pocket. "In order to achieve that end, the heiress hired a young woman in whose debt, coincidentally, I am, to secure the rental of North Cross."

"Another young woman? What young woman?"

"Evelyn Cummings Whyte."

Bernard ruminated a moment before his face lit with realization. "Good God, Jus, Lally's granddaughter?"

Jus slanted Bernard a curious look. "Yes. Do you know her?"

"Only by reputation. Her grandfather is an acquaintance. He calls his grandaughter *Her Preternatural Formidableness.* Swears his entire family runs in terror of her."

"Terror?" Justin tried out the word. "She's as big as a minute and looks like a schoolgirl. In fact, I mistook her for one. Now, 'strange,' I might concede you, but I must disagree on 'terrifying.' "

Bernard lifted his hand in a gesture of exasperation. "I'm sure you know best."

"Normally I wouldn't be so presumptuous," Justin demurred. "But it's amazing the camaraderie that can develop between housebreaker and house owner."

"What in God's name are you talking about now, Justin? Is this your idea of a joke? Your sense of the absurd has always been your Achilles' heel. Speak plainly, man. What has a housebreaking to do with the Duke of Lally's granddaughter and an American widow?"

"I thought I'd been clear," Justin said. "Lady Evelyn broke into my house in order to collect on a favor I owed her. She felt it necessary to gain illegal access because legitimate routes had been closed to her by Beverly, who, acting upon my orders in an apparently futile attempt to keep my presence in the city from being known, told her I was not in."

"Does it ever worry you that you play the part of an absentminded muttonhead too well?" Bernard asked, winning a brilliant smile from Justin.

"No, but I thank you for your concern. Again, where was I? Oh, yes. Apparently, her aunt—Lally's daughter—arranges," Justin groped for the right term, "matrimonial fracases or fetes or banquets or such."

"Ah, yes, I recall," Bernard mused.

"Well, the aunt has eloped, leaving Evie—Lady Evelyn—minding the store. Unfortunately, she seems to have been making a hash of it. She is certain this American widow is her last chance to save the family business from disgrace. And, I suspect, herself from humiliation." His expression grew pensive. "I don't think the word 'fail' is a part of that young woman's lexicon."

Bernard retained his good humor. He'd learned from long past experience not to bother trying to rein in Justin's conversation. Eventually, Justin would get to the point. But Bernard once more was overtaken by the suspicion that Justin did it on purpose, to distract and trick a fellow into revealing more information than he intended to. "You are getting to your actual *plan,* are you not?"

The puzzlement vanished from Justin's expression. "Everything in its given time," he said. "The reason all this is material, Bernard, is that in order to transform my dusty inheritance into a suitably impressive stage, fit for the widow's wedding, my little housebreaker will have to import a great many things. Which means—Bernard, are you attending? Good—which means that the abbey will receive shipment upon shipment, crates upon crates of accoutrements, flowers, food, trimmings, equipage, and various and sundry wedding paraphernalia."

"Ah!" Bernard released his breath.

" 'And thus, the veil lifted from his eyes,' " Justin intoned. "That's right, Bernard, your mysterious foreign agent can ship the even more mysterious 'diabolical machine' to the abbey without anyone remarking it. What's one crate amongst dozens? Then, after it arrives, we slip your pet scientist in to do a quick little anatomical survey, so to speak; trash the prototype and back off to Oxford he pops to report in to the rest of the brain bank. It's perfect."

"What if Lady Evelyn opens it?" Bernard asked dubiously. "The hell of the situation is that we don't know exactly when the bloody thing will arrive. It isn't as if it's being shipped legally, you know. It might arrive a few days after it leaves port or a few weeks. I can't see any woman leaving a crate unopened for a full day, let alone an entire week—regardless of whom it is addressed to."

"She won't open it, Bernard—and here I wish you to pause and appreciate the magic I have worked—because I'll be there to see that she doesn't. It's the one stipulation that I put on renting her the place: I must be allowed to reside there while it's being readied for the wedding."

Bernard stroked the side of his jaw thoughtfully.

"Look, Bernard, since you gave me this commission, I have been racking my brain trying to figure out some means to get this thing into the country and into your hands without exciting curiosity. My plan meets all the criteria you set forth. The wedding preparations serve as perfect camouflage. Once the shipment arrives, I'll send word and we'll be able to slip your scientist in as a tradesman or repairman, to have his peek at the device without rousing suspicion. Added to which, I can control the environment there in a way I never could in London. North Cross Abbey is thirty-five miles outside London, which means the crate can be shipped with a great deal less possibility of something unfortunate happening to it than there would be amidst London's myriad byways. In the country, everyone knows everyone else and the roads are few and easily watched. Should unfriendly forces get wind of where you've had it sent and a stranger shows up, I will hear of it at once. With Beverly watching the goings-on at the abbey and me keeping an eye on the locals, we'll have the situation pretty well attended. In London, the Kaiser could move in next door and I might not know of it until next year."

"It sounds good," Bernard allowed. "It might do."

"It's a godsend and you know it, particularly as we don't know precisely when your man on the continent will be able to send it across the Channel. This way we will have as much control as can be hoped."

"But what about this young woman, Jus?" Bernard fretted. "Won't she get suspicious?"

Justin relaxed again. "She is single-minded in making sure this wedding comes off. Besides, any contact between us is likely to be limited to her attempts to keep me away from the female wedding guests."

Bernard blinked, surprised. "Why is that?"

Justin's eyes danced with delighted memory, but his tone was quite bland. "Lady Evelyn is convinced I am the last word in womanizers."

Bernard stared, trying to gauge whether Justin was joking or not. When it became apparent he wasn't, he burst into such spirited laughter that Justin had to thump him on the back.

"Oh, dear," Bernard said, wiping his eyes and sniffing. "Forgive me, Jus. It's just that—*you,* of all people, a womanizer."

"My sentiments exactly," Justin replied pleasantly.

"However did she get such a notion?"

"Oh, she has reasons. Based on erroneous assumptions, but reasons, nonetheless."

Bernard was still dabbing at his eyes. "Is she addled? Her father is rumored to be rather eccentric."

Justin pulled a wounded expression. "My dear

Bernard, surely a woman doesn't have to be addled to consider me a—what did she call it?—a wolf."

"God, she *is* addled. What's she like?" Bernard asked, curious in spite of himself.

Justin shrugged. "Says the damnedest things. Whatever pops into her head, in very nice accents, of course, without appearing to have the least idea how they might sound. Nor does she have any idea of what she looks like, I should imagine. Very cavalier about her appearance. She'd dressed in boy's clothes for our interview."

"Gads. What *does* she look like? Her mother was Francesca Cummings, you know. Stunning beauty. And the oldest daughter is Verity Hodges." Bernard nodded as though picturing her in his mind. "Heard the younger one was as different as night to day."

"Night?" Justin tested the word. "Yes, maybe. A rollicking, moonlit, wind-scoured summer night."

"You're growing poetical in your old age, Jus," Bernard said in interested tones.

"Am I? How tiresome. A momentary aberration," Justin apologized and then, "What does she look like? Small, dark. Hiding behind a hideous pair of spectacles. Masses of black hair."

"Obviously, she is not very perceptive if she thinks you're a libertine," Bernard said. "But that can only be a plus for our purposes, eh?"

"I wouldn't dismiss Lady Evelyn."

"No. Just hope she keeps busy with her end of the show as you attend to yours." He paused and chewed on his lip, his face slowly screwing up with worry.

Justin nodded readily enough, which did nothing

to reassure Bernard. Justin Powell was inevitably agreeable, until the moment when he decided not to agree, and then ... But he was here to persuade Justin to take this mission, not to worry about how he'd react if things went awry.

He liked Justin. He knew how much the young man had sacrificed to work for them. In order to join Bernard's clandestine company, Justin had ostensibly left the military because "the company was boring, the food atrocious, and the enemy simply too well trained."

His grandfather, General Harden, had thereafter been tireless in his criticism of his only grandson and, while Justin had maintained a sweet disregard, Bernard was certain the continued slights and sneers of Harden and his myriad John Bull pals must have caused Justin some pain.

The notion that he was using a man who had given up so much for his country pricked at Bernard's long-dormant conscience, and he waved his hand irritably, as if to rid himself of the pest. "It's a workable plan," he allowed.

"Yes," Justin said slowly, his light gaze touching and holding Bernard's. "I can't think of another. I just don't want Lady Evelyn penalized by involvement with me."

"Neither do I! Gads, Lally belongs to my club," Bernard declared. "If you're worried she'll be tainted by simple proximity to you, stay away from her!"

The lopsided smile, so charming and rueful, appeared once more on Justin's lean, clever face. He rose with the loose-jointed grace of the natural athlete and picked up his hat.

"Well, that shouldn't be too hard," he said, putting it atop his head. "She's probably out buying bolts and locks for all the chamber doors this very minute."

An hour had passed since Justin's departure and still Bernard sat, his hands folded across the top of his silver-knobbed cane. Near twilight, a nondescript man in worn Ulster, his cloth cap pulled low over blunt features, limped up the promenade. Beside him a little terrier danced on the end of his lead. When he drew close to Bernard, the man unclipped the leash and the terrier bounded off into the mist.

"Aren't you afraid he'll go missing?" Bernard asked.

"Not Captain," the man replied. His voice belied his common appearance, having perfect public school accents. "He'll set a perimeter and let us know if anyone approaches."

Bernard nodded. "Even your pets have duties."

"We all play many roles, Bernard," the man replied. He remained standing, his hands clasped lightly behind his back, rocking gently back and forth on the balls of his feet. "You handled Justin?"

"Yes." Quickly, Bernard told the man about his conversation with Justin.

"And he suspects nothing?"

Bernard gave a short snort. "I wouldn't go that far. He's asking questions. He wondered why we chose him for a simple courier job."

"What did you say?"

"I told him this invention could change the way wars are fought. That we couldn't use any regular routes. That we weren't even sure when the thing could be got across the Channel. That though we expected nothing untoward, under the slim chance that something does go wrong, we need someone with his experience and expertise at hand when we import our scientist for a quick study of the device before destroying it," Bernard said grimly, looking down at the toes of his boots. He looked up and caught his superior's eye with a flat look of frustration. "I certainly didn't tell him the truth, if that's what you fear."

"And what is the truth?" the blunt-featured fellow asked quietly.

"That we need him because in order to catch a big shark you have to use big bait. What bigger bait than one of our best agents? Damn it all!" Bernard pummeled his fist into his open palm in uncharacteristic ire. "I don't like having leaked a rumor about Powell's identity without giving him any warning. He's too good a man to throw to the wolves this way."

"You've done what you had to do," the blunt-featured man answered. "If you'd warned Powell that we were setting a trap at the abbey, he wouldn't have agreed to the plan. He would never place innocent people at such risk. This girl, Lady Evelyn, the wedding guests... he would think there too much potential danger to innocent bystanders. It's why we've never made as good a use of him as we might have; he lives by his own code, not ours."

He was right. Powell was notorious for making his own rules, and there was no room for improvisation in this game.

It had taken months to set up this house of cards, months to plot a way to lure the secret agent into revealing himself before he could identify the Agency's own master spy, a spy who, according to all their information, this enemy spy was in close association with, even if he had yet to realize it.

So, in order to lure him into revealing himself they'd offered a substitute—an agent high up in the echelons but who, because of his unfortunate conscience, was growing more and more intractable.

They'd made up a story about a history-altering device, leaked the rumor that this top field agent would be receiving it, and trusted that the enemy spy would not be able to resist the combination of two such powerful enticements.

"You weren't too subtle about Powell, were you? This man *will* realize that he needs only follow the device to its destination to discover Powell's identity?"

Bernard shook his head. He was getting too old for this. Sentimentality had crept into his reasoning. He did not want Powell hurt. "I think it will work."

"It has to work," the other man said in a low fervent voice. "We cannot lose."

Bernard had always known his superior's interest was not wholly indifferent. Still, he was surprised by the passion in his voice.

"Powell inadvertently gave me an idea of how we might chum the waters further. Just in case the rumors we let slip *were* too subtle."

"How?"

"Lady Evelyn. She might serve in that capacity, too."

"Oh?" The man mused again. It was one of the reasons he was so good at what he did. He never pressed. He simply waited.

Bernard told him.

Ten minutes later their meeting was at an end. The rough-looking man whistled his little terrier in from the fog and bent to clip his leash back on. He straightened. "We have no concerns about Powell's loyalty?"

"That, at least, is unquestionable and absolute," Bernard assured him. "If he does suspect something is amiss, he will still do his duty. It just might not be in a manner we foresee."

"Then make sure he doesn't suspect, Bernard. We can't take any chances."

"But Powell can." Bernard regretted the words as soon as he spoke them.

"Well, yes." The man turned and the little dog fell into step beside him as they walked past where Bernard still sat, staring out at the river. "That's what he's always done."

# Chapter 5

"WE HAVE EVERY CONFIDENCE IN YOUR good sense, dear. But are you certain a chaperon wouldn't be a good idea?" Francesca, Marchioness Broughton, had dropped by to see if she could persuade her younger daughter to lunch with her in Pall Mall.

She'd found Evelyn seated in Agatha's Louis XIV chair, competently managing a stream of deliveries and tradesmen. Evelyn had declined the offered meal on the excuse that she had too many details to address before she left for East Sussex. At which point Francesca, who knew nothing about any such plans, decided to keep her daughter company until the arrival of the American lady on whose behalf Evelyn was traveling to some place called North Cross Abbey.

She'd seated herself on the plump yellow chaise,

pulled her tatting from her chatelaine, and proceeded to draw from her daughter a recital of her adventures over the past few days.

If she felt any disapproval of the means her daughter had used to gain access to Mr. Powell's town house, she hadn't voiced them. She only looked up when Evelyn mentioned the cut on her leg and, after having been reassured that the wound was healing nicely, returned to her tatting.

"Why?" Evelyn replied in response to her mother's mild query. "We both know it would only be to satisfy convention, and I don't think there's enough convention in East Sussex that it needs satisfying."

"Do we?" her mother murmured, frowning over an intricate knot.

"Yes, we do," Evelyn replied, jotting down the projected costs of shipping five hundred hothouse gardenias to North Cross Abbey.

"If you say so, dear," Francesca said. "I suspect you know best. Besides, Justin Powell doesn't strike me as the sort of gentleman who would take advantage of a lady."

Evelyn, in the midst of her calculations, didn't think before speaking. "Oh, he would. He has."

The sudden termination of movement from the chaise alerted her to her mistake. She looked up and met her mother's startled eye. *Oops.*

"You aren't listening to rumors, are you, dear?" Francesca asked. "You know how unreliable they can be."

Unhappily conscious of her vow to remain mum on the Underhill matter, a vow she had just come perilously close to breaking, Evelyn regarded her mother mutely.

Francesca set her lacework down in her lap. "I can't quite believe it. Justin Powell, a cad."

Evelyn attempted not to squirm. Her mother would be enlisting her father's aid to stop her from going to North Cross Abbey if she didn't quickly remedy her blunder. "I didn't precisely mean *that*. I only meant that he has a Certain History where women are concerned. But before you get upset, Mama—"

"I'm not upset, dear." And truthfully, Francesca looked perfectly composed, as opposed to Evelyn.

"Besides," Evelyn said, "all that is in the past. Mr. Powell assures me that he is reformed."

"He does?" Francesca said. "Well, I suppose that's nearly an admission, isn't it? I mean, you can't reform if you haven't done anything worth reforming, can you?"

"Er, yes. I mean, no."

Francesca shook her head. "Who'd have thought it? I mean not that he's not perfectly yummy and all—and you needn't look at me like that, Evelyn, I'm not so ancient that I can't appreciate a handsome young man—but he never seemed in the least bit *interested*, if you take my meaning."

"Not really," Evelyn said wryly, thinking of Justin's interest in Mrs. Underhill.

"Your father and I run into Mr. Powell occasionally in town. And though he has very sweet manners, he always seems a bit, well, *vague*." Francesca smiled and shook her head. "He struck me that way at Verity's coming-out, too. I distinctly remember commenting to your father how unlike the other young gentlemen he was."

"I don't think he seems vague," Evelyn said.

"No?"

"No. Perhaps you mistake his extreme ease of manner for a lack of interest in what's going on, but I feel confident that very little goes unnoticed by Mr. Powell. He just doesn't conform to the usual pattern, you see, and I expect that can be misinterpreted." She found herself remembering very distinctly the manner in which his eyes crinkled at the corners when he smiled, and the feel of muscles moving beneath his shirt as he picked her up. She also recalled his laughter, and she smiled in response to it, even if it was only a memory.

"To be honest, I found him likeable," she said. "And clever. In a bohemian sort of way. A sort of careless way. But not an objectionably bohemian careless way."

"You did, did you?" her mother murmured, regarding her closely.

"Yes."

"And you are perfectly satisfied he will not attempt to importune you?"

Evelyn gave her mother a wry look. "I am certain he'll find the wherewithal to resist me. He's only there to plot the migration of some odd little bird he discovered."

"You could take Merry with you," Francesca suggested, startling Evelyn. The idea of the perennially 'entangled' Frenchwoman playing the part of chaperon was too delicious. She burst into laughter.

"Merry? You're teasing!"

"Not at all. Granted, Merry's morals are somewhat lax, but only in reference to herself. She believes herself to be cursed, or blessed, with an artistic soul. Which she is, the darling!"

Evelyn wasn't nearly so sanguine about the direction of Merry's moral compass, but as she'd planned to send for the dress designer soon after her arrival at North Cross Abbey anyway, she might as well make her mother happy by toting her along right from the start. "All right," she agreed. "I shall ask Merry to come along with me."

"Ah, good. The more help you have with the wedding, the better."

Evelyn nodded. "Mother, *this* wedding will be a success. I have arranged for every possible contingency. I have hired backup delivery people, contacted alternate suppliers for various items, and ordered double quantities of everything.

"Added to which, I shall be at hand from a month before the wedding until the final guest has left. This time, I swear I will not fail. The Vandervoort-Cuthbert wedding will be spectacular."

An odd expression crossed her mother's face. "Evelyn, darling, isn't 'spectacular' asking rather much?"

"Not at all," Evelyn said. "People seek Aunt Agatha's services for the spectacular. They have every right to expect it, and I will deliver it."

"And what would happen if you couldn't deliver on that worthy goal?" her mother asked softly.

The question caused an unpleasant twist in Evelyn's stomach. She frowned. "Don't you think I can do it?"

Her mother laughed at her expression. "Oh, Evelyn, my darling. I don't doubt your ability for a minute. If you told me you had decided to fly, I should expect to see you soaring about the rooftops by sunset. But that doesn't mean I wouldn't wonder what lured you into the sky."

Her mother was regarding her with uncharacteristic earnestness. Usually Francesca was a font of tranquil encouragement, unquestioning in her faith in Evelyn's intelligence, abilities, and resourcefulness. The ache in Evelyn's stomach deepened.

"Please, Mama. I *can* do this. Don't worry."

"But, darling, I do worry. Perhaps I—"

A knock on the door interrupted her, and Evelyn turned with a guilty sense of relief. "Come in," she called.

The door opened and Mrs. Vandervoort entered, followed by Merry, who had also just arrived. The Frenchwoman greeted Francesca and retreated to the side of the room to wait.

"Good day, Mrs. Vandervoort." Evelyn rose and greeted the American woman. "May I introduce you to my mother, Marchioness Broughton? Mama, Mrs. Edith Vandervoort."

The two ladies looked one another over with open interest. On the surface they looked a great deal alike. Both were statuesque beauties, having reached the full bloom of their looks in their middle years. Both had dark blond hair and striking blue eyes. Both were dressed in the height of fashion, though Francesca's buttercream wool serge had been made over in order to achieve its chic while Mrs. Vandervoort's dark blue lace dress featuring the new pigeon-breast style was brand new.

Both were quiet women, but where Francesca Whyte's stillness evoked a sense of tranquility, Edith Vandervoort's offered only silence. Francesca's looks charmed and invited; Edith Vandervoort's beauty held one at arm's length.

"I am pleased to make your acquaintance, Marchioness," Mrs. Vandervoort said.

"And I yours, Mrs. Vandervoort." Francesca tucked her tatting back in her chatelaine and stood. "Evelyn, dear, I am so pleased about your good news." She turned to Merry. "Merry, if I might have a word with you outside, we can leave these ladies to their business."

"Of course, madame," Merry said.

"Good day, then. And," Francesca paused on her way through the door and pinked up prettily, "may I wish you every happiness on your upcoming marriage, Mrs. Vandervoort."

"Thank you, Marchioness."

After Francesca and Merry left, Mrs. Vandervoort turned to Evelyn. "Your mother is a charming lady."

"Thank you," Evelyn said proudly, gesturing toward a chair. "Won't you be seated? May I ring for some tea?"

"Thank you, no." In one fluid, economical movement, Mrs. Vandervoort took the offered chair and placed her jet-beaded purse in her lap.

"I have wonderful news," Evelyn began without preamble, retaking her seat behind her aunt's desk.

"Mr. Powell is willing to let us rent the abbey for April."

Mrs. Vandervoort nodded calmly. She was a woman used to having her wishes granted. It probably seldom occurred to her to wonder about the difficulties she posed for those to whom she gave the task of fulfilling her wishes. "Excellent."

"There is only one caveat."

"And that is?"

"Mr. Powell insists he be allowed to remain at the abbey."

Mrs. Vandervoort betrayed no discernable reaction. "I see. And you have explained that this is my wedding?"

"Yes, but Mr. Powell is an ornithologist."

Her brows angled sharply up. "Is he? I fail to see the connection. There are presumably other areas in Great Britain where one might see birds?"

"Not the bird Mr. Powell is interested in, a very rare species he discovered himself."

"Oh? And what is the name of this newly discovered species?"

Luckily, in spite of not actually knowing Latin, Evelyn had an excellent memory. "*Bubo Formosa Plurimus.*"

Mrs. Vandervoort, in the process of opening her purse, looked up, startled.

"You have heard of it?"

"I? No, indeed." She did not offer an explanation for her look of surprise and, after a second, Evelyn went on. "Mr. Powell is adamant that he must be at the abbey for the spring migration, but he promises to be completely undetectable." He'd actually promised nothing of the sort, but she'd see to it that he remained out of sight even if she had to lock him in his room herself.

"I see." Mrs. Vandervoort tilted her head. "What is your opinion of Mr. Powell's offer, Lady Evelyn?"

"I think it is very likely your only option if you wish to be wed at North Cross Abbey."

"A hardheaded man, then? Rude, domineering, arrogant? His grandfather was."

Evelyn did not hesitate. "No. I found him quite amiable, actually."

"Surely, if he's so easygoing he might be . . ." Mrs. Vandervoort trailed off suggestively.

"Amiable, not tractable," Evelyn said. "I don't think he's likely to change his mind once it's made up."

"Then we shall accept his terms." Mrs. Vandervoort opened the small beaded bag and from it she withdrew a bank cheque. She held it out to Evelyn. "This should cover your expenses for the next few weeks."

Evelyn stood and reached across the desk. "Thank you. And please, don't concern yourself with Mr. Powell. Everything will be lovely."

Mrs. Vandervoort stood, also. The interview was at an end. "I depend on it. And on you."

"I won't fail you, Mrs. Vandervoort. You will have a wedding people will talk about for years to come."

"Bunny will be pleased. Now, I shall send you a guest list at the end of the week. You can expect a small but exclusive number. Fifty or thereabouts, including the servants."

"I shall look for it in the post." Evelyn came round from behind the desk.

"When will you leave for the abbey?"

"As soon as possible. Ten days or so. Mr. Powell led me to understand it is in substantial need of attention."

"Then I leave everything in your capable hands. And thank you for introducing me to your mother. Her style is internationally acknowledged." Mrs. Vandervoort moved to the door. Her hand on the brass doorknob, she paused. "You say Miss Molière dresses her?"

"Yes," Evelyn said enthusiastically. "She is true genius."

"Does she dress you, also?"

The question took Evelyn by surprise. "No."

"If she is as good as you say and your mother's example testifies, why not?"

Evelyn blinked. "I have never had an occasion to make use of her talents. I don't go to balls."

For a brief instant, Evelyn had the oddest feeling that Edith Vandervoort almost smiled, but the instant passed, and when the American spoke, her voice was perfectly cool. "A ball isn't the only occasion upon which a woman might wish to look her best."

Evelyn found this personal turn of conversation uncomfortable. Besides, of what possible concern could her wardrobe be to Mrs. Vandervoort? Being Evelyn, the journey from thought to vocalization was a short one. "Of what possible concern can my wardrobe be to you, Mrs. Vandervoort?"

There was no chill of reproach in Evelyn's voice, only honest curiosity, and Mrs. Vandervoort reacted accordingly. "You will be present at my wedding and its preliminary celebrations. No matter in what capacity you are there, your appearance reflects on me. I should like it to be unremarkable, and for you to be unremarkable amongst my friends, you must be dressed in the most au courant styles."

"I see." And she did. But she didn't see what she could do about it. Her family was comfortable but by no means wealthy, which was one of the reasons her aunt Agatha had gone into business in the first place. Evelyn's income did not extend to a frivolous, expensive, and unserviceable wardrobe. "I'll do my best to remain out of sight."

Mrs. Vandervoort released a little sigh of impatience. "And how much more comfortable would my friends be, Lady Evelyn, with you dodging behind potted palms whenever they entered a room? Besides, your pride would never suffer it."

"Oh?" Evelyn said a trifle stiffly.

"Come, Lady Evelyn. I see pride in you only because I'm so familiar with its company myself."

The admission surprised Evelyn. She wouldn't have thought Edith Vandervoort a perceptive woman.

"What do you suggest, then?" she asked, mindful that the pride Mrs. Vandervoort had perceived was even less likely to allow her to admit she couldn't afford such clothes.

"That we have your Merry Molière create a suitable wardrobe for you. Of course, as it is I that require you to dress in a particular manner, I assume you will add the cost of the gowns to my bill."

"I could never—"

Mrs. Vandervoort held up her hand, a shadow of impatience crossing her face. "I am not giving you a gift, Lady Evelyn. I am telling you, *as your client*, that this is what I want and expect of you, and that I am perfectly satisfied to pay for the privilege and presumption of demanding that you refurbish your wardrobe."

Mrs. Vandervoort had such a lucid way of thinking, Evelyn could not help but admire it, even though her pride disliked the conquest.

She wished fervently she knew how to accept. "You've made a very reasonable argument and you win" didn't seem proper and "You are generous and logical" sounded asinine. Ultimately she was left murmuring, "Thank you."

For the briefest instant something akin to compassion flickered in the arctic blue depths of Mrs. Vandervoort's eyes. "Good. Three day dresses, two skirts, five waists, and two—no, best make it three—evening gowns. That should do," Mrs. Vandervoort said, opening the door.

Francesca and Merry were sitting on the small divan in the outer office, their heads together in a profoundly conspiratorial manner. Doubtless, they were plotting Francesca's new autumn wardrobe.

Francesca gracefully unfolded from her seat. "And you'll keep me well apprised of how things get on?"

"You will be as if on my shoulder," Merry assured her.

"Good." Francesca smiled before turning her attention to Mrs. Vandervoort. "Ma'am, I hesitate to act on such short acquaintance, but would you care to join me for lunch?"

"Why, Marchioness," Mrs. Vandervoort said, "how kind. I'd be delighted."

# Chapter 6

NORTH CROSS ABBEY OCCUPIED A SMALL fold in the forest on the East Sussex–Surrey border. The church itself was gone except for a few skeletal arches and only the monastery still stood, expropriated long ago to the domestic purposes of the Powell family.

Looking at it, Evelyn wondered about the original opportunist who had finagled Henry VIII out of this prime piece of real estate. Now, however, time and taxes were finally having their way. The house was built roughly in the shape of a *U*, the moss-covered eastern façade housing the main entrance before which she stood.

"Isn't it lovely?" Merry breathed. "Isn't it?" she insisted, clambering down to stand beside Evelyn and staring round-eyed. Merry felt keenly that all romance was better shared. In spite of being raised by stolid Parisian parents, Merry was prodigiously impressionable. It had been her curse.

Unfortunately, Evelyn had no romantic inclinations. She eyed the structure critically. Having spent her childhood in similarly picturesque places, she had a good idea of what to expect inside: Cold and dark. Maybe mold. She studied the green base again. Definitely mold.

Still, there was no reason to disillusion Merry. She put her hands on her hips and nodded. "I am confident we'll be able to produce a wedding worthy of the Whyte name."

Though just how they were to accomplish that remained to be seen. Only a bit over thirty miles from London's outskirts, North Cross Abbey might as well have been two hundred. The area was severely depressed. For years the farming population had been migrating to the city, lured by the promise of work. She hoped Justin Powell had a decent staff—though, as the stairs were upswept and leaves piled against the outer walls, that seemed unlikely.

"Where'd you like your luggage, Miss?" Buck Newton, their driver, asked.

"That depends. Do you know whether Mr. Powell has arrived yet?"

"Aye," Buck replied.

"Ah. Good. Wait here, while I find him," she said, "and then you can bring those inside. If you'll wait with Mr. Newton, Merry?"

Merry bobbed her head and giggled, drawing

Evelyn's alarmed glance. Ever since Mr. Newton had met them at the railway station, Merry had been primping and tittering. Now Evelyn, in spite of a dearth of firsthand experience, wasn't naive. Merry was, she recognized, in the process of winning yet another "admirer." Apparently men were fatally drawn to women who acted feeble-minded.

She only hoped Merry would keep her priorities well established. But as there was nothing Evelyn could do about it now, she approached the front door, her step muffled under a layer of decaying leaves. She rapped sharply. She waited. No one answered. She rapped again.

Five minutes later, when there was still no reply, she took hold of the handle, twisted, and shoved. The door swung inward on a groan. Apparently, country habits dictated that doors remain unlocked. How charming!

" 'Allo!" Evelyn called. Her voice echoed down a dim corridor. She stepped inside. Silence, ripe and stagnant, retreated before her. Her heel struck the barren flagstone with cacophonous impatience. Something furtive scuttled in a far-off corner.

She felt her spirits fall. She could not envision a more dismal setting for a wedding party. Unless one was a ghost—*"Dear heavens!"* A dark figure in murky robes materialized before her.

"Ah, the intrepid Miss Whyte," the apparition said. "Silly me. I should have realized I needn't bother answering the door."

"You!" Evelyn gasped.

Beverly regarded her stoically. "Perhaps you'd prefer to enter through the window? I could leave one open and pretend I never saw you, if you wish."

"Evelyn!" Merry appeared breathless in the doorway, Mr. Newton hovering close behind. "*Mon Dieu!* Are you all right? I thought I heard you squeak, and . . ."

At the sight of Beverly she trailed off, looking askance at Evelyn.

"This is *him,*" Evelyn pronounced coldly.

"*Beverly* him?"

"Your servant, mademoiselle," Beverly stated dryly. "May I be so bold as to suggest that you try 'Beverly' should 'him' fail to elicit the desired response?"

"Where is Mr. Powell?" Evelyn asked haughtily, ignoring his sarcasm.

"I don't suppose 'not here' would suffice?" Beverly suggested morosely.

"No, it wouldn't."

"Well, he isn't here. He's gone."

"Where?"

"Bird-watching." He offered each ort of information as reluctantly as a glutton gives away cake.

Normally, Evelyn would have simply waited for her host's return. But the idea of sitting in this dank place under Beverly's basilisk glare was distinctly unappealing. "Which way did he go?"

"Out there." Beverly's accompanying gesture encompassed roughly one hundred and eighty degrees.

"Where out there?" Evelyn felt tension setting her jaw.

"In the woods."

"Listen, Beverly. If you—"

"Evelyn!" Merry launched herself between Evelyn and the stone-faced butler. "Perhaps we should have Mr. Newton bring our things in, and Mr. Beverly can tell him which rooms he has readied for us?"

Evelyn recovered her aplomb at once. "Capital notion, Merry. You and *him,*" she glared at the butler, "see that all's shipshape in our rooms. *After* he points out the direction in which he saw Mr. Powell go. And be advised, Beverly," she continued, "I am an accomplished woodsman. I will not get lost. I will, however, know if I am being deliberately misdirected, and your employer will hear about it if I am."

Beverly sniffed. "Madame, I resent the inference that I would deliberately conspire at your discomfort." Without awaiting a reply, he pointed. "Mr. Powell went that way."

"Thank you, Beverly," Evelyn said, gliding serenely in the opposite direction he'd indicated.

It was with decidedly piquant pleasure that she heard him mutter, "Drat!"

Evelyn had lied. She wasn't much of a woodsman. Happily, the area around North Cross Abbey wasn't much of a wood. After stumbling blindly around for half an hour, certain landmarks began to seem familiar even to her: a patch of bluebells; the beech whose doubled-up trunk reminded her of Quasimodo; a flinty shelf above the path.

She considered going back to the abbey—she was relatively certain of the direction—but ruled against it as being far too likely to delight Beverly. Instead, she took measure of her situation and began a slow, methodical sweep.

Thus she went, finally reaching the edge of the weald. The latticed dome of budding branches overhead gave way to bright sky, and a gentle slope unrolled before her like a carpet. She stopped and raised her hand, shading her eyes and scanning the dell.

Not far below, a tidy little cottage stood at the end of a primitive lane. As she watched, the door opened and a heavy-limbed man emerged, pulling on a cloth cap. Good. Perhaps he'd seen Justin, or at least could tell her how to get back to the abbey.

She raised her arm to hail him. "Yoo—!" A hand clamped over her mouth and an arm lashed around her waist, snatching her against a hard body. She struggled, and her glasses flew off as the man dragged her beneath the forest canopy.

She tried to scream, to bite him, but he was too powerful. Suddenly he dipped, caught her behind the knees, lifted her in his arms, and dumped her flat on her back on the soft forest earth. The air left her lungs in a whoosh and her hair tumbled over her face as he followed her down. Once more his hand covered her mouth—as the rest of him covered her. She could *feel* him, over her, on her, his body hard and tense.

"Quiet! He'll see you!"

She twisted frantically, trying to free her mouth. If she could just scre—She frowned. His voice had seemed familiar. She jerked her head, dislodging just enough hair to be able to see, and found herself staring up at Justin Powell.

He was so close she could see the grain of his skin, even to the pale skin behind his ears that betrayed a recent haircut. He was looking out past her, his expression fixed, his hand all but cemented in place.

"Mider Powwow, ta yo han offma me," she commanded. He glanced down and lowered his head until his lips were mere inches from her ear.

"You must promise not to make a single sound. Not one." His breath was as soft as a sigh. "Do you promise?"

She nodded, and he slipped his hand from her mouth.

"Good girl. Now lie very, very still for a moment. Just a moment more . . ."

He wasn't looking at her anymore. He'd lifted his head again, captivated by whatever it was he was studying. He groped by her side and came up with a pair of binoculars. He lifted them to his eyes. He tensed, and dramatically her attention shifted to the rest of his body.

He was *lying* on top of her. One of his legs sprawled across her thighs; the other knee was planted by her hip. His elbow was braced on the ground alongside her head to support the binoculars, and his free hand, the hand that had been clamped over her mouth, rested on her shoulder, his fingertips brushing her collarbone. He didn't appear to notice her. She wished she was similarly unaffected.

All right, she told herself, struggling to marshal her scattering thoughts. It wasn't unusual that she'd find this unsettling. After all, she'd never had such close contact with a man before. No wonder he roused—*ah*!

*Bad choice of words!*—piqued? Yes, yes, no wonder he *piqued* her interest.

And why *not* learn something from the encounter? If God provided an experience, who was she to deny it? Yes, she thought virtuously, clearly the Good Lord meant her to be lying under Justin Powell's large, hard body, soaking up knowledge.

Knowledge such as that his breath was unexpectedly sweet. That up close, his skin was clean and fine-grained. That the tips of his lashes gleamed bronze in the slanting afternoon light. That he smelled soapy and heated and living and masculine. And he was warm. He *radiated* heat. It seeped into her, as potent as a drug.

"Mr. Powell?"

Without looking, he pressed his forefinger gently over her lips. "Quiet."

The finger on her lips was lightly callused. She fought an overwhelming urge to touch it with the tip of her tongue to see if "masculine" was a taste as well as a scent. It was certainly a tactile quality, for she felt a change the instant whatever had held his attention vanished. He relaxed, no less hard, but somehow more pliant.

He lowered the binoculars and looked down at her. "Why, 'allo, Evie," he said in a tone of pleased discovery. His gaze played over her face, hesitated at her eyes, and moved to her mouth. It was interested and amused. It unnerved her, the way he looked at her mouth.

"What was it?" she asked faintly. He hadn't taken his finger from her mouth yet. The corners of her lips had begun to tingle.

"Hm?" It seemed—and she wasn't at all sure of her perceptions; everything seemed a bit confused—but it *seemed* as if his fingertip swept along her lower lip.

"Whatever you were watching. What was it?"

"Oh." His gaze sharpened. He gave her a lopsided smile before tapping her lips once and withdrawing his hand. "Lesser Bolshevikian Toadeater."

"Is it rare?"

"Rare enough in these parts," he replied, rolling away and leaping to his feet. He held out his hand and she placed hers in it. Unceremoniously, he hauled her to her feet.

He pulled her toward him, twirling her like a dancer and bringing her to a halt with her back pressed against his chest. She looked up over her shoulder at him, startled. He winked and let go of her before bending down and casually slapping the leaves and bits of grass from her skirt.

She went still as stone, astounded.

Finished, he came round the front and studied the effects of his endeavors. He put his hand under her chin and tilted her head this way and that.

"Something's different," he murmured. "Something's not..."

"My glasses," Evelyn suggested with a touch of alarm. She hadn't brought a spare pair and, while she wasn't blind, she felt naked without them.

"That's it!" He spun around, spotted them gleaming amongst the fiddleheads, and retrieved them.

She held out her hand for them, but he bypassed her hint, opening the wire bows and hooking them over her ears. He stood back, reached out, and straightened them on the bridge of her nose.

"There," he said with satisfaction. "Now I recognize you. Evie, that is you, isn't it? But what is this you're wearing? Is it a dress?"

She blinked. "Why, yes."

"Should have stuck with the knickers."

"You find something wrong with my dress?" she asked, wide-eyed.

"No, not a thing," he said. "I just thought you utterly fetching in the knickers is all. Perverse, ain't it? What is that color, anyway? Puce?"

"I don't know," she replied. "It just seemed like a good, serviceable shade. One that wouldn't show dirt."

"Being the color of dirt, you mean."

"I guess so."

"Aren't you hot under all those layers and buttons and such?"

"A little," she allowed.

His expression grew suddenly pitying. "Is this . . . do you . . . do you *like* that dress?"

*Like?* She'd never thought about *liking* a dress. One liked a friend, liked a pet, liked a child, liked a book, liked one's chances. One did not *like* a dress.

"It serves its purpose."

She glanced up and caught him regarding her strangely.

It suddenly dawned on Evelyn that *he* didn't like her dress, and that caught her very much off guard. Except for Mrs. Vandervoort, and some very occasional and very mild advice from her mother, to her knowledge no one had ever noticed anything about what she wore or how she looked. But Mr. Powell clearly thought her dress was ugly.

She felt an odd combination of emotions, a little gratification that he'd noticed her, a little embarrassment that his notice had been uncomplimentary, and a touch of affront that he was presumptuous enough to be uncomplimentary. Added to which, she was struggling against the urge to explain how silly it would be to dress in one of the lovely gowns Mrs. Vandervoort had insisted upon her having just to ride in a dusty train.

"I am sure it is most utilitarian," he said kindly.

She frowned at his patronization. He wasn't exactly a picture of sartorial splendor himself. Once more, he'd eschewed his jacket and wore a rumpled dun-colored shirt and a pair of dark, grass-stained trousers held up by brown suspenders. His hair was tousled and there was a red scratch on his hand and *why* did being unkempt look so delicious on him when it would only look slatternly on her? It wasn't fair.

"I don't design the dresses. Merry does," she explained grudgingly.

"Your aunt will be prostrate with gratitude," he said under his breath. But she'd heard him.

Her head snapped up, her momentary abashment fleeing before righteous indignation. "Is this an example of your way with words, Mr. Powell? Because if it is, I am amazed you should *ever* have had any success as a womanizer."

It was his turn to be affronted. "I could turn a pretty phrase if necessary."

He frowned. Then, as if something pleasing had

suddenly occurred to him, he announced righteously, "Besides, I told you I had reformed. Honesty, candor, and frankness are my bywords. 'The truth, blemishes and all,' is my motto. Flattery, blandishments, and sweet talk be damned."

"Hm." Her tone was far from impressed. "Are you sure you don't mean 'blunt, tactless, and brusque'? And what was that motto? 'The truth, bludgeon them with it'?"

He almost gave in to a smile; she saw it in his eyes. But then he gave her a wounded look. "I am a changed man, Evie. I thought you'd be relieved Mrs. Vandervoort's lady friends will be safe from me."

"I wasn't overly concerned," she replied dryly. "I begin to suspect that your past conquests were of unsophisticated females. The women at the Vandervoort wedding will be mature, worldly, and sophisticated."

His eyes widened. "My, Evie. That sounds awfully like a dare."

Her father often claimed she was constitutionally incapable of backing down from a challenge. She knew she ought to keep mum, to let this pitiful example of masculine posturing slide by without comment. Instead, with a faint feeling of doom, she heard herself say archly, "Did it?"

To Evelyn's heightened imagination, it seemed little copper flashes exploded in the blue-green of Justin Powell's extraordinary eyes. He smiled wolfishly and cocked his head. "Did you hear that?"

She hadn't heard a thing. "What?"

He cupped his hand around his ear. "I distinctly heard the sound of a gauntlet being thrown down."

He sketched an elegant, old-fashioned bow. "And, of course, I accept the challenge."

Dear heavens, were all men such competitive little boys at heart? she wondered, ignoring the fact that she'd deliberately goaded him. The answer was clearly "yes." And knowing that, she decided she'd best do what she could to fix the situation. "Need I remind you, Mr. Powell, that you have made a promise?"

"Ah, yes. I recall. I promised not to import or importune any guests with the purpose of—how did you so quaintly put it?—'tryst, rendezvous, criminal converse, or liaison.' I am more than willing to renew that vow."

She sighed with her relief. "Good. Now, might I suggest we return to the abbey before poor Merry sends for the local militia? I've been gone over an hour."

"Of course," he agreed pleasantly. "It's not far as the crow flies." He ushered her forward. "After you."

She smiled, pleasantly surprised by his gracious attitude, and moved ahead to a thinly marked footpath. She hadn't gone ten steps, however, when she heard him say in light, reasonable, and perfectly conversational tones, "You know, Evie, strictly speaking, there is one potential—what shall we call her? Victim? Beneficiary?—who, by the terms of my vow, is not precluded from my attention."

She should have realized he wouldn't back down so easily, not with all that male ego on the line.

"Oh?" she asked. "Who?"

"Why, Evie, you."

# Chapter 7

JUSTIN WATCHED EVELYN BOLT LIKE A RABbit up the path. In a few seconds, however, dignity overcame impulse and she settled into a half-trot, her heavy skirts sweeping the path as she launched into garbled speech, pointedly ignoring his provocative statement.

Not that he had *any* intention of seducing her. But she needn't know that.

"We must be nearing the house. I seem to recall passing these toadstools," she babbled. "I remarked them because they were such an unusual color and their gills are so deep. But perhaps all toadstools are of such a hue in this area, and all toadstool gills are equally deep. In my native county we have several varieties of toadstools, their color ranging from..."

He let her go on without interruption, reflecting

that a few more minutes of uncertainty would probably do her a world of good. He smiled. He only wished his sisters were here to see how effectively he'd rattled Evie.

Justin was not given to self-delusion. In his profession, a man needed to be certain of his strengths and equally aware of his weaknesses. Thus, while he knew a susceptibility to members of the fairer sex was *not* one of his weaknesses, he also knew that charming them was just as assuredly *not* one of his talents.

But then, he'd never tried to be a ladies' man. Men who used women were cads. So why, he asked himself thoughtfully, had it provoked him so much when she'd snickered at him? Now, there was a poser.

"... will be wondering where I am." Evelyn was still chattering frantically on. "I hope she's not too distressed, but wouldn't you be distressed if a friend of yours disappeared in an unfamiliar woods for over an hour? I would. I would be having kittens, as I very much fear Merry is. Oh! Look! There's Merry!"

Evie burst from the edge of the wood like an agitated partridge, arms flapping, skirts snapping, her thick black hair brandishing leaves and twigs. "Yoo-hoo! Darling! Here we are!"

Justin trailed her into the clearing, looking in the direction she pointed. On the back of Buck Newton's farm wagon a buxom, redheaded woman sat swinging her legs. She was not having fits. She was blushing and giggling as if she'd been named Queen of the Dairy at some county fair.

The object of all this girlish attention was shuffling

in place, crushing his soft-brimmed hat in his huge paws and swatting it against his thighs.

Evelyn, either ignoring or failing to recognize a flirtation when she saw one, raced the last ten yards and grabbed hold of the older woman's hands. "Oh, Merry! I am so sorry, darling!" she cried. "You must have been scared out of your wits! Forgive me for frightening you! I..."

She stopped. Her tinted lenses magnified the widening of her eyes. She looked like some sort of bug, what with those huge eyes and the twigs sticking out of her hair like antennae.

"Oh!" She laughed nervously. "See, Mr. Powell? I told you not to fret!"

"I never fret."

She ignored him. "And we weren't gone as long as you thought. But then, time can drag so when one is lost."

"I wasn't lost."

"Misplaced, then," she muttered.

"Perhaps you were misplaced, but I certainly—"

"Mr. Powell!" She swung around, smiling at him with determined brightness. "I don't believe I've introduced you to Miss Merry Molière, the *couturière* genius behind Whyte's Nuptial Celebrations. Merry, this is Mr. Powell, who has so graciously rented us his abbey."

"Pleased to meet you, Miss Molière," Justin said.

The redheaded woman slid off the back of the open wagon and bobbed once. "*Enchanté,* Mr. Powell."

"Did Beverly tell you which rooms we are to have?" Evie asked.

"I haven't asked him yet," Merry answered in a small voice.

"Oh? Why didn't . . . ?" Evie stopped. "Oh! Well, maybe you could ask him now?"

"I will at once," Merry agreed, and steamed off in the direction of the abbey, leaving Evie smiling uncomfortably at Buck Newton.

She was altogether unexpected, this Evelyn Cummings Whyte, thought Justin. She was so painfully unadorned. To the point where one was almost embarrassed for her, she seemed so naked.

None of the usual physical embellishments for Evie, none of the froufrous and gewgaws most women stuck to their persons, no frippery or frills or lace or bows. No enhancements of any kind to draw a chap's eye and get him to offer the sort of gallantries ladies liked. It might have been rather pitiful if one didn't realize that Evie had other weapons, potent ones, like intelligence and imagination and enterprise.

And *why,* Justin asked himself as Evie began dragging a valise toward the front door, why was he spending so much time thinking about Evelyn Cummings Whyte when—he took the valise from her without asking permission, tossed it over his shoulder, and carried it into the front hall—he had more important fish to fry? Like the pair of eelpout currently occupying the Cookes' cottage.

Yesterday, Justin had spent the afternoon chatting up the local lads at the town pub, where he'd heard the interesting news that the Cookes had rented their summer cottage to a pair of foreign brothers who'd come to partake of the fresh country air.

When Justin voiced his surprise that the Cookes had advertised their cottage for rent, he'd been quickly corrected. The Cookes hadn't advertised; they'd been approached and offered a windfall, if you like. And just where had that wind originated? Justin wanted to know.

The "brothers" could be foreign agents sent to intercept the crate being shipped to the abbey. As long as he knew where they were, they posed little danger. One of the wisest adages that fit his profession was an old one: *Keep your friends close and your enemies closer.*

Just to make sure they were staying put, each day he'd spent an hour or so in the woods "birding." Evie's arrival this afternoon had nearly betrayed his presence.

After he'd trapped her beneath him and effectively stifled her yells, he had been too distracted to pay much attention to the men he'd spent days trying to catch a glimpse of. He still couldn't explain why. Yes, he found the young woman attractive. All right, desirable.

Still, he'd experienced desire before and managed to keep his focus. But then, he'd never had the focus so formidably challenged. He could still feel her beneath him, the slender body, light, tensile, but still pliant and accommodating, the fragrance of her hair, the velvety texture of her lip under his fingertip.

When she'd stood up, he'd been surprised that something so feminine and womanly was clad in something so hideously conventional, dowdy even, not nearly as attractive as the boy's knickers and blouse she'd been wearing when she'd broken into his house.

Who'd have recognized the small, bright-eyed hoyden in this drab little wren in tinted glasses? It wasn't that he was all knowledgeable about fashion, but he did know a lot about disguise: Evelyn Cummings Whyte was definitely wearing one, and he could not help but wonder why.

And he had no *right* to wonder anything about Evelyn Cummings Whyte. He had to get on with the job at hand. He was a spy. His soul had already been spoken for. No good could come of playing games with her.

He hefted the last trunk from the wagon bed and staggered under its weight to the door. He'd apologize for twitting her as soon as an opportunity presented itself.

Physical activity had always helped Evelyn put things in perspective. By the time she, Buck Newton, and Justin Powell had unloaded the wagon, she was feeling quite herself.

Clearly, Justin had been teasing her. Since their return he'd barely glanced her way, and when he had, he looked far more contrite than predatory, which, for some reason, irritated Evelyn.

Did he regret his flirtatious banter? Because he *had* been flirting, hadn't he? *Drat.* She wished she'd more experience with those playful exchanges between the sexes that novelists celebrated.

Perhaps—an even darker thought took root—perhaps Justin Powell looked like that because he was worried *she* thought *he* was serious about pursuing her. And if he thought she took him seriously, that meant he also thought she considered herself a serious candidate for his attention, and *that* she most certainly did not.

She knew her shortcomings. She knew that she was categorically *not* the type of woman men like Justin Powell noticed. She understood quite well that he'd been having a little joke with her, and she wasn't so self-important that she couldn't join in on the fun. Ha-ha. See?

After all, she was twenty-five years old. She's been around a bit herself. Well, maybe not *herself*, but she'd been around women who'd been around. Like Merry, she thought, as the Frenchwoman emerged from the house and dimpled at Buck Newton.

Merry had been around, well, a lot. And from all appearances, it looked like she was ready to take another turn. The trouble with dear Merry was that, while she owned a Frenchwoman's passion, she had none of a Frenchwoman's practicality. It had been because of this, being so often at the mercy of an undiscriminating heart, that Merry had been expulsed from M. Worth's Parisian workrooms.

Luckily, Evelyn's mother had been in Paris acquiring a new wardrobe at the time of Merry's dismissal and, thinking of her sister-in-law's new enterprise, had snatched up the budding designer and shipped her back to London. That had been ten years ago. Since then Merry had been "in love" with a florist, a pastry chef, a draper, a haberdasher, and who knew who else.

"Did you find Beverly, Miss Molière?" Justin Powell broke Evelyn's reverie. She looked around and found Merry had approached.

"Yes," Merry said, coyly swishing her hem back and forth.

"And?" Justin prompted.

"And? Oh! And he said," Merry frowned in concentration, "he said that he didn't prepare any rooms for us because he knew that as soon as Miss Evelyn arrived she would only go snooping about and take the ones she wanted anyway."

Evelyn's skin warmed. "I suppose that as he is a legacy from your grandmother, you must keep him?" she asked Justin.

"It's kind of you to be so understanding."

"Well," she allowed, graciously letting go of the hope that Beverly would be sent packing, "I have been accused of my own set of idiosyncrasies."

"No!" Justin's face registered satisfying incredulity.

Behind her Merry snorted. There was no use asking her what was so amusing; the French had the oddest notions about humor.

Evelyn turned back to Justin. "May we have a look at the available bedchambers?"

"By all means," Justin answered. "If I might lead?"

"Please. And, Merry, could you find a place to use as a workroom while I go see about the sleeping arrangements?" She glanced at Buck. "Perhaps Mr. Newton might be persuaded to wait and, once you find a place, take your things there?"

"Oh, aye, ma'am," Buck agreed. "Pleased to oblige."

"Splendid." She turned. "I am ready, Mr. Powell."

He led the way into a corridor where the dust had been collecting for years. Dust motes climbed and swirled in the thin light as they walked and Evelyn carefully took stock of the abbey.

They passed what looked like a library of sorts on their left, while on their right was a closed door. They continued down the hall, past various disreputable-looking rooms, Justin explaining that this corridor contained the public rooms and the opposite side contained the sleeping chambers.

Near the end of the hall he pointed to a corridor that led to the other wing. They proceeded a short way and he turned and led the way down a few wide, shallow steps into a tall, cavernous room that he called the great room. It had once been the monastery dining hall, he told her. Evelyn looked around, trying to imagine a wedding reception here.

It was bright but grimy and drafty, clusters of mismatched furniture standing on threadbare carpets. On one side, wide French doors looked out on a dilapidated courtyard and weed-filled fishpond. Evelyn craned her head and looked up. Dark beams crisscrossed the vaulted ceiling like a fat spider web.

It was going to be hell to clean.

"Can we find women to come in?" she asked.

"I should imagine so, though I've never asked."

She bit back the word "obviously."

"Economy's so rotten, I wouldn't be surprised if even some of the chaps hire out for cleaning as well."

"Good." She picked up an ancient, dented helmet

resting near her feet and wrinkled her nose when she discovered a pile of cigar stubs in it. "What do you call the decor? Early Draconian?"

He smiled. "The rest of the place isn't quite so bad. It's been strictly bachelor quarters since I inherited it a few years back and before that, well, the General wasn't keen on spending money."

She tried to look reassured.

"Everything considered, I should say the best course would be to keep the lighting as low as possible," he suggested helpfully.

"Oh, Lord," she murmured.

"It was an abbey," he said a trifle defensively. "They were *supposed* to lead simple, cloistered lives, which means simple quarters and great, plain common rooms."

"Why ever would your ancestors want to make such a place their home?"

He grinned disingenuously. "It was free, given to my ancestor for his faithful service to Queen Bess. My maternal line's motto is: *Never pay for what one can get gratis*. I believe it's actually written somewhere on the family crest."

"And is your family very political?" she asked curiously as he started into the room.

"Only when we feel threatened. Then we howl 'King and Country' with the best of them. Ergo North Cross Abbey."

"If it's as unappealing as you suggest, and I've yet to see anything which contradicts you, it doesn't seem much of a reward for a good and faithful servant."

"Perhaps the service wasn't so good, or the servant

so faithful," he said cheerfully. "Incurably lazy lot, my family. Not to mention opportunistic and predisposed toward artful behavior." There was a touch of pride in his voice.

"I suppose I ought to thank you for yet another warning."

"Warning?" He stopped so abruptly she plowed into him. He caught her elbow, steadying her. The moment he touched her, she had a distinct physical memory of his fingertips brushing the side of her breast.

"Listen, Evie—"

"Evelyn," she corrected him faintly. He was standing too close. She had to tilt her head up to see him and it felt bizarrely as though she were lifting her mouth for a kiss. She flushed at the notion and dropped her chin.

"About what I said earlier..." He scowled, and in the dim hallway his features looked angular and severe. "About pursuing you. I apologize."

"Apologize?" He had a beautiful mouth, long and chiseled looking, the bottom lip deep and full.

"I would *never* press my attentions on you."

"You wouldn't?" His words slowly penetrated. "No. Of course you wouldn't! You were teasing. I know that."

She flushed hotly. Justin must have sensed what she'd been thinking and was desperate to dispel the notion.

True to her suspicion, he breathed a sigh of relief. "You're a sensible woman, Evie."

His fingers dropped from her elbow. She smiled,

trying to look sensible, which shouldn't have been that hard, because she *was* sensible. Sensible, smart, good at everything she laid her hand to—except planning weddings. Because weddings were about love.

*Pull yourself together, Evelyn! You have work to do here and you can't afford to spend the days dodging Justin Powell.*

"What an ass you must take me for," Justin said.

He put one hand flat against the wall at her head level, and leaned against it, subtly hemming her in, looking down into her eyes, smiling pleasantly. His shirt stretched tightly across his broad shoulders, the rolled-up sleeves pulling farther up his arms, exposing the start of a bulging biceps muscle. Careless, cavalier, no sense of decorum.

And fascinatingly, casually, extraordinarily, unconsciously masculine.

"Imagine me, flattering myself that you'd take me seriously." He said. "Can you forgive me?"

But whatever he was, he was also truly a gentleman, Evelyn thought with bittersweet admiration. With a few words, he took the onus off her.

"I don't see that there's anything to forgive," she replied, and hurried away.

# Chapter 8

EVELYN WATCHED AS JUSTIN DREW A diagram in the thick dust that had settled on the library table. It took a concerted effort, but in three weeks Evelyn had not only forgiven Justin for teasing her but had vanquished the unfortunate incident from her mind. In the interim she'd discovered that a reformed "wolf" was not such a difficult friend as one might have imagined. In fact, he was quite an easy man to have around . . . *when* he was around.

Most days he went off "birding," sometimes not returning until late in the day. Not that she was keeping track of his comings and goings, but when one lived in the same house with another person, that person's presence or absence was bound to be noted. And with Merry diplomatically dividing her free hours between Buck Newton and another local man, well, Evelyn was a bit at loose ends when she wasn't working. It was only natural that she should look forward to her time with Justin. As a friend, of course. Nothing more.

How could there be more? He was a confirmed bachelor, having renounced the pleasures of illicit relationships, while she was a confirmed spinster, doomed never to know such pleasures, licit or il-.

"There. Perhaps now you see what I mean," Justin said, sitting back in his seat and waving his hand at the diagram.

Evelyn slid her chair closer to his. "*But* if they'd posted their men like so," she dotted in some men, "and come down the field thus," she traced a thin arc, "they would have carried the day."

"My dear Evie." For some reason, Justin called her his "dear Evie"—she'd quite given up trying to get him to call her Evelyn or, God forbid, Lady Evelyn—whenever he pontificated on a subject he considered solely a male province. There were a lot of them. "You are wrong."

He covered her hand with his own and, using her finger as his stylus, sketched a fat line straight through the middle of the impromptu map. That was his manner; he was utterly insensible of personal boundaries. If Justin had need of a finger, he was as likely to co-opt hers as use his own. It was an uncomfortably intimate sort of thing—uncomfortable for her, that is. He didn't appear to realize anything untoward in it.

"And *that* is why," he was saying, "the men on the left flank kept them from doing so."

With a smile as kindly as it was annoying, he dug a

handkerchief out of his trouser pocket and dabbed her finger clean before returning it to her.

She, however, was not done. "Not if these men," she said, pointing, "had secured the area. With the opposition's attention diverted, the center could have advanced."

He shook his head. "Impossible. They weren't strong enough to clear the center."

She drew a deep breath. "If they had used their heads rather than their—"

"Ahem." They both looked up. Beverly stood over them, looking annoyed. "Perhaps I misheard your directions, but I was under the distinct impression that you wish this room cleaned. All of it."

Evelyn looked around, surprised to find that while she and Justin had been debating, the library had filled with an army of workers. A pair of girls were scrubbing the floor, chatting amiably to one another, while three men fitted new panes of glass into the mullioned windows; overhead, a plasterer worked diligently on the coved ceiling. She'd been so absorbed with Justin she hadn't noticed them come in.

"Forgive me, Lady Evelyn," Beverly drawled as she stared about in bemusement. "Clearly I slipped into a foreign language for a moment. Let me repeat my question."

Beverly's gibe awoke her from muteness. "Yes, I asked you to have this room cleaned."

"And might I suppose that edict included this table? Or is the grime on it part of the intriguing 'Midsummer Night's Folly' decor?"

The man was an incorrigible troll. Evelyn glanced

at her timepiece. Gads, she'd been here an hour. She stood. Justin rocked his chair onto its back legs and hung a long arm over the back of it.

"I am sorry to inconvenience you," she told Beverly.

Justin's mouth curled with amusement. Let him be amused. She would have given Beverly a handwritten apology to keep him at his job. There were plenty of people willing to work and work hard, but finding someone capable of organizing all that energy into productivity had been another task altogether.

She'd asked Justin for the loan of his butler after witnessing Beverly grab his chest in horror when one of the workmen had dropped a dingy old ginger jar Beverly later claimed had been a Ming dynasty vase. Justin had obliged, ordering Beverly to submit to her direction.

Beverly had acceded, assuring Justin that he was not only qualified to perform the task but indubitably more qualified then anyone else present. He'd been looking straight at her when he said it.

To do him credit, he'd done a wonderful job, coordinating the workers into a smoothly oiled engine that rolled doggedly from one end of the abbey toward the other, leaving in its wake a series of clean rooms.

All in all, everything was going swimmingly. The abbey was quickly being repainted, replastered, and repaired; the various trim and trappings for the wedding were being assembled; supplies were arriving daily.

"Mr. Powell and I will get out of your way at once. We were just going anyway, weren't we?" Evelyn gave Justin an encouraging smile.

"Dear me, yes," he agreed, standing up, and then adding, "Remind me. Where were we just going?"

"I'm going to town to fetch the ribbons Merry ordered," Evelyn said, "and *you* were going to look for birds."

"So I was." He plucked his jacket from the back of the chair and shrugged into it. "But before I go . . ."

"Yes?"

"The Marlborough rugby team would have lost the Nationals no matter what strategy they employed. And that's the end of the matter." With that pronouncement, he strolled off, before she could frame a reply, leaving her stifling a laugh she knew would only encourage his hubris. She watched him with unwilling admiration.

He'd donned his "birding jacket," a wrinkled and disreputable-looking tweed, so he must have been planning to go out before he'd stumbled upon her ordering the removal of debris from the entrance's circular drive.

Not that he ever looked appreciably different dressed for birding than he did for dining. Apparently, he didn't own a pair of cufflinks, for his sleeves seemed to be perennially rolled up over his forearms. He seldom bothered wearing a tie, or buttoning his collar, or sometimes even putting on a collar, for that matter.

She might be dowdy, but at least she was a neat dowd.

"Lady Evelyn, if I might have a word?" Beverly said.

"But of course, Beverly," she replied with an inappropriate sense of anticipation. Trading barbs with

Beverly had become one of her daily pleasures. And Beverly's baggy little eyes were positively twinkling. "What is it? You feel the siren pull of a magnum of Lafite-Rothschild and wish to abdicate your current responsibilities in order to pursue it?" she asked.

"Not at all, madame," Beverly said smoothly. "I am simply on tenterhooks to see if you approve my choices in the main corridor."

She followed him out into the hall, stood, and looked about admiringly. Overhead—miracle of miracles—Beverly had discovered a skylight so choked with leaves and mold it had gone unnoticed for years. Now it glistened, pouring sunlight down on a brilliant antique Oriental runner he'd found rolled up in the cellar. On the freshly waxed sideboard, shaggy-headed parrot tulips amassed in a huge silver urn. A series of paintings he'd discovered in a closet hung sentinel on the freshly painted walls. "It looks fine, Beverly."

"I grow faint at such praise."

"Don't let it go to your head. We still have, what? Another six rooms to ready before the wedding guests arrive?"

"Yes," Beverly replied. "*We* have six rooms left to arrange. After which *we* will have to make haste to see that the kitchen is well stocked for the arrival of *our* chef."

She smiled winsomely. "I'm delighted you've come on board so enthusiastically, Beverly."

He was such an unbridled wretch, but such fun to trade unpleasantries with. No wonder Justin kept him around. The thought brought with it curiosity.

"Beverly?" she said.

"Lady Evelyn."

"Are you a confirmed misogynist or am I special?"

His smile was sublime. "My appreciation of the fairer sex is universal, madame."

"Mr. Powell must find it rather disconcerting to have such a confirmed woman-hater about," she said, "being a ladies' man and all."

"Mr. Powell? A ladies' man?" He snorted.

Why should that phrase provoke such a reaction? But then Evelyn recalled that Justin had reformed. Perhaps he'd reformed before taking Beverly into his employ.

"Perhaps I should have said 'having *been* a ladies' man.' Didn't you know?"

Beverly stiffened. "I have been in Mr. Powell's service since he entered the army fourteen years ago."

She frowned, doing the math. It didn't add up. She'd caught Justin with Mrs. Underhill a mere decade ago. But then, whatever Beverly's faults—and they were many—he was extremely loyal.

"Mr. Powell comes from a military family on both sides of his family, doesn't he?" she asked, fully aware she was being nosey, but unable to let an opportunity to learn more about Justin go by.

"Yes, indeed." A hint of pride had crept into Beverly's usual ironic tones. "Mr. Powell's maternal grandfather was with Wolseley in Africa, and his father saw action in India."

She would have been in the army if she'd been born a male. The adventure, the danger, the excitement, and the opportunity to organize all sorts of people under her command would have been just her forte.

"I'm surprised Mr. Powell didn't pursue his career." She thought of Justin. He could barely stand to correct his butler, let alone a stranger. Besides, with his hair in permanent disarray and his ill-fitting jacket askew, he was hardly a model for those popular "war hero" cigarette cards. "On second thought, maybe I'm not surprised," she said. "I suppose his grandfather and father were disappointed when he cashiered out.

"My uncle Hugo was a military man. Thought the sun rose and set on his regiment. He was stiff with pride." Evelyn smiled. "Only thing that could have made him prouder would have been if he'd had a son to enlist, too. Though cousin Mary Elizabeth could have easily passed as..." She trailed off. Beverly's usual bland countenance had turned grim.

"What is it?" she asked.

"Nothing, ma'am."

"Out with it, Beverly. Why are your eyes growing bloodshot?"

"I don't know what you're talking about, Lady Evelyn."

She sighed heavily, as one would when challenged by a recalcitrant four-year-old. "You know what I'm capable of."

"I recall, yes."

"You know I will badger you until I have an answer. You know how persistent I am when I want something."

"Unhappily, yes."

"Then don't you think you ought to just give over graciously and be done with it?"

He vacillated. She could see it in the minute shift of his eyes. She pressed on. "Something to do with Mr. Powell's grandparent and the army. What of it?"

"It's the injustice of it is all." The words burst from between his compressed lips, his virulence catching her off guard. "It's so unfair. The old ba—goat had no idea what was what."

"Yes?" she prompted softly. This was not simply the verbal scrimmages she and Beverly usually engaged in. For the first time, Beverly was speaking sincerely to her.

"Eleven years ago, at the family Christmas celebration, Mr. Powell announced he was leaving the army," Beverly said. "The Brigadier General didn't even wait for him to finishing speaking before standing and declaring that he would rather Mr. Powell had died in Africa than live a coward. He never spoke to Mr. Powell again."

Evelyn stared, stricken. To be called a coward in front of your entire family . . . ! "How horrible."

Beverly's eyes shifted. "I am sorry I spoke. I have been indiscreet. Mr. Powell would be most annoyed. I only told you this because you seem to have an empathy with him."

"Did they never reconcile? No? How terrible. How he must hurt," Evelyn said, shaking her head.

"Pray do not concern yourself. Mr. Powell is not the sort to waste time looking back, is he? And he's made of sterner stuff than to allow his grandfather's blustering bigotry to ruin his life. Besides, it's a long time ago. A lifetime."

She smiled sadly and, for a fraction of a second, Beverly returned it. Then he cleared his throat.

"Now, if you are entirely finished with the interrogation, Lady Evelyn, perhaps you'd let me return to my work?" He didn't wait for a dismissal before hastening off.

She followed him at a more sedate pace, wondering if it was possible Justin really hadn't given a rap for the Brigadier General's opinion. It was an interesting thought.

Evelyn had spent her entire life enjoying the approval, deference, and esteem of her entire family. If that were to be taken away, what would she have left?

A little frisson of panic speared through her at the very thought. It wasn't *going* to be taken away. She wasn't *going* to fail. Not her family name, not her aunt, not Mrs. Vandervoort. Things were going exceedingly well.

Calming herself, she ducked into the great hall and appreciatively studied the work being done in the courtyard. The weeds had all been dug up and the flagstones scoured clean. The romantic moss creeping up the stone urns had been allowed to remain and the small, stagnant fishpond was being cleaned out and restocked with large goldfish. A few gardeners were busily nesting flowering plants into crevices while a diminutive latticed and arched bridge was being erected over the pool, the center topped by a tiny, intricately wrought gazebo.

It would be a wonderful. It would be a success.

"The gray worsted, again?" Merry hailed her from the French doors. Evelyn turned.

Thank heavens, whatever her personal susceptibilities, Merry had a magnified sense of duty. She had not only completed Mrs. Vandervoort's wedding dress but was almost finished with the veil. Yesterday the plush satin for the table bunting had arrived ahead of schedule, albeit a bit wrinkled—Justin had admitted he opened it, mistaking it for something or other he was expecting.

"Merry," Evelyn said, ignoring her question, "I am going to bicycle into town. Can I get you anything?"

"Another five hundred straight pins."

"Lovely. I'll be back in an hour or so."

"Take your time, Evelyn. You've earned yourself a bit of a holiday," Merry called, watching Evelyn leave.

Merry went back to her workroom and sat on her stool, still shaking her head with Gallic mournfulness. "If only she would put on one of the dresses I made . . ."

"Aye?" Buck asked, entering with his arms piled full of bolts of materials. He deposited them and wandered over to where she sat.

"Lady Evelyn. Poor pigeon. You would not think it to look at her now, but in my creations . . ." Merry paused and kissed her fingertips, her eyelids swooning shut with self-congratulation.

"I'm sure she'd be a treat."

"Treat." Merry pronounced the word with distaste. "She could be more than a 'treat.' She could be a lover." She looked at Buck thoughtfully. "You have not failed to see how very taken she is with the unkempt Mr. Powell."

Actually, Buck hadn't noticed but he didn't want to admit that to Miss Merry. "Oh, aye. Poor puss."

"She doesn't need those hideous tinted spectacles she wears, you know," Merry revealed.

"Go on," he said, trying to sound suitably impressed. "Then why does she wear them?"

"She says she feels naked without them. Oh!" She covered her mouth with her hand and giggled. "I have used a not nice word."

"No matter," he said gruffly.

Merry set down the piece of satin she'd been working on and peered up at him. "She hasn't any notion of how to attract Mr. Powell's notice. Why, the little goose acts like she thinks a man wants a friend or someone to trade *sallies* with." Her face scrunched up in repugnance. "But what to do about it? What to do?"

Buck nodded, though he wasn't listening very carefully. Merry had twisted on the stool and the motion had rucked her skirts up, revealing a neat pair of ankles.

"A man wants someone he can be proud to have on his arm," Merry mused. "Not someone he always has to be on his toes around, because she's that sharp-witted."

She regarded him seriously with her big brown eyes. “Don’t you agree, Mr. Newton?”

“I do, indeed, Miss Merry.” He bent over and kissed her.

And, for the next hour or so, all conversation stopped.

# Chapter 9

EVELYN STOOD ON HER BICYCLE PEDALS and took off down the drive, heading for Henley Wells. Though she half expected to see Justin stomping around in the shrubbery, other than a pair of placid cows lifting their heads to watch her sail by, Evelyn had the road to herself. It was a glorious afternoon for a ride. The apple orchard was in full bloom, scenting the brisk spring air, while overhead grand heaps of white clouds sailed sublimely through a cerulean ocean.

She loved cycling: skimming along above the earth under her own power, her legs pumping the pedals, her body canted above the handlebars, the sound of her bonnet ribbons rippling behind her. All too soon, the lane curved around a hill and dropped into Henley Wells.

She parked her bicycle in front of the dry-goods store and righted her bonnet before entering. A few minutes later, she returned with a paper parcel. She'd just secured it to the front fender of her bicycle and was about to start back when the train station's portly manager, Mr. Silsby, stepped out of his office and hailed her.

"Lady Evelyn! A moment, if you please!"

Curiously, she walked her bicycle across the road.

"Thank you," Mr. Silsby greeted her, mopping at his face with a bright paisley handkerchief. "Glad I am to have caught you, Lady Evelyn. The afternoon train came in late today and delivered four crates for you. Leastwise I think they're for you. I'm not rightly sure."

"I don't take your meaning."

"Well, they be addressed to North Cross Abbey but they don't have any name posted anywhere on them."

"Perhaps they're Mr. Powell's?"

"Nah." Mr. Silsby tucked the handkerchief in his jacket pocket. "Anything comes for Mr. Powell, it says 'Mr. Powell' on it."

"Maybe there's been some mistake," she suggested as the station door opened and a stocky, pleasant-looking blond man wearing a trilby hat emerged.

"The label is as clear as day," Mr. Silsby said. "And you're the only one what's been getting crates and such."

"But I've already received everything I've ordered thus far, and I only telegrammed in my latest orders yesterday afternoon. They couldn't possibly be shipped so quickly."

The man in the trilby hovered nearby, waiting patiently.

Mr. Silsby shrugged. "I don't know what to tell you. But these have the abbey address posted on them and that's where they need to go. Here. Take a look, why don't you?"

"All right," she agreed. The blond man leapt forward to hold the door open for her, drawing Mr. Silsby's attention. "Oh, Mr. Blumfield. I got your shipment inside. If you can just wait for a few minutes, I'll have you sign for it."

"Please," Mr. Blumfield agreed. "You must, of course, see to this young lady first."

A foreign accent flavored his speech. Evelyn smiled at his excellent manners as he doffed his hat to her, thinking that Justin might have retained at least *some* of the more charming aspects of a Don Juan. Not that this young man seemed in the least bit slick. He looked shy and eager. Which was very nice.

She preceded both men into the station, where four square crates stood stacked against the wall. Beyond these was a tall wooden box.

"There's your order, Mr. Blumfield," Mr. Silsby said, nodding toward the wooden box and pointing to a large flat label on top of one of the crates. "See, Lady Evelyn? Clear as day. North Cross Abbey, Henley Wells, East Sussex."

"Well, they're not mine, so I suppose they must belong to Mr. Powell. He'll have to send someone back for them."

The manager pulled out his pocket watch and

tapped the face significantly. "That's the problem. Mr. Powell has left explicit instructions that if anything, and he said *anything,* arrived addressed to him I was to straight off send someone to fetch either him or Beverly. Now, this ain't addressed to him, but you say it ain't yours, and the station's closing in half an hour."

"Tomorrow, then."

"Have to wait 'til Monday, I'm afraid. I'm taking my wife to see her mum tomorrow, and the next day be Sunday."

She hoped Justin didn't need whatever these crates contained. She hesitated. "Perhaps you could stay open a bit later today?"

"My Elsie'd have my skin. Today's Friday." At her flummoxed expression he explained. "Sausage day."

Heaven forbid that she should come between a man and his sausage, Evelyn thought, eyeing the manager's girth.

"Excuse me."

Evelyn and the manager looked around. Mr. Blumfield had taken off his hat again and was turning it by the brim in his hands. "I cannot help but overhear that perhaps the young lady is in some difficulty?"

"No. Just a spot of inconvenience, is all."

"It has to do with transporting these crates?" he asked.

"Yes."

"But I can remedy!" His smile transformed his ordinary features. "I have a wagon, by which means I will transport my own shipment. I would be most honored if you allowed me to be of assistance."

"You are very kind, but I couldn't impose on you."

"But it is no imposition. Perhaps you hesitate because we are not properly introduced? Then let us remedy this. I am Ernst Blumfield, who has, with my brother Gregory, rented the Cookes' charming cottage. And you are Lady Evelyn Cummings Whyte of North Cross Abbey."

"How did you know that?" she asked.

His gaze fell to the floor, disarming her. "Because I have seen you, Lady Evelyn, sometimes when I am walking by the abbey, and I made so bold as to inquire."

He looked up, as eager to please as a spaniel pup. "So you see it will be my very great pleasure to offer you this small aid." He glanced at the stacked crates. "Though I fear my wagon is not sufficient to hold all of these. Two, perhaps. But there will be room for your bicycle, too."

"If you're sure it won't be too much trouble?"

"Not at all." Ernst Blumfield's face lit with delight. He replaced his hat. "If you please, Mr. Silsby, will you have these loaded into my vehicle?"

"Aye." The manager pulled open the door and shouted that he had a quid's worth of loading to do. A minute later two teenage boys slunk into the office, looking about warily, as if the odds of their being in trouble were about as likely as their being hired.

While they loaded the wagon, Ernst picked up her bicycle and stowed it behind the seat. Then, bowing, he gestured for her to precede him.

He had a lovely way about him, so respectful and

modest. And while his dress was inconspicuous, it was well cut and the fabric good.

He assisted her into the seat and climbed in after her, visually checking the arrangement of the articles in the back. Then he clucked to the pony and they were off.

"It is a most beautiful day for bicycling," he said after a few minutes. "I, too, am an enthusiast. In fact, the box in the back contains my newest acquisition, which is a bicycle."

"Really?" she asked.

He nodded excitedly.

"Well, then, I would be most interested in hearing just what manufacturer you chose. I am considering the purchase of a new machine, myself."

He smiled again, quite clearly tickled that she wanted his opinion. "I would be pleased to be of whatever service I can. You have simply but to ask."

"Ah. Then let me begin. Is it an American machine? Because I have heard that..."

The drive back to the abbey went quickly. Ernst was quite scholarly on the subject of bicycles and had done a good bit of research before committing to the purchase of a Dursley Pederson machine that she was simply dying to see. Not only was it the newest thing in bicycle manufacturing, but it cost a small fortune.

They were still discussing the pros and cons of his new bicycle's triangulated tubing construction when they arrived at the abbey. Ernst reined in the pony. "We are here."

"So we are," Evelyn said.

He climbed down out of the carriage and looked around. There was no convenient place to tie the pony. "If you would kindly wait with the beast, I shall go find some men to unload these things."

"Of course." She picked up the reins, though she seriously doubted whether the pony, who stood head down, desultorily swishing its tail, was thinking of bolting.

Idly, she flicked the reins back and forth across her lap, chasing an annoying fly. She wondered if she would be too bold if she asked Mr. Blumfield if, after he'd unpacked his bicycle, she might come by and see—

"Plotting the overthrow of some nation?"

Startled, she looked around. Justin had emerged from the edge of the forest. His jacket was slung over his shoulder, and his binoculars swung from a strap around his neck.

"Oh. Hello, Justin."

" 'Allo, Evie." He walked to her side of the carriage and took the reins from her hand, wrapping them around the brake. "Want out of there?"

She nodded absently and stood, reaching down to place her hands on Justin's broad shoulders. He was warm under the white shirt, and the sun-toasted scent of bleached linen rose like perfume, bright and pleasant. He put his hands around her waist and lifted her straight off her feet, holding her aloft as he looked around for a likely spot to deposit her.

She waited, suspended in midair.

He'd done it before, picked her up when a simple

hand to offer balance would have sufficed. Knowing him as she now did, she believed he did that sort of thing because he just didn't see the difference between a friendly hand and this far more substantial effort. He really was, as her mother had suggested a few weeks ago, a bit oblivious.

At first she'd been a shade uncomfortable with such physical familiarity. But it soon became clear it was only his way, like the laxity of his dress, the rumpled locks, the easygoing manner. If she were to resist his friendly overtures, she'd look a silly, prudish spinster.

And as for holding her aloft, well, in spite of his lackadaisical manner, Justin was an extremely fit man. He walked to the edge of the grass and set her on her feet. He peered down into her face.

"What?" she said, touching her cheek and wondering if she'd driven with Mr. Blumfield all the way from Henley Wells with a smudge on it. "What!"

He moved closer, bending so that he was eye level with her. His breath was warm on her mouth, and sweet. He'd been chewing mint leaves. "Is that dirt on your nose, or are they freckles?"

"I do *not* have freckles."

He laughed at her huff of indignation. His eyes danced, his smile broadened. He adored teasing her.

"Lady Evelyn?" Mr. Blumfield's voice startled her. She'd forgotten him.

"Here I am, Mr. Blumfield," she called cheerily. She had to stand on tiptoe to look over Justin's shoulders. She waved. Justin went quite still.

"Ah! My dear Lady Evelyn, I was worrying that perhaps I had imagined our delightful drive, and that you were but a happy figment of my imagination," he said, his tone jocular.

"Mr. Blumfield?" Justin whispered, his back to Ernst. "Now, where did you find Mr. Blumfield? And however did you manage in so short a time to become *his* dear Lady Evelyn?"

Smiling determinedly over his shoulder, she said between her teeth, "Behave!"

Mr. Blumfield was coming toward them, a tentative smile on his face, as though he were uncertain of his welcome. Behind him, a man began unloading the cart.

"I am. That's the problem, damn it," Justin replied with a hint of frustration before turning. He eyed Ernst pleasantly enough, but Evelyn wasn't comfortable. There was something *off* about the way Justin regarded him.

He looked rumpled and mild enough, and yet Evelyn could not get rid of an impression of—she grappled with a word to express what she sensed—danger. He didn't *look* dangerous; he *felt* dangerous.

Which was totally and completely mad. Justin Powell was the least dangerous man she knew. He was an ornithologist, for heaven's sake. And oblivious, nonchalant, bohemian. A one-time ladies' man who'd most likely given up the endeavor as being too strenuous.

Dangerous, indeed! She was going to have to stop reading those penny dreadfuls she'd found in the library.

"Justin, this is your neighbor, Mr. Ernst Blumfield,"

she said. "He generously offered me, and these crates," she pointed at the boxes, "a ride home."

"Did he, now?" Justin asked.

"Yes, and a good thing, too. Mr. Silsby has closed the office for the next few days. As it is, there are two more crates still down there. But they'll have to wait until Monday now to be fetched."

"Did you need them, Evie?"

"I don't think they're mine," she admitted. Nothing in his manner or expression changed, but she could have sworn her words startled Justin. "I thought they might be yours."

He shrugged. "Doubtful. Unless... One of them might be some taxidermy equipment I ordered. Fancy it's getting here so soon. I guess I owe you my thanks, Mr. Blumfield—"

"Taxidermy equipment!" Evelyn gasped. "Justin Powell, if you think I've had this abbey scrubbed top to bottom so you can fill it with the vile scent of chemicals—"

"Please, Evie," he said, holding his hand up and shooting an apologetic look at Ernst, "not in front of the *kinder*. Besides," he added, "there are no chemicals."

She breathed a sigh of relief before noting the look of confusion on Ernst's face. She forged on with introductions. "Mr. Blumfield and his brother have rented the next cottage down. Regrettably, his brother is unwell. It was suggested that the cool, damp evenings and warm days of the countryside might aid his recovery."

"Ah! Jolly damp nights, jolly warm days," Justin said, nodding wisely. Evelyn could have throttled him.

"Mr. Blumfield, this is Justin Powell. He owns the abbey."

Ernst stuck his hand out and Justin shook it. "I am so pleased to finally make your acquaintance, Mr. Powell. You are spoken of most highly in Henley Wells."

"As well I should be," Justin replied lazily. "The local scoundrels at the pub tap me for a round of drinks every time I venture into town."

Ernst blushed, unused to Justin's odd humor. "No, no," he demurred. "Everyone says only good of you, sir. The Powell family is most august. Most respected."

"You must have been chatting the lads up *after* closing time, when they were feeling all friendly and congenial," Justin commented.

"Chatting up? I am unsure of your meaning," Ernst replied, looking to Evelyn for guidance.

"He's being tiresome. Ignore him. He doesn't mean any harm," Evelyn explained. "He fondly imagines that by rebutting any suggestion his family is respected, he might be perceived as modest. Despite appearances," she shot a telling glance at the open throat of Justin's shirt, the rolled-up sleeves, and the scuffed shoes, "he has a most lofty opinion of himself."

During the course of Evelyn's explanation, Justin had leaned against the wagon and was smiling at her encouragingly. Poor Ernst only looked more and more confounded. He glanced appealingly at Justin.

"She knows me too well," Justin admitted cheerfully.

"You are maybe her brother?"

"Good God, no!" Justin burst out, causing a sharp

jab of pain somewhere in the vicinity of Evelyn's... pride.

"No, no," she added her voice to his denial. He looked at her strangely.

"I did not *think* so," Ernst said. "But when I saw how—"

"How cavalier I was with her, you imagined that the relationship was fraternal?" Justin suggested mildly.

"Yes. That's correct," Ernst replied.

"No. No blood relation at all," Justin said with odd emphasis.

Evelyn felt a betraying burn race up her throat. Impossible to pretend she didn't understand. "Ha! It is purely a business relationship."

It dawned on her how this must look to an old-fashioned gentleman like Ernst Blumfield. "And, of course, I am chaperoned," she ended, demurely dropping her gaze.

"You are?" Justin asked incredulously, making Evelyn want to strangle him. "By whom?

"Merry," she said tautly.

"Oh. Merry. Didn't realize she was the chaperon. From the goings-on I've witnessed between her and Buck, I'd say she's the least—"

"Ha, ha," Evelyn interrupted, forcing a laugh. "Mr. Powell is a great tease."

"Not I. Now, *Merry*..."

She turned her back on him, her skirts snapping. Securing Mr. Blumfield's arm, she dragged him away from Justin and whatever other horrible, indiscreet things he'd been about to say.

Ernst beamed. "Lady Evelyn, perhaps you might do me the honor of coming to our cottage tomorrow afternoon that I might show you the bicycle?"

"Without a chaperon?" Justin asked from close behind. The scoundrel was following them! "I shouldn't think that would be bloody likely."

Ernst turned beet-red and Evelyn swung around, mortified that Justin should have embarrassed Mr. Blumfield. "*You* have a very nasty mind," she said. She turned back to Ernst. "I was hoping you would ask, Mr. Blumfield."

But Ernst wasn't looking at her, he was gazing penitently at Justin. "I have made a terrible faux pas. My ignorance is unforgivable. Of course, she must not come unescorted. You are right to protect her reputation."

"You meant no harm," Justin proclaimed magnanimously. It was too much.

"Just when," Evelyn said to Ernst in the calm, careful tones that would have alerted her family to a brewing storm, "did you first perceive that I had lost my reasoning abilities?"

Ernst stared at her, round-eyed. "Lady Evelyn?"

"Because clearly something must have alerted you to the fact that I am incapable of making decisions for myself and thus must rely on another."

"I . . . I . . ." Clearly, Ernst's mastery of the language did not extend to sarcasm. He looked at her, unhappily detecting that she was angry. "May I ride the bicycle *here* tomorrow, perhaps?"

"Oh!" She gave up being angry. It did little good when one was dealing with children; apparently the same was true of men. "Fine. Ride it over here. I shouldn't take much time away from the bridal preparations, anyway."

Justin smirked. Ernst breathed a deep, heartfelt sigh of relief. "Good. I look forward to it, so much. And now, my brother awaits me. It is a pleasure to make your acquaintance, Mr. Powell." He bowed formally.

Justin touched two fingers to his brow in a mock salute. Evelyn wanted to shake him and was so busy envisioning it that she was startled when Ernst suddenly clasped both her hands and lifted them, clasping them to his chest.

"Until tomorrow then, Lady Evelyn. I bid you adieu." He gave her hands a little squeeze.

"Huh? Oh. Yes." She smiled. "Adieu."

He didn't let her hands go, but stood gazing into her eyes. "I am so glad we met."

"Me, too."

"I wish my brother could meet you. He would find you as charming as I."

"That would be the brother that's waiting?" Justin asked loudly.

"Yes. Gregory. I am reminded he awaits." Ernst released her hands. "Until then."

He climbed aboard, snapped the reins lightly, and waved. "Good-bye!"

"Good-bye!" Evelyn said, waving back.

Justin stepped away from the wagon and lifted a hand in farewell. "Must be Prussian," he muttered out of the side of his mouth, watching the cart disappear.

"Now, why do you say that?" Evelyn asked, turning to him, her hands on her hips.

"They never leave until they've said good-bye at least half a dozen times. Must be a national trait." He screwed his face up, clearly in love with the idea. "In fact, if you consider it in that light, Mr. Blumfield's reluctance to be the first to turn around might be culturally ingrained."

He'd piqued her curiosity. "And why would that be?"

He grinned, gratified. "Quite simple. A matter of 'Do unto others as you would do unto them.' In other words, 'Never be the first to turn, lest your host stab you in the back.' "

"And that host would be you?" she asked sweetly.

He burst out laughing, and after a second, she joined him. She couldn't help it. He completely undermined any attempts to remain angry at him.

"You're a fool, Justin," she said fondly, shaking her head. Without waiting for a reply, she started up the steps.

"I know, Evie," he said quietly, watching her go. "I know."

# Chapter 10

THOUGHTFULLY, JUSTIN WATCHED EVELYN disappear.

The Blumfields, he knew, had been in the cabin for just under two months. Not much longer than Justin had been at the abbey. There was no possible way they could be enemy agents awaiting the arrival of Bernard's infernal machine. When they'd rented the cottage, Justin hadn't even known where he was going to take delivery of the shipment. Logically, he knew they were just what they appeared to be. But logic did not always play a role in espionage. And more and more often of late, Justin had been on edge, his instincts screaming that something was not right.

And yet, on the face of it, nothing could be more right. There was nary a whisper of anything sinister in the air. Indeed, he'd seldom had an assignment so straightforward and harmless. And yet . . . and yet . . .

It was this waiting. It made him edgy, likely to jump at shadows . . . or bluff Prussian neighbors.

But now maybe the waiting was over. One of these crates might hold the device. It was certainly time the damn thing made its appearance.

With that thought, he went in search of Beverly. He found him around the back of the abbey, supervising the placement of a modern oven in the kitchen.

Soon after Justin had entered the army, Beverly had surreptitiously joined his unit at the request of Justin's maternal grandmother, who had apparently felt less than confident in Justin's ability to stay alive in the field.

He had worked for Justin ever since. The two had formed a good team, and if Beverly had discovered in the easygoing young man a spine of tempered steel and the intellect and cunning to make use of it, he'd never let on that he'd expected anything different. And for his part, Justin had soon enough discovered that Beverly's talents extended far beyond a batman's or butler's arts.

But their interesting experiences did not keep Beverly from forgetting his butlering. Not for a moment. Nor did it keep Beverly from expressing his morose, misogynistic and puckish personality.

"Beverly, I want you to hie yourself off to the stables and have one of the lads hitch me up a cart."

Beverly looked at him mournfully. "The stables, sir? Where there are horses and thus horse excrement?"

"Walk carefully, Beverly."

"Thank you for your concern, but don't you think that taking into account your current state," he shuddered delicately as his gaze swept over Justin, "you might see to this little task yourself?"

"No. I'm going to dash inside and pry the tops off the crates Evie and her new boyfriend have just delivered and at the same time keep an eye out the front window in case Mr. Blumfield should *happen* to drive by on his way to Henley Wells where he *happened* to have forgotten something. Like a crate," he said with heavy irony. "I doubt he's a secret agent for another country but God knows I've played harmless pups myself enough times not to risk trusting to appearances.

"I have extremely good vision, sir."

"You have terrible vision. Worse than a mole in sunlight. Look at you. You're squinting right now."

"It's a tic, sir."

"No wonder Evie thinks you a difficult creature."

"Does she?"

"Terribly."

"How delightful of her to consider me at all."

"Enough of your slathering after my good lady, Beverly. Off to the barn with you."

"Of course, sir," Beverly said before offering a dignified little salute.

Justin headed to the library, where Evie had taken to storing incoming paraphernalia, and examined the two crates. Both were large and stoutly made. He found a claw hammer and within five minutes had jimmied the lids off, fully expecting to find another, better secured box inside.

Instead, he found a great deal of ladies' luggage, trunks and valises monogrammed with the initials *E* and *C*, which Justin quickly deduced was Mrs. Vandervoort's future monogram.

Alas, there was nothing inside to gladden the heart of an expectant recipient of diabolical machines. Still, two other crates awaited him in Henley Wells. He couldn't afford to assume that they, too, held Mrs. Vandervoort's trousseau. He'd just finished nailing the lids back on when Beverly appeared. "The beast waits without."

"Good," Justin said, heading outdoors. He climbed aboard the waiting wagon and whistled up the horse to a trot.

Despite Evie's claim that the station had closed, he knew better. He would like to have seen Sully Silsby's face when he realized Evie didn't have the vaguest notion that when he said "sausage day," she was *supposed* to offer him a quid to stay open past hours.

No, Justin had no fears that he could rouse the manager and bribe him into releasing the boxes. But he did have to get there before any other, yet to be identified, interested parties got there. He'd always been clear-sighted, focused on his goal, absorbing pertinent data, filtering out the extraneous, always one step ahead of the opposition. It's what had made the game fun.

But recently, he'd begun second-guessing his motives. Being clear-headed, he decided, was deucedly inconvenient when one's personal bias started to creep into the equation. The fact was that he didn't like Mr. Blumfield. Mostly because Evie did, but also because in spite of what he knew, he was still suspicious of the Blumfields.

Their sudden appearance in this sleepy little hamlet, the manner in which they'd secured the strategically located cottage, Ernst's attentions to Evie—which coincidentally gave him an excuse to visit the abbey—it was all just too convenient.

And yet, if Blumfield was after Bernard's device, why offer to haul two of the crates most likely to contain it here? No. He was tilting at windmills.

He was too good an agent to make assumptions without any evidence to support them, he reminded himself.

Justin arrived in town at dusk. The chink of cheap china, the high pipe of children's demanding voices, and the low drone of the parents' patient replies drifted in the air. The smell of frying bacon and onion perfumed the dusk. Henley Wells was settling in for the evening.

Only the pub was crowded and raucous. Its double doors stood open and the shutters were flung wide, spilling light and noise into the twilight.

Justin drew around to the back of the dark train depot, set the brake, and leapt to the ground. He took the steps up to the back door and peered through the sidelight. Inside, he could just make out the dim shapes of several crates. The office door was shut and the gas jets had been turned off. He knocked lightly, just in case, and, when no one answered, tried the doorknob. It was locked.

Not that a locked door would stop a determined thief. Or spy. Or even a one-time spy, Justin thought, dipping into his pocket and extracting a penknife. He flipped up one of the blades, a very slender, flexible blade.

Carefully, he inserted the slender blade into the catch. Picking a lock was a matter of finesse and delicacy, a task more appropriate to touch and hearing than sight. A little jostle here, the slide and click of a tumbler there, a gentle tug, a sleek tickle and *voilà*!

With one last, careful look around, Justin turned the knob and slipped into the office, quietly closing the door behind him. Once inside, he made for the manager's office.

He found a crowbar on a shelf just inside the door and went to the crate. As quietly as possible, he wedged the end of the bar under the wooden lid and pushed. Nothing. He looked closer at the crate. The damn thing had been nailed shut every four inches. Bloody hell. He jammed the crowbar more securely under the lip and heaved down. He'd just heard a recalcitrant groan when the office gaslights flared to life. Blast!

"Is that you, Mr. Powell? Whatever are you doing?"

Justin turned his head. Sully Silsby stood in the front doorway, weaving slightly on his feet. Hovering behind him stood Archie Flynn and two others Justin didn't recognize.

Many years ago, Justin had learned that the best reaction to being discovered in a compromising situation was to play put-upon. He sighed in exasperation.

"I'm trying to get this blasted thing open," he said. "What does it look like I'm doing?"

It worked. Sully nodded as if indeed, now that he

thought of it, of course that was what Justin was doing. "So you are. But how'd you get in here, sir?"

"Through the door." Justin rolled his eyes, the picture of exasperation. He dropped to the ground. "What does your wife put in those sausages, anyway?"

Sully flushed guiltily. "I haven't been home yet. I stopped by the pub and was just about to leave when Archie here come back to say how he seen a cart behind the station."

"And you rounded up this stalwart band to see who'd breached the sanctity of your office?" Justin asked.

"That's right." One of the men in the back hiccuped.

Justin lifted his hands, palms up, at his sides. "Just me, I'm afraid. Lady Evelyn informed me that if I didn't hurry, the crates would be doomed to wait here until Monday. Couldn't let that happen. So hither I flew."

"But how'd you get in, sir?" Sully insisted.

"I tried the door. It was open."

"I could have sworn I locked it."

"Maybe the latch didn't catch," Justin suggested.

Sully nodded, convinced. "Needs replacing."

"But if you was coming to get the crates, why're you trying to break 'em open here?" Archie demanded, blast him.

"To determine just who owns the bloody things," Justin explained with exaggerated patience. "If they're mine, I figured I'd leave them until Monday and save myself the effort of loading them myself. But if they are Lady Evelyn's, well, she'll need them." He didn't miss the wink Sully sent his nearest mate.

"So, that be the way of it?" Sully asked with all the subtlety of a twelve-year-old. "And whose crates are they?"

Justin shrugged. "Haven't found that out yet."

"Ach! We can get that lid off for'n you," one of the strangers, a rabbity-looking fellow with a sunburned complexion, offered. "Can't we, Jim?"

His friend, stouter and already sporting a stunning map of capillaries across his bulbous nose, nodded.

Justin didn't want an audience when the contents of the crates were revealed. He wrenched the iron bar out and dropped it on the floor. "Thanks for the offer, but I'd just as soon wait until I'm back at the abbey to open them, since I seem to have found some fine fellows to lend me a hand loading them. That is, if you wouldn't mind helping?"

"Sure thing, Mr. Powell," Sully agreed. Justin always paid well for any effort expended on his behalf.

Justin looked over the strangers. "I don't think I've had the pleasure. You are . . . ?"

"New to town," Sully answered for the pair. "Come down from London only a few days ago. Salesmen for a new line of combine harvester. They've decided to make Henley Wells their 'center of operations.' Leastwise that's what they said, and right official-sounding, too, don't you think?"

"Very," Justin murmured.

"Good fellows," Sully said, which, in Sully's lexicon, meant they'd paid for a round of drinks. "We're quite chummy over to the pub. You stop by, Mr. Powell. Got us a merry little crowd. The deacon's cousins—what he didn't even know he had afore they appeared on his doorstep last night—they're over to the pub, too."

"Sounds grand. But first things first, eh?" Justin said. Salesmen, ailing Prussians, long-lost relatives—was there no end to his possible adversaries? He suddenly felt tired. If there *had* to be an enemy within, why couldn't the fellow have the good grace to don a black cape and twirl pointy mustachios?

"Right. You and me, Archie," Sully clamped a paw on little Archie Flynn's shoulder, "we'll take this one and you lads take t'other."

Amidst general camaraderie, the men hoisted the crates to their shoulders and shuffled out into the street, where they made quick work of loading them. Then they stood back and gazed expectantly at Justin.

"Well, I'd say you've earned yourselves a well-deserved round or two."

Justin fished some money out of his pocket and flipped the coins to Sully.

"Now that's right kind of you, Mr. Powell. Don't say you aren't going to join us?"

"Not tonight, Sully. Lady Evelyn—"

Archie dug his elbow into Sully's side. "Never thought to see you struck by Cupid's arrow, Mr. Powell."

Justin regarded him dryly. "Not to worry, Archie. I don't think it's an arrow so much as a dart."

He winked as the men broke into laughter, and swung up into the carriage. But as he drove he could not help but consider how easily the local men accepted this role of unwilling lovesick swain. Perhaps because it wasn't far from the truth. . . . Ruthlessly, he hauled his thoughts back to the task at hand.

He wouldn't think of her. He spent far too much time thinking of her as it was. Thinking of her, wanting to be with her. Wanting her. Damn it, next thing he knew, he'd be mooning about like that fool Blumfield!

Thirty minutes later he was back at the abbey, rousing the poor stable boy to help him manhandle the crates into the library. By the time the boy left, the grandfather clock had struck sonorous notes that echoed down the deserted corridors.

Justin shrugged out of his jacket and turned up the gas jets. The claw hammer lay where he'd left it. He picked it up.

"Well," he said softly, "I suppose there's no time like the present—"

*Swoosh!*

He ducked. The blackjack caught him a glancing blow behind the right ear. The hammer skittered across the floor as he went down hard, driven to his knees by the explosion of pain.

Out of the corner of his eye he glimpsed movement and rolled. The second blow missed his face, pounding with nerve-numbing force into his shoulder. He turned to face his adversary just as the room went black.

Blast! The man must have come in earlier and hidden when he'd arrived. Justin froze. Listened. By turning off the lights, his enemy had leveled the playing field. The sudden darkness would be more to his enemy's detriment than Justin's—which meant his assailant didn't want to be seen.

Footsteps slid along the floorboards. Justin crouched, holding his breath. A figure slipped across the rectanglular murk of the doorway and dissolved into the darkness to his right. Dressed for the occasion, had he? Justin thought, bitterly aware of his own white shirt. This would teach him to ask Providence for villains in black.

A floorboard creaked close by. He waited. Felt more than saw the looming presence behind him. Tensed. Heard his assailant's breath catch, and at that instance pivoted, driving up with a clenched fist. His knuckles connected with bone-crunching force.

"Ahh!" His assailant bellowed.

"Bloody hell!" Justin swore, violently shaking his injured hand and ducking the wild swings of an all but invisible arm.

One should never, *ever* hit something without being able to see it. *Bloody* hell, that hurt!

Justin ducked another swing, glimpsed a black, featureless face, and, gritting his teeth, drew back his fist and drove straight from his shoulder. But this time the man saw his arm coming and ducked in time to avoid it. Then, just when Justin was vulnerable, the figure plunged headfirst into Justin's unprotected belly.

"Uff!" Justin gasped and stumbled backward, knocked to the ground. He curled, protecting his head, but the man was apparently now simply intent on escape. Before Justin could regain his feet, his enemy had stumbled out of the door, slamming it closed behind him and pitching the room into even deeper darkness.

Justin leapt to his feet, intending to give chase, but tripped over the sodding hammer, flung open the door, and collided straight into Evie Cummings Whyte.

# Chapter 11

IT HAD BEEN A LONG DAY. EVELYN HAD supervised the hanging of a new chandelier, started the workmen on the papier-mâché boulders, finally located the source of a noxious odor in one of the guest rooms and dealt with the rat's disposal. By the end of the day, she was exhausted but too keyed up to sleep.

She took dinner standing up in the kitchen and spent the rest of the evening going from room to room, checking the progress of cleaning and repairs. She ended her tour in the room across from the library, one of the last that needed cleaning, and decided to take a little break.

The Brigadier General had used it as a trophy room. The walls were covered with photographs of him in various uniforms, the tables piled with scrapbooks, ledgers, and diaries from various generations. Idly, Evelyn sat down and began leafing through them. If Justin came in she would hear him and they could . . . talk. No one came. Justin least of all.

Soon even the General's amazing record of tight-fisted domestic tyranny failed to hold her attention and she fell asleep. Almost at once she began to dream.

She was driving a carriage, and Mr. Blumfield stood in the road behind her, applauding. All at once, the road turned into a track careening down the side of a steep mountain, and the carriage became a bicycle. She was losing control, going faster and faster, when her wheel hit a rut, hurling her out over the cliff face.

Terrified, she plummeted, screams freezing in her throat. And then she saw Justin hanging from a gnarled tree root halfway down the cliff face. Her terror vanished. She stretched out her hands and he caught her round the waist. The moment they touched, the air turned balmy and soft.

Gently, he gathered her in. "Evie," he whispered. "What did you think you were doing?"

Somehow his shirt had come off and her hands were pressed against a chest as satin-smooth as Italian marble. He pressed a kiss on her brow and slowly, tenderly, sweetly, trailed it down her cheek. He was going to kiss her lips. . . .

A crash brought Evelyn rudely awake.

She lurched to her feet as a man's voice rained curses outside the room. Confused, still half asleep, she groped for the door handle and stumbled into the dark corridor. The library door swung open and a tall figure in a ghostly white shirt bowled straight into her. She cried out and he grabbed her arms, steadying her.

"Evie, are you all right?" His voice was tense, having lost its usual insouciance. He gave her a little shake. "Are you all right? Evie!"

She steadied herself with her hands splayed against his chest. "Yes, yes, of course I am."

His hands raced over her face and down her torso with even more outrageous impropriety than usual, but before she could react he stepped away and with a short, "Wait here," he quickly disappeared out the front door.

From outside she heard the sudden sound of a man's shout followed by the thunder of a horse's hooves. Her heart raced. Had the house been broken into? Had something been stolen? A second later, a dark figure reappeared beside her and Justin turned up the lights in the hall sconces. He peered at her intently. What he saw must have relieved him, for he released a deep breath.

"Good heavens, Justin," she whispered, pushing her spectacles up her nose. His hair fell over his brow and the top buttons of his shirt were missing, the throat gaping open well below the sternum. She tried, and failed, to keep her gaze from that wholly masculine expanse. "Were we robbed?" she whispered.

"No." He shook his head. "I came in and caught him before he got away with anything."

"But you're not hurt?" she asked.

"I'm fine. Absolutely fine."

Her relief gave way to a burgeoning awareness of him. His masculinity. His athleticism. Dark swirls of hair covered heavy shelves of pectoral muscle in a V, narrowing to a line that disappeared beneath the rest of his shirt. And he was dense and hard, like a well-toned animal, but not like stone. Nothing at all like stone.

He took a step closer, gathering both of her wrists in one of his hands and pulling them flat against his heart. It thundered, vibrating through her palms, spurring her own pulse. Shivers trembled through her limbs.

"Are you sure you're all right?" he demanded. "You're shaking like a wet dog."

She couldn't move her hands, so instead she patted him awkwardly with her fingertips. "Yes," she said shakily. "I was dreaming and I thought I heard you cry out. . . ."

He said, "I was in the library when the lights went off. I saw a figure run out of the room and ran after him, only it seems I ran into you. Did you see him?"

"No." She frowned. "Was it a burglar, do you think? Shouldn't we alert Merry and Beverly and send for the—"

"It's all right, Evie," Justin said soothingly. "I'll get Beverly to join me in a look 'round but I doubt we'll find our man had an accomplice. I saw the man mount a horse he'd obviously tied earlier to the bushes and ride off. There wasn't another. Poor sort of chappie he'd be to make his cohort go afoot when he came astride."

"But shouldn't we send for someone? Maybe they

could track him to his . . . his lair?" Evelyn suggested, the idea of a culprit getting away offending her sense of justice.

A gleam of amusement had entered Justin's eyes. "In the dark? And him with a lead. I'm afraid he's gotten away, Evie. For now. We'll see what daylight brings."

He relaxed. "Probably some poor chap carrying more liquor than sense thought to pinch a bit of silver," he said. He let go of one hand and reached up, capturing a lock of her hair and testing it between thumb and forefinger. It must have come down while she slept. It would look a fright, twisting about her shoulders like witch locks.

He coiled it about his finger, then slid it free, releasing a perfect bouncing little corkscrew. "Pretty."

Awareness simmered along her nerve endings, pulsing in her lips and fingertips, working their way to other places, long-neglected places.

Once awoken, dormant passions were not easily driven back into subjugation. But Evelyn tried. She couldn't risk misreading the situation and looking like a pathetic fool.

"However," she began, trying to sound like the sensible, unflappable Evelyn Cummings Whyte she knew herself to be. "However, if a London thief got wind of Mrs. Vandervoort's wedding plans, he might see a trip here as potentially worthwhile."

"Very true," Justin agreed distractedly. "You are, as always, entirely logical."

"I shall have to warn Mrs. Vandervoort. Perhaps she can hire some private guards."

The gaze that had been fixed thoughtfully on her hair snapped to meet hers. He really had the most beautiful eyes. "Oh, I don't think that's necessary."

"Oh?" she whispered. She was having a hard time attending to what he was saying with him standing so close, his gaze fixed on where her hands were spread against his bare chest.

The shadows cast by the gaslight cut the contours of his face into sharp relief. He didn't look like a dilettante or idler anymore. The angle of his jaw was too uncompromising, the shape of his nose too autocratic; even the hollows beneath his cheeks, hollows she never noted in daylight, looked worn bone-deep.

"Why did you leave the army?" The question surprised her even more than him.

He lifted one brow. "You've been talking to Beverly."

She wasn't going to tattle on Beverly. "I remember when you were at our house for Verity's coming-out, my mother wondered why you'd left Her Majesty's service. And seeing you now . . . I was reminded of a soldier."

That brokered a laugh from him. "God help the country if I'm an example of what's keeping our shores safe."

"I don't know. You look capable to me." At this, the corner of his mouth lifted. She flushed. "Why did you leave?"

"I had a better offer." He seemed amused.

From Mrs. Underhill? It was only a few months after he'd left the army that she'd found him coming out of the diplomat's wife's bedroom. "But—"

He tipped her chin up with his fingers and pressed his thumb to her lips. "No more questions. Not tonight. I can't think how to answer them."

What an odd thing to say, and why was he looking at her like that, so rueful and apologetic? A gaze that was fixed on her mouth. Or was it hers that was fixed on his? The full curve, the small dark line of... blood.

"What happened to your lip?" She glanced away, despising her knee-jerk aversion. But he saw it. And it was that, finally, that broke whatever strange spell held them. He released her wrists, stepped back, and wrenched his shirttails free, using the end to dab at his lip. "Gads, I *am* sorry, Evie. Forgot I had this."

Her eyes widened. In holding up his shirttails, he'd exposed his stomach. Oh, my! She'd never seen a man's naked stomach before. It was beautiful. At least his was.

A shallow valley separated the abductor muscles that bunched as he bent forward. The dark V of hair that had narrowed beneath his shirt grew even thicker before it disappeared under his waistband.

Her breathing grew shallow. Fascinating. And provocative. Entirely. And mysteriously, wholly masculine.

He shoved his shirttails back into his pants, casually fastening up a few of the undone buttons on his shirt. But not all of them. Happily.

*Stop it!* She had to stop thinking in one-word sentences. She wasn't an idiot. She was an intelligent woman, not some uncouth female operating on a sexually primordial level.

Hopefully.

"You are hurt!" She forced herself to look him in the eye. "And don't tell me you cut your lip opening a crate. And why were you opening it so late at night?"

She simply loved the way his smile started in his eyes and turned up one corner of his lip before the other, making his smile a little lop-sided, a bit chagrinned, and entirely appealing.

"Those lids are devils to get up."

"Yes?" she prompted.

"Well, it's not a very manly thing to admit, but after trying every other means, I finally stuck an old crowbar under the lid and heaved down on it. The drat lid splintered and I fell and, well, bit my lip."

He wasn't going to admit the burglar and he had fought. He would hate to be fussed over. So, she let it go.

"What is it with you and my crates, anyway?" she teased. She was relaxing now. The odd undercurrents she'd sensed must have been leftover bits of her dream, unsettling but essentially meaningless. She was all right now. "It seems every time a shipment comes, you're the first to open them. Do you have a mania for all crates, Justin, or just mine?"

He stared at her blankly. "I'm sure I don't know what you mean."

She shook her head. "Must be my imagination," she said. "Now, bend down and let me look at that cut."

She nearly laughed at his reluctant expression. "I'm all right. I promise not to faint. It's *my* blood I can't stand to see."

"Most understandable."

Gently, she cupped his cheek, and as she touched him her heartbeat tripped over itself in its haste to mock her recent declaration of self-possession. His beard abraded her palm. The rise and fall of his chest fascinated and beguiled. He edged closer.

"Will I live, do you think?" he asked. Though his voice had gone lazy and warm as melted candle wax, there was nothing in the least casual about his gaze. He looked hungry and cautious and determined, like a man approaching the enemy's banquet table with a drawn sword in his hand.

"Well?" His voice was a seductive lure, a low caress.

She swallowed, retreating an inch. He followed three. "No one dies from a split lip."

She'd startled him, doused the fire that had been kindling in his eyes, and brought self-mockery flooding back into his expression. He laughed.

"Are you always so truthful?"

She should be relieved, not disappointed. "Mostly."

"Why are you?"

"If you tell people the truth, they learn to be careful what questions they ask."

Once more he laughed. "Begads, you have more defenses than any woman I know."

"Defenses?" she asked indignantly. "That's preposterous. What do I need to defend myself against?"

"Me, I suppose," he suggested, crossing his arms over his chest.

"Ha! I'm afraid this time you've outmatched your own vanity, Justin." She sniffed. "Why, you probably think every woman you meet dreams about you."

His expression grew interested. "Do you? Did you?"

"No!"

He smiled lazily. "Liar."

"Peacock!"

"Coward."

"Swaggerer!"

"Owlet."

"Moose!"

He burst into laughter, chucking her chin as if she were a crabby little girl who needed cajoling, and making her unaccountably irate. She slapped his hand away. Had she actually been thinking about *kissing* him? She'd rather kiss Mr. Blumfield's pony.

"That's what I like most about you, Evie, your scintillating wit. A veritable tour de force of the English language. What descriptive term will you next grace me with? Cow dung?"

Amazingly, she giggled. Her hand flew to cover her lips as if she weren't sure where the sound had come from. And she wasn't. She never giggled. Not since childhood.

"Are you still angry with me?" Though he asked easily enough, his gaze was watchful.

She sighed in overblown exasperation. "It's too much trouble staying irritated with you, Justin Powell."

He sketched an overexaggerated court bow. "I am profoundly in your debt, madam."

"Again? I'm thrilled. Do you have any other abbeys I might put to use?"

She smiled cheekily and heard him catch his

breath. He took a single step toward her and then, as though recollecting himself, deposited a brief kiss on his fingertip and tapped it against her mouth.

"Nope," he said. "You've seen the extent of my ecclesiastical holdings. Now, you'd best find your bed, Evie, my dear. I'll wait here a bit and see if our intruder returns, though I doubt he will."

"I'll stay and keep you company, then."

"No," he said quickly. "You need your sleep. Much to do around here yet, and Mrs. Vandervoort's wedding celebration deserves your wakeful best. Besides, it's late."

She frowned, unwilling to leave him. "It's not that late."

He laughed, the sound a little mocking, and, turning her by the shoulders, gave her a gentle push. "Oh, my dear, not only is it *that* late, it's *too* late."

At the far end of the hall, standing across from each other on opposite sides of the corridor, two figures dressed in night apparel peered at the unfolding tableau with equally interested eyes. They spotted one another at the same moment and withdrew to their respective corners, each listening until they'd heard Evelyn pass before peeking out again. A glance told them that Justin was gone too, leaving them to creep out and confront one another.

Merry hadn't had much to do with Beverly. Her province and his rarely overlapped. Likewise, Beverly had managed to avoid the Frenchwoman, certain she represented the worst of her gender. But now, a common thread brought them together.

"Well, Mr. Beverly," Merry said, crossing her arms under her large bosom. A silly puff of lace squatted atop her red curls like some fantastical, highly inbred roosting chicken.

"Mademoiselle Molière."

"What do you make of that?" she asked, jerking her head toward the library.

"Interesting." He didn't pretend to misunderstand.

"And just what should we do about it, do you think?" she asked with that saucy French impertinence that some men found appealing. Not him, however.

"Do about it?" he echoed. True, he had been considering what, if anything, ought to be done about it, but he certainly hadn't intended to have an ally.

"Yes, do about it. *Sacré bleu!* I know the English serving class is dull, but why must you all wear reticence like a virtue?"

Beverly stiffened, attempting to look outraged, which was difficult in a tassled bed cap. Anyway, she ignored him. "Your master is much enamoured of Miss Evelyn. Miss Evelyn is not averse to his attention. And Lady Broughton, her good mother and my savior, is not averse to her daughter being not averse."

"And how do you know Lady Evelyn is not 'averse'?"

"Because," Merry said, "I am much attuned to the quiet whispers of the female heart."

"Oh?" Beverly looked down his nose at her. "If the noise coming from the general vicinity of the rose arbor this afternoon was any indication, those 'whispers' aren't all that quiet."

"Eavesdropper!"

"Hardly, mademoiselle. A deaf man wearing cotton batting in his ears and seated in a padded room would have been hard pressed to ignore the sounds—"

"Enough! We are not speaking of me, but of your *louche* master."

"*Louche*?" At this insult, Beverly grew rigid. "My master, Miss Molière, is one the finest gentleman in England."

She waved away his indignation. "*Mais oui*. What has that to do with being *louche*? To the Frenchwoman, a little experience, a few affairs, serve to refine the skills a man later brings as a gift to his true love."

She sighed, her eyes growing misty with recollection. Then her lips puckered. "In England, everyone must be, oh, so naive. No experience, no seasoning, no skills. Everyone must come to their first lovemaking like a fumbling teenager. If fumbling has appeal, it is only to the inexperienced. Or the very anxious."

She eyed him as if she thought he might very well fit in the latter category.

Beverly closed his eyes, reminded again of why he detested females. "Is there a point to this lewd monologue, mademoiselle?"

"Yes. Your master, is he truly reformed? Or will he break my Evelyn's heart?"

"Will *he* break *her* heart?" Good God, were women constitutionally incapable of understanding that a man might be as susceptible to being hurt as a woman? "Mademoiselle, Justin Powell is as decent, honorable, and worthy a man as you will find. Now, I might ask you the same? What of Miss Evelyn?"

He felt a smidgen of guilt about asking. He wouldn't be standing here if he hadn't already determined that Miss Evelyn was in all likelihood the best the female gender had to offer. It was a deduction confirmed when she kept his indiscretion about the Brigadier General from Mr. Powell. She was bona fide, all right.

In fact, if he hadn't for some time now been convinced that Justin ought to have sons, he wouldn't be standing here. That Lady Evelyn's mother had had a similar thought, and had apparently enlisted this harridan to encourage any developing relationship, only made his job easier. But it did mean working with *her*.

"Miss Evelyn is better than *worthy* and *decent* and *honorable*," Merry mimicked his haughty tone. "She only awaits a man able to see beyond her terrible spectacles and stiff, ugly dresses, which would be easier if she ever donned the perfections that I have created for her—" Seeing Beverly's bored expression, her lips snapped together. "*Does* your master possess the imagination to see what is beyond his eyes?"

How dare she intimate that her mistress was better than his master! Beverly thought. He longed to tell her about Justin's secret life, his espionage career, his intellect and cunning. "Don't you worry about Mr. Powell's vision. He sees everything just fine. *Everything*."

She suddenly smiled, as sunnily as if they were bosom mates. “So, we are agreed. They suit.”

He eyed her warily, finally admitting, “They suit.”

“Good. Now, the first thing we must do is this…” she began, and Beverly had the unhappy suspicion his life was about to be turned upside down.

# Chapter 12

BACK IN THE LIBRARY, JUSTIN ROLLED HIS forehead against the door. Thirty-two years he had lived unscathed, and now this woman, this Evelyn Cummings Whyte. How did one prepare for a woman like Evelyn? Shrewd and green, autocratic and shy?

One didn't.

She broke in unexpectedly and stole things you valued: your peace of mind, your sense of purpose. Her touch brought you to your knees, laying self-sufficiency and years of emotional liberty to waste. And she didn't even know it. Hadn't a clue, this worldly innocent.

Such a small woman to cause such large problems. He swung around, stalking to the two newly delivered crates. Hell and damnation. He didn't need this. Not now. He had too much to do, too many other things to consider, and all of them would only be harder with her mucking around in his thoughts. In his heart. *Blast*!

He slammed the side of his fist against the nearest crate, and pain exploded in his injured hand. He grimaced with caustic amusement. That would teach him to leave the romantic outbursts to the chaps who didn't mind getting hurt. At least, it cleared his thoughts.

He had a job to do and he had always done his job very, very well. Before, his lack of personal attachments had been one of his greatest assets. None of his actions or observations were clouded by emotional issues. And they weren't going to become clouded now. He wouldn't allow it.

In the last hour everything had changed. Somehow the enemy had discovered where the device had been sent. The simple delivery he'd anticipated had turned into something dangerous.

Justin had little doubt that the man with whom he'd fought was an enemy agent, for while he was willing to concede that the intruder in the library had been the half-drunk lout looking for a quick bit of ready he'd described for Evie, he was not willing to trust that speculation. Particularly when Evie's safety was at stake.

And the assignment. Not that it held precedence. Not over Evie.

At least, Justin told himself, he no longer needed to concern himself with getting Bernard's scientist into the house. As the point of the entire operation had been to take possession of the device secretly, it was now moot. It was too damn bad that it was too late to have the shipment diverted.

He still needed to take delivery of this thing. But then he would send it straight off again to Bernard.

He retrieved the crowbar and wrenched the tops off the crates. Inside, he discovered nothing remotely diabolical—unless you counted a dozen hatboxes. He replaced the lids on the crate and stood back. His eye caught a glint on the carpet. He bent over and picked up a kitchen boning blade.

Useless as a means to pry something open, its presence here was disquieting. Whoever had brought it in here had carried it as a weapon. If he was an agent... Well, that wasn't the way the game was played.

Clandestine operatives depended on their ability to blend in with the local community in order to accomplish their fact-gathering. Some spent years making themselves invisible through habituation. Others, like Justin, openly entered an area and assumed a harmless persona. A spy rarely offered physical violence, because to do so called attention to him; a man running from authorities has little chance to accomplish anything else—like stealing a diabolical machine.

Besides, covert operatives didn't go about killing one another. They were seekers of information, not assassins.

No, Justin disliked this knife intensely.

His lips tightened. He thanked God it had been him and not Evie who'd entered that room. The very thought of her running into the assailant and his boning knife set a clamp tightening around Justin's gut.

He'd send her away. Tell her he'd rethought their arrangement and it wasn't working. As soon as he thought it, he dismissed the idea. He couldn't do that to her.

The things she'd done with the abbey in the space of a few weeks had been extraordinary. The transformation from a moldy, dusty old tomb to—how had she put it?—"an adequately picturesque country house" had been astounding. No, he couldn't reasonably argue that she'd interfered with his life. And she wasn't going to know how she'd interfered with his heart.

Over the course of the years, he'd sacrificed a great deal for his position, for his cover, for his country; while he had never stopped to tally the cost, he had occasionally felt it. He honestly hadn't cared what opinion his grandfather had of him, but he would have liked his grandmother to know he hadn't been a useless idler.

He loathed the thought that because he was a successful spy, Evelyn must come to a similar assessment. He should hate to see disappointment in her dark, muted eyes. But that was his problem, not his country's and certainly not Evie's. He couldn't tell her he was not just some aggravating, unmotivated social parasite. He'd taken oaths of silence, and he well understood the necessity of absolute secrecy. Not only his life but the lives of others relied on his staying mute until such time as his superiors released him from his vows.

But none of this solved his current problem, and that was what to do about Evie. And just what did he *need* to do about her? he asked himself, forcing his thoughts to be clear and unemotional.

Now that he knew for certain that there was an enemy about, he could be careful, take every precaution. No one was after Evie, he reminded himself. He only needed to keep her away from any likely-looking crates and stick close to her, to keep her safe.

Besides, his assailant had revealed himself. He wouldn't risk another frontal attack. Until he was certain the thing was within reach, he wouldn't make another move.

But though reason and experience told him one thing, his gut refused to believe it. Fear still dug its talons deep. There was only one thing he could do: He would find a man with a face bruised from where he'd struck him.

He left the library without bothering to lock the door and headed for the bedchambers, noticing the change the abbey had undergone. The ceiling had been fixed and the water-stained walls freshly painted. An Oriental carpet muffled his footsteps. On the wall, a portrait of some saucy eighteenth-century Powell wench smiled at him.

He went on and entered the corridor that led to the sleeping quarters. Evelyn's was the farthest down, a corner room with windows affording reasonably easy access on two sides. Surely, no one would assault her? Why would they?

He stopped at the room opposite hers and hauled out an armchair, which he slid beneath the window at the end of the hall. He had to start looking for his assailant somewhere and Blumfield's place was as good as any. Tomorrow, he'd pay the Blumfields a neighborly visit. And if by chance the invalid brother wasn't around, or big brother Ernst had mysteriously disappeared, well, then, certain deductions could be made—such as one of them was hiding a black eye. With that thought, Justin flopped down in the chair, his legs sprawled out in front of him and his head tipped back. He stared at Evie's door, waiting to fall asleep.

Though every bit of common sense declared there was no reason anyone would hurt Evelyn, and every shred of experience pronounced her safe for the rest of the night, his gut wasn't buying it.

And a spy slept when his gut was satisfied, not his head.

# Chapter 13

"WHO PUT THIS CHAIR OUTSIDE MY DOOR?" Evelyn asked Merry, who'd emerged from her room in her nightdress. "It wasn't here last night."

"Can't say," Merry answered in a bored voice. She peered at her more closely. "Did you sleep well? You look a bit done for this morning, Evelyn."

"I do?" Evelyn's hands flew to her hair. It took only a few pats to determine that every strand she'd bullied into submission was still in place. Admittedly, she hadn't had a very restful night. She'd had more blasted dreams, and though she didn't remember them specifically, she knew Justin had figured prominently in them.

Justin's eyes. She remembered now. She'd dreamt about Justin's eyes. And kisses, only in her dream those kisses had been the beginning of an end she couldn't quite recall and wasn't sure she wanted to. She fidgeted and glowered at Merry. "Nonsense."

"If you say so." Merry grinned. "But you are as red as cherry jelly. Who've you got in there with you, anyway?" She stood on tiptoe, pretending to peer into Evelyn's bedroom.

"Merry!" Evelyn gasped.

Merry's eyes twinkled. "I was just teasing you, Evelyn. I know you are alone. More's the pity."

"You are incorrigible!"

"What is incorrigible? To think that you have finally enjoyed the uncommon pleasures of the common woman?"

"Merry Molière, your parents would be aghast."

Her lips compressed with scorn. "Probably so. The French bourgeois are so conforming. But I am an artist. It is only in heightened passion I find inspiration."

"Then, on the evidence provided by Buck Newton's ever-rapt expression, I may deduce that Mrs. Vandervoort's wedding dress will be the product of near delirium?"

Merry laughed. "You try so hard to be the good girl, Evelyn, when the naughty woman suits you so much better."

This didn't bear further conversation. Evelyn *was* a good girl, and had no intention of becoming a naughty one. It was all very fine for Merry to espouse free love, but a duke's granddaughter had standards to live up to. Though those standards *did* seem unfairly restrictive.

Why, she'd never experienced more than the few

clumsily executed kisses that the boys at coming-out parties had talked her into allowing—not that it'd been all that hard to talk her into them. Those certainly hadn't been the stuff of girlish dreams. They'd been wet and slobbery, like smooches from Stanley's bloodhound.

She didn't imagine Justin kissed like that. Now, if Justin were to want to kiss her, maybe she would be a little naughty. And that happenstance, she was loath and excited to admit, actually might arise.

She knew Justin liked her, and if evidence could be gathered from his own lamentable lack of style, he might not require ravishing good looks from a woman in order to be attracted to her. He might be satisfied with intelligence, industry, and competence. . . .

*Whatever was she thinking*?

She returned her wayward attention to Merry. "Never you mind my love life, Merry. I should think yours would be more than adequate to keep you busy."

"But I am fond of you!"

"I appreciate your interest and I promise that the next time a man throws himself at me, I will immediately seek your counsel." She smiled wryly, certain Merry would join in her joke. Merry only shook her head.

"Evelyn, sometimes you are such a fool!" she pronounced angrily and marched back into her room, stopping in the doorway. "And it is a *sin* that you leave my dresses to rot!"

With this non sequitur, Merry slammed the door shut, leaving Evelyn staring at it in bemusement. She didn't stand there long. She struck out for the library, deciding to find out what had been in the crates Justin had picked up yesterday. She was nearly there when Justin came in the front door carrying the daily post.

For once his hair was brushed and his chin had the smooth sheen of the freshly shaved. His shirt even had a collar attached to it, which was as close to sartorial elegance as Justin came.

"Are you going somewhere special?" she asked, trying to quell the fluttering of her heart. It would be best for everyone if they just returned to their former comfortable relationship.

"Going somewhere special?" he repeated, looking at her as if she'd gone daft. "Where the blazes would I be going, Evie? We're in the middle of the country, for crying out loud, and the last time I looked they hadn't erected any opera halls in Henley Wells."

She smiled serenely. She needn't have worried about any awkwardness on Justin's part after their harmless intimacy last night. "Are any of those for me?"

He looked at the correspondence in his hand as though he was trying to make up his mind whether or not any were, indeed, for her, before thrusting a little stack of letters in her hand. "Here. These."

"Why, thank you."

He stood looking at her expectantly. "Aren't you going to read them?" he demanded gruffly.

She studied him. If she hadn't witnessed him coming from Mrs. Underhill's room herself, she would never have believed he was a debonair lady-killer.

He just didn't fit the mold. Not at all. He'd crossed his arms over his chest and was regarding her impatiently. There was nothing in the least suave about him.

"Tell me, Justin. At some point in the last few years did you sustain a knock on the head?"

"What?" he asked, looking tellingly at the letters she held. "I think you ought to read your posts. One looks as though it was written in a foreign hand."

"It would have to have been a hard knock, I imagine," she mused. "Perhaps enough to render you unconscious."

"Whatever are you talking about, Evie?" he asked. "No, I was never hit in the noggin. Why?"

"Well, I've heard that being hit on the head can in some instances actually alter a person's personality so much that after the blow he is unrecognizable as the person he was prior to it."

"And what," he asked, "has this to do with me?"

She shrugged. "Oh, nothing. It would just explain so many things."

He regarded her suspiciously. "Have you been drinking, Evie?"

"No." She sighed, reluctantly giving up on the notion that a brain injury had ended Justin's lady-killing career. "No. I haven't been drinking."

"What sort of woman are you, then? My sisters can't leave a letter alone for ten seconds, and here you are holding the blasted things as though they were bills from the coal steward. Aren't you interested?"

"Of course I am." She slipped her finger beneath

the flap of the first one and withdrew several sheets of paper.

She thumbed to the last page. "Aunt Agatha must be employing a secretary for her correspondence. I didn't recognize this as her handwriting," she murmured, going back to the first page to read. "Ah! They've abandoned Paris for the Alps, and are thinking of taking a ship down the African coast, of all things—"

"Yes, yes," Justin said, pointing to another letter. "You'll want to study it at your leisure. Best look at the next one and make sure it's not creditors."

"I suppose." She opened the next one and read the short note with increasing pleasure. "Another cheque. Again presumably from Mrs. Vandervoort," she murmured and stacked it beneath her aunt's letter before opening the last one.

"Why, Justin, what an eye you have! It is, indeed, a foreign hand. It's from Mr. Blumfield. He asks me to join him on a picnic this afternoon and, listen, he apologizes most profusely for not respecting my independence and autonomy."

Justin craned his neck to look at the letter. She hid it against her chest.

"Go on," Justin sneered delicately. "The poor blighter didn't actually write 'independence and autonomy,' did he?"

"He most certainly did," Evelyn sniffed. "*I* find his formality charming."

Justin made a derisive sound. "Sounds like my father's aunt Bessie. Pinched of nose, thick of skull. You're not going, are you?"

"Why wouldn't I?"

"You have things to do."

"No I don't. Everything is running along smoothly, and I should like a picnic."

"Well," he said, looking blustery, "if you don't think the wedding will suffer from your dereliction of duty."

"Don't be an ass, Justin. For some reason you dislike Mr. Blumfield. I suspect it's because he's foreign."

"Are you accusing me of being a xenophobe, Evie?" he asked haughtily.

"If the phobe fits..." She trailed off with sweet smile. "Now, if you'll excuse me. I have things to see to before I leave, and I know you wouldn't want me to be derelict." For once, she had the last word.

It wasn't the best day for a picnic. It was cloudy and humid and still. Ernst had picked her up promptly at eleven o'clock, respectfully admiring her tidy brown worsted dress and neatly plaited hair. He'd already picked the picnic site, proclaiming it the prettiest place in East Sussex.

For a while, it appeared that Ernst's only contribution to the conversation was going to be an occasional mumble, and Evelyn had begun to feel a shade alarmed at the prospect of spending an entire afternoon in monologue. Then she'd asked about his bicycle, and he'd launched into a comprehensive discourse on the benefits versus the practicalities of the new vulcanized tires. From there on, they'd had no troubles.

Soon, Ernst drove the wagon off the road, hopped

out, and unhitched the pony. Evelyn descended, waiting while Ernst unloaded his bicycle and two large, cumbersome-looking wicker hampers.

"I will use my machine to transport these one at a time to my little idyllic place," he said.

Oh. So they weren't there yet. Well, good. A bit of exercise before a meal always stimulated the appetite and invigorated the spirit. "Mr. Blumfield—" Evelyn began.

"Ernst, please."

She dimpled. Well, she would have dimpled had she owned them, but she could have sworn she felt little dents developing in her cheeks. "Ernst. You must allow me to carry one of the hampers. I am perfectly capable."

"As I am well aware," he answered solemnly.

She picked up one of the hampers and immediately listed forward. Gads! The man must have packed a stove. Still, she smiled valiantly and shifted the weight to her hip, happy to note that he didn't try to appropriate it from her. He sincerely respected her independence and autonomy. Heavens!

It took twenty minutes to hike to Ernst's picnic site. Most of it uphill. And through a creek. Clouds of midges swarmed up from the grass as they trudged across a rutted field and up a steep slope toward the edge of the forest. Her boots had not been intended for cross-country meets and soon rubbed blisters on her heels. The brown worsted she'd worn as least likely to show grass stains wasn't up to camouflaging the dark rings spreading under her arms.

Ernst, on the other hand, looked perfectly at ease.

He pushed his new bicycle with the wicker hamper affixed to the handle, chattering gaily about the contraption's braking system. Finally he stopped. "Here. It is a lovely place, yes?"

"Yes, it's charming," Evelyn said. It didn't look appreciably different to her from any of the other half dozen places they'd passed.

"I think that in the hamper you carry I have packed a nice blanket. If you would be so kind?"

"Gladly." She gave her heartfelt assent. She could use a spot of respite. She flipped open the hamper and withdrew a heavy wool blanket. She gave it a sharp snap and settled it on the grass beneath a huge oak.

Gratefully, she sank to her knees while Ernst carefully leaned his bicycle against the trunk and returned with the other picnic basket. He sat down beside her and said shyly, "Perhaps you would do the honors, Miss Evelyn."

Evelyn looked at him blankly. "Excuse me?"

He wagged his finger in a jocular fashion. "I always loved watching my mother make the preparations for our meals. There was something so feminine about the way she arranged things and set things out. I have missed a woman's presence in my life."

"Oh." Flattered, if a trifle doubtful, she dutifully began pulling things out of the hamper. She unloaded and arranged cutlery, plates, napkins, glasses, and several items wrapped in waxed brown paper, found a thermos and mugs, and, after looking at Ernst, who said, "Please, do," filled them with iced coffee.

Ernst sighed happily and lay back on the blanket.

Evelyn gave a mental shrug and unwrapped a loaf of bread, a quarter round of cheese, several apples, and a haunch of ham. After another encouraging nod from Ernst, she sawed through meat and bread and created heroically proportioned sandwiches, one of which she then presented to Ernst.

Ernst, who'd been dreamily studying the cloud configurations overhead, came to with a blink and accepted the plate.

"How restful it is here, is it not?" he asked, leaning on his elbow and gazing blissfully into her eyes. "Everything is perfect."

Evelyn had been on the cusp of responding that she would give him her opinion regarding the restfulness of the setting after she'd actually experienced a few minutes of it, but the look in his eye forbade her. He looked so content. And so young.

"Just peachy," she said, taking a bite of sandwich.

Ernst talked while he ate. He spoke of his mother and father, of the little castle in Bavaria where he'd grown up—Gads, not another moldy white elephant, thought Evelyn—and his brother's ill health. He asked her about her family, was suitably impressed that her grandfather was a duke, but not so impressed that it was awkward, and remarked how amazing it was that someone as accomplished as she was not yet some man's treasured wife. Clearly, she had high standards, as well she should, but was there someone who, perhaps, had some hope of making her his?

It was the last that broke through Evelyn's pedestrian concern with blisters and jettisoned her right back into the realms of romance. She'd never had one offer of marriage and here Ernst took it for granted that she had had several offers, all of which she'd turned down. And he was serious!

She finished the last bite of her sandwich and put down her plate, cupping her chin in her palm and staring raptly into his eyes. "No. No one."

*Except Justin.*

Her eyes widened in horror. Where had that come from? And it wasn't even true!

"Is something wrong?" Ernst asked solicitously. "You look surprised. Unhappily surprised. A bug, perhaps?"

"No. Oh, no." Evelyn tittered nervously. "Now, you were saying...?"

"I was saying how surprising it is that a woman with your qualities, so capable and so charming, so little, yet so very..." She never found out what he'd been about to say because at that moment he leaned forward and kissed her.

A real, honest-to-heaven kiss.

He pressed his lips firmly against hers and made an appropriately kissy sound. His mouth was warm and his mustache tickled a little. And that was about it.

It wasn't bad. It wasn't wet. It was even pleasant. But it was not anything she was going to lose sleep over. Or dream about.

"I am sorry," Ernst exclaimed worriedly. Trying to read her expression. "It is only, well, I was carried away."

Perhaps kissing was an acquired taste. Like Roquefort cheese. Well, she was certainly willing to give it another go and from the look on Ernst's face, so was he. She smiled encouragingly and he reached out, gently clasping her shoulders. He closed his eyes. Should she close hers? He leaned in, closer, closer . . .

Something rustled loudly in the limbs of a nearby oak.

Her head snapped up, Ernst's kiss went amiss, and Justin Powell fell out of the tree.

# Chapter 14

"JUSTIN?" EVELYN STARED DISBELIEVINGLY. Even though the tree he'd fallen from was forty feet away, she could see his face was red. As well it should be.

She rose in a flurry of serviceable brown worsted and unadorned cotton petticoats and marched over to him, Ernst hastening after her. A few feet away, she stopped, set her hands on her hips, and tapped her toe. He didn't look up until he'd finished dusting himself off. And why *now* he should evince interest in his personal appearance when he hadn't shown any before could only be construed as suspicious.

"Well?" she demanded.

"I've torn the knee in these trousers," he said severely, as if this were somehow her fault. "I liked these trousers."

"Are you all right, Mr. Powell?" Ernst asked anxiously. Dear Ernst, trust him to show kindness in the face of such monstrous intrusiveness. "That was a nasty fall."

"I didn't fall," Justin said with quelling hauteur. "I jumped down and lost my balance. Jumping being my only recourse given the goings-on I unwillingly witnessed."

She opened her mouth to respond to such patent swill but all that came out was a choked sound. "Ah!"

Poor Ernst turned pale. "I assure you, I have—"

"Save your assurances, Blumfield. What you and Miss Powell do is none of my concern."

"We weren't doing anything!"

Justin managed to look superior and bored and disbelieving all at once. No small feat for a man who'd just fallen from a tree. "Hm. As you say. Regardless, it is no concern of mine. My only concern is *Bubo Formosa Plurimus. Minor*."

Ernst's eyes widened. "Excuse me?"

"It's a bird, Mr. Blumfield," Evelyn explained, eyeing Justin. He raised his brow defiantly, daring her to disbelieve him. She wavered in her indignation. She supposed it wasn't *inconceivable* he'd been up that tree watching birds.

"I was so close to the female I could have touched her," he said. "Then *you* two came along. I did my best to ignore you, hoping that you'd tuck into your dinner and be off. But as soon as it became apparent that things of a private nature were taking place, I made myself known."

"By falling out of the tree?" Evelyn asked.

He turned an injured expression on her. "By *leaping* from the tree. And scaring poor little *Bubo* in the process, I might add. You should have seen her ruffled feathers."

"You mean to say that you'd been up that tree since before our arrival?" she asked.

"No," he rejoined sarcastically. "I crawled on my stomach through the grass and then scaled the tree, all without your noticing."

She began to feel a tad foolish, and perhaps a shade embarrassed. "Hm."

"I am afraid, Lady Evelyn," Justin turned a cursory glance toward Ernst, "and Mr. Blumfield, that it is *you* who impinged upon *my* solitude. Not vice versa."

"I am most sorry, Mr. Powell," Ernst apologized.

Justin inclined his head graciously. "You didn't know."

"Oh!" *When* Justin went up that tree was beside the point. A gentleman would have made his presence known at once. And even though she understood that the proximity of his bird might have made him wish he could ignore that social edict, he still shouldn't have done so.

And Ernst shouldn't be standing there in stalwart misery, wringing his hands. He should be demanding an apology. Yes, she knew she should make allowances for him as a foreigner, but she wasn't in a very charitable frame of mind. In fact, she was *damn* irritated.

Her gown was glued to her with perspiration. It itched. Her face was sunburned, and she'd a bruise on her thigh from where that blasted basket had banged it. And *The Kiss, The First Kiss,* the focal point of years of fantasies and conjecture, had been nothing more than a . . . a *canapé.* Not even a delicious canapé. It had been more like a carrot stick. Deplorably wholesome.

In his heyday as a skirt-chasing scoundrel, Justin had probably doled out the caviar of kisses. The good Russian beluga stuff, too, not shad roe.

The more Evelyn thought about it—the interminable hike, her sweat-stained dress and sunburned cheeks, making sandwiches like a farmhand while Ernst snoozed, and then having her first kiss not only be so anticlimactic, but having the anticlimax witnessed! By him . . . !—the more enraged she grew.

"Ah!" the high, tight cry escaped from deep in her throat.

Both men immediately stopped making conciliatory sounds at one another and stared at her in alarm.

"Ah!" She flounced around and stalked off down the hill.

"Miss Whyte?"

"I say, Blumfield," Justin said, "it looks to me like she's decamping."

"Miss Whyte! Please, Miss Whyte! Come back! There are so many things to carry!"

"Ah!" The cry escaped again before she could strangle it. She stomped down the hill, crossed the foully idyllic creek, and clambered up the ditch to where the pony grazed. By the time she'd caught him, Ernst arrived breathless and red-faced, his bicycle buried under blankets and hampers.

"Here! You sit, Miss Whyte. I will attach the pony."

He then threw the paraphernalia into the back of the wagon, hitched the pony, and climbed in beside her. "I am so sorry, Lady Evelyn. Only what is wrong? Please, you must tell me!"

"What is *wrong*?"

He flinched. At once her outrage shrank. He smiled weakly, his expression so filled with apprehension and contrition that the rest of her anger withered and died. He honestly hadn't any notion of what was wrong.

It wasn't his fault she hadn't dressed for an overland expedition. Nor was it his fault that Justin had been in that tree. And it certainly wasn't Ernst's fault that his kiss had been a carrot stick. She liked carrot sticks. She'd just been expecting caviar. She owed him an apology.

"What is wrong is that I was embarrassed Mr. Powell witnessed a private moment. Unfortunately, when I'm embarrassed I sometimes act childishly. I am sorry."

He blew out a sigh so replete with relief that she couldn't help smile. "I thought perhaps it was something I had done."

"No," she assured him. "Can you forgive me for acting like a spoiled brat?"

"You? Spoiled? Never," he said. "You are a very special lady. It was unfortunate, the occurrence with Mr. Powell."

She glanced at the trees, expecting to see Justin climbing back up one of them, and was surprised to see him leap lightly across the creek and saunter toward them. Accusingly, Evelyn turned to Ernst.

"He says his little bird is gone now and there is no reason for him to stay," Ernst explained. "So, I thought it neighborly to offer him a ride."

Justin arrived wreathed in smiles and vaulted into the wagon bed. He sat down, threw his arm over the back of the front seat, and looked at her. "Damned good sport Blumfield is, eh, Evie?"

"Very."

Justin was the picture of bland aristocratic camaraderie, all "good-chap" and hearty "heigh-ho's" when only a short while before he'd been filled with stuffy indignation. Her expression smoothed as she turned around, her thoughts in a whirl.

Justin rode all the way to North Cross Abbey studying the back of Evie's head. Just as well.

He had the uncomfortable suspicion that Evie had uncomfortable suspicions and that, in and of itself, rattled him a bit. He was very good at being a chameleon. His life had often depended on his ability to slip seamlessly into one of a half-dozen guises. The one he most oft wore was that of the harmless, thin-blooded dilettante. But she wasn't buying it.

Fascinating. He wondered why.

He was sure he'd convinced both Evie and Blumfield that he'd been sitting up that tree hours before their arrival. The truth was that he'd gone round to Blumfield's rented cottage earlier. When his knocks went unanswered, he decided to go aloft.

A handy trellis allowed Justin to silently hoist himself eye level with the bottom of the upstairs window's sill. Sure enough, a young man lay abed facing Justin. His eyes were closed and the side of his face not pressed into the pillow was completely unmarred. And the other?

Letting go of the sill with one hand, Justin had dug in his pocket for a tuppence piece. He found one and tossed it through the open window, hearing it skitter across the floor. Then he'd lifted himself back up and looked in. The young man had raised himself up and was looking in the direction of the penny, giving Justin a clear view of his other profile. Flawless.

Disappointed, Justin climbed down. So, it hadn't been Gregory Blumfield. It could still be Ernst. The thought perked him up considerably and, not wanting to waste time waiting for Blumfield to return Evie to find out if he sported a bruise, Justin had decided to go in pursuit of them.

With that in mind, he cut across the field and went toward the part of the forest where earlier he'd seen Blumfield unhitching his wagon. He looked around until he spotted Evie and Blumfield trudging up a distant hill, heading for the huge old oak atop it.

Now, he hadn't actually crawled through the grass on his hands and knees. At least, not much of the way. Most of the distance, he simply crouched.

Once to the wood, it was easy going. A quick scramble up an obliging tree and he'd settled his binoculars against his eyes and peered at Ernst Blumfield's face. Unfortunately, with all his flushing and blushing, it was nearly impossible to tell if there was any discoloration on his jaw. And when the

Prussian bounder had the temerity to put his hands on Evie's shoulders...

Justin sat back, forcing his jaw muscles to relax. It had been a pitiful kiss. Instead of acting as if he'd insulted her, Evie should thank him for falling—er, leaping—out of that tree.

So, he'd spied. He was a spy. It was what he did. And he'd achieved his goal. Close but surreptitious scrutiny revealed that Ernst Blumfield had no bruises on his face. Not that he wouldn't look damn good ornamented with a few manly lumps.

Justin's mouth twisted sourly. Besides, he wasn't ready to cross Ernst off his list of suspicious characters quite yet. Blumfield could have hired someone to raid the abbey. Just as he could be pretending to be an anxious, lovelorn ass.

Justin was enjoying imagining a scenario in which he personally obliged Ernst in the acquisition of a more manly patina—specifically, one that encircled both eyes—when they reached North Cross Abbey. Evie, who hadn't said a word to him since they'd started out, allowed Blumfield to help her from the carriage. The young man made way too much of it. Fussing and beaming and... Disgusting.

Justin jumped out, landing beside Evie. "Say thank you to the nice gentleman, Evie."

She ignored him, giving her hand to Ernst. "Thank you for the picnic, Mr. Blumfield. I enjoyed it."

"It has been my great pleasure," Ernst said, bowing over her hand and kissing the back of it warmly.

Justin yawned and, catching Ernst's eye, waved him

on. "Sorry. All that sunshine has made me positively inert. Please, don't mind me. You two go on."

"You might consider that," Evelyn said sweetly. "*Going,* I mean."

"Oh? Am I de trop?" Justin asked, wide-eyed. "Sorry. Frightfully dull of me, what? Just want to slide in my own spot of thanks, don'tcha know? Thanks so awfully, Ernst, old boy. You're a corker!"

Evie closed her eyes briefly. Her lips trembled. When she opened her eyes, she looked firmly away from Justin.

Justin smiled vacuously at Blumfield. "Well. Ta, old bean! Oh! That's right, *I* was going. Ha!"

Evie's cheeks dished in and Justin would have bet ten pounds she was biting them, holding back laughter. He clapped Blumfield on the shoulder and walked to the front door of the abbey, turned as though he were about to wave good-bye, and froze. He let his mouth drop open, staring at the bushes beyond the wagon. With every indication of excitement, he raised his binoculars to his eyes.

Blumfield cleared his throat and regained Evie's hand. "Lady Evelyn. I am so pleased we have had this chance to get to know one another—"

"Please!" Justin whispered frantically, snatching the binoculars from his eyes and glowering at them. "It's *Bubo*! Right here! Now!"

"Oh!" Ernst answered. He glanced at the bushes, swallowed, and drew nearer to Evie. "Lady Evelyn," he whispered, "if I might have the honor of calling again—"

"I beg you, *please be quiet!*" Justin whispered urgently, keeping the binoculars glued to his eyes, one hand clasped to his heart in supplication. "She is getting *agitated*!"

With a harassed and unhappy air, Blumfield bobbed his head, crept on tiptoe past Evie, and eased himself into the wagon. Carefully, he gathered the reins.

"Thank you!" Justin mouthed.

Blumfield nodded, quickly whispering, "I bring the bicycle another day for you to ride!" to Evie, and set off down the drive.

Evie watched him go until he disappeared before turning. Her gaze found Justin with targetlike precision. He spat out the blade of grass he'd stuck between his teeth as soon as Blumfield had left, and smiled.

"You ought to be ashamed of yourself," she said, coming toward him.

"Oh, I am," he assured her. "Most of the time. But today," he paused, considering, "no, I don't think so."

She mounted the two steps. She was so small she had to angle her head to look him in the eye, exposing the graceful length of her throat. It was most lovely. "You owe Mr. Blumfield an apology."

"Forget it."

She didn't reply but reached for the doorknob. He got there before her, opening the door for her.

"Okay, why do I need to apologize?" he asked.

She preceded him into the front hall. He followed her.

"Why?" he insisted.

She didn't even bother looking around. "If there was a bird, *Bubo* or otherwise, in those bushes, I'm the Queen of Siam."

Beverly chose that moment to emerge from a door midway down the hall. He saw Evelyn and started to beat a hasty retreat, but she'd spied him. "Beverly! A moment, please."

"Only a moment, madame? Usually your forays into these employer-servant exchanges last a good deal longer."

"I'm going down into the wine cellar, Beverly," Evelyn said. "Kindly give me the keys."

"The cellar is not locked, madame," Beverly answered. "There is nothing in the cellar worth stealing. Perhaps some barrels of antique cider. The Brigadier General's palate was not highly developed. Indeed, I believe he considered his Indian cook's curry the highest form of culinary art."

Beverly looked at Justin as if he suspected him of sharing likewise low tastes and sniffed.

"Fine," she said to Beverly, ignoring Justin, which he disliked. "You won't mind if I check myself?"

"On the contrary, miss. It would seriously undermine my belief in the natural order of things if you didn't."

Evelyn didn't bother replying. She cut around the butler and entered the drawing room, Justin hard on her heels. "Evie, do you really want to go creeping about in a musty old dungeon?"

"Yes," she replied, heading for a small, low door tucked beside the cavernous fireplace.

The door was, indeed, unlocked and easily swung

open. A little ledge affixed at the top of a flight of stairs held a small brass lantern. Deftly, Evelyn lit it and started down stone steps so ancient they dished in at their centers. Justin started after her.

"You needn't come with me," she said in that infuriatingly cool voice, a voice that only made him more determined to discover what was going on behind those tinted lenses and that thoughtful expression.

"I daresay, you won't mind if I indulge myself, will you? I have a pash for cider." He grinned. Charmingly. Winningly even. She only eyed him coolly.

"Suit yourself."

As wine cellars went, it was a bust. A rickety network of shelves held a scant few dozen bottles of indifferent Italian wines, a cask or two of undistinguished brandy, and a moldy old bottle of Madeira. And, true to Beverly's predictions, a half-dozen barrels lined one crumbling wall.

"Guess old Beverly was right."

"No, he wasn't," Evelyn replied, holding the lantern aloft and looking about. The stark, golden light limned her features and gilded the lenses of her spectacles. An errant curl had escaped and cast a capricious shadow on her cheek.

"Ah!" She hurried over to a barrel that stood by itself, its lid tipped upright beside it. She set the lantern down on the ground and reached in. She was so small that her upper torso disappeared inside.

"Drat!" her voice echoed from the interior.

She gave a little hop, kicking her feet, and, making sounds of strenuous activity, rustled inside the barrel.

"Can I help?" Justin asked.

"No!" Her voice drumrolled up from the depths. "I almost... There!" She emerged triumphant, a pair of wine bottles held aloft in each hand, her face smeared with dust, and cobwebs caught in her fast-escaping locks.

"And what have you there?"

"Here, Mr. Powell? Here I have two of ten bottles of Château Lafite-Rothschild. Bottles your grandfather hid here just prior to your father's visit to the abbey in 1886."

"I say, sounds like something the old dog would have done. But how did you know about it?"

"I read his journal. He was very much the military man, wasn't he? Everything accounted for, each tactical action—particularly domestic ones—documented, even those that following generations might consider reflected poorly on him."

Justin laughed. "I doubt the notion that anyone would disagree with his reasoning, let alone see his actions as being other than shrewd, ever occurred to him."

Evelyn hesitated, slowly setting her prizes down. Her expression was difficult to read, a little anxious, a bit resolute, a trace embarrassed. "Do you... It must be so difficult. Being you. And him. Being him."

"A great deal less difficult than the other way around, I imagine, say if he was me and I—" Justin started jocularly but broke off when he saw her expression. By God, she was truly troubled.

"My dear girl," he said softly. "It really isn't a family tragedy, you know."

"But he expected you to be someone different than

who you were. It couldn't have been easy knowing you didn't measure up to his idea of what you should have been."

Justin frowned, seeking some way to comfort her, bemused and startled that she was so troubled. His own family didn't know about the odd turn his army career had taken, but though they had been disappointed he'd cut with the tradition of generations by ostensibly leaving the army, they had never forsaken him. The only one for whom it seemed to truly matter had been the Brigadier General and his potty old army mates.

He had to make Evie understand that. Because there was more to her concern than simple empathy. She'd a personal stake in his answer. And he wanted to reassure her. He wanted that very much.

"I never cared what the General thought, Evie." Justin leaned over the barrel toward her, bracing his hands on the rim. She moved closer, searching his face.

"How could you not care? He was your grandfather."

He considered. "I was lucky. My father stood between us. He wouldn't let his father-in-law browbeat me, make choices for me, or humiliate me into acquiescing to his ambitions.

"My father had spent years trying to make his father-in-law proud, you see. Succeeded, too. But he made himself miserable in the process. Then one day, or so he says, he woke up and realized that, in the process of being what the General wanted him to be, he'd nearly lost track of the ideal he held of himself."

"Ideal?" Her lips had parted a bit, like a rapt child listening to an amazing story.

"Yes. The person we know ourselves to be if we can only find the courage and honesty and strength to become that person."

She'd moved incrementally closer as he spoke, drawn as if by a magnet. "And your father taught you to hold to this inner vision?"

He reached out, barely aware he did so, and brushed that errant curl from her cheek with the backs of his fingers. Her skin was warm and smooth. "Yes," he murmured.

Her eyelids drifted partway closed, her lashes brushed her cheek. He started to reach out again, to turn that gentle brush into a full caress.

Her lids slowly raised. Her revealed gaze was sharp and assessing. "And this inner image you hold of yourself is that of an indolent, affable, supercilious fainéant?"

His hand dropped. He'd given away the game.

"I don't think so, Mr. Powell," she said. "In fact, I don't think you're what you appear to be at all."

# Chapter 15

SHE'D CAUGHT HIM OUT. SHE'D USED HIS need to comfort her in order to decipher him and see behind his mask. In the process, he'd all but confessed to having ideals, principles, and values for which he would fight.

Unfortunately, in order for him to do his job, the world needed to assume that Justin Powell had a dearth of those things. He had to embody the quintessential eccentric English gentleman: a dilettante and dabbler, overbred and faintly ridiculous. Thanks to his blunder, she'd never believe that of him. Not after that charming and impassioned little soliloquy.

Unless he did something to prove otherwise.

Though it felt as though he'd faced her probing gaze for minutes, in reality his hesitation lasted only a few seconds. Then, like ice dissolving under a warm rain, he lolled back against one of the kegs. He turned his hand over, studying his nails. "Can you think of a worthier goal?"

"Sorry, m'boy. It doesn't wash."

"Oh? What's that?" he asked mildly.

"The old Irwin the Idler act. You can't be all huffy moral superiority one minute and an easygoing noodle the next."

"I don't take your meaning."

She tapped him lightly on the chest, her eyes sparkling with exultance. She was utterly adorable.

"Oh, you know," she said, dancing back. " 'Jumping being my only recourse, given the goings-on I unwillingly witnessed,' " she said, imitating his earlier speech.

"Gads! Did I really sound so pompous?"

Her lips stretched in a sweet, victorious smile. "Uh-huh."

"Well, I would hate for you to think I'm a prig."

He pushed off the barrel rim and came round its side. He loomed over her, his pose suddenly, subtly predatory. He angled his head slightly, as if he were trying to scent her, dissect her with senses other than sight. His gaze slipped down her features, her throat, to her bosom, and rose to her face again. His lips parted as if tasting the sudden change in the atmosphere between them.

It worked. The assurance in her expression wavered. Her eyes dilated behind her lenses. She backed away a half-step, and her hand stuttered to her throat and fidgeted with her collar's top button.

His success was bittersweet. He'd needed only to

reveal more of the truth in order to obscure it. He needed only to let her see how much he wanted to touch her, kiss her, in order to make her forget what he'd told her about himself. He'd thoroughly rattled her. He should let it drop at that. But he couldn't. He couldn't stop, not yet. He had an excuse now, a reason to do what he wanted to do.

"If I seemed outraged, Evie, it was solely on your behalf."

"Mine?" she whispered, her eyes riveted on his, big and worried. So damned worried. She shouldn't be. He wouldn't hurt her. He didn't want much.

"Yes," he said, moving a step closer. "That kiss Blumfield gave you. What a poor piece of work."

A flicker of affront darkened her eyes. Her lashes beat against their glass lens cage. Her lips pursed. They shouldn't purse, they should be soft and relaxed.

"You had no right to watch," she said. "And don't hand me that feeble excuse about not wanting to startle your drat bird."

She was even more delicious vexed and combative, her skin blooming with ire, her eyes flashing.

"You're right," he agreed. "But then, I'm a cad, don't you remember?"

"A cad," she scoffed, but she countered his forward step with one backward. His conciliatory smile turned vulpine.

"Yes," he affirmed softly, stalking her across the small wine cellar.

"You're no more a cad than Ernst."

The name sent a tremor of jealousy through him.

He hated the intimacy implied by her use of his Christian name. "Oh, I agree Ernst is no a cad," he said. "Why, I'll bet he even apologized for kissing you, didn't he?"

She stopped, her back against the chill, damp rock wall. The light played in her dark clouds of hair, lacquered her profile with amber light. Her nervous fingers had worked the button at the top of her high-necked dress free, unwittingly teasing him by revealing the vulnerable little hollow at the base of her throat.

"He said he was carried away," she declared.

"Carried away?" Justin laughed. He didn't need to feign amusement. The poor bastard didn't know the first thing about being carried away.

An irresistible torque of attraction dragged him nearer until he'd cut off any chance she had of escape. He bent over her, breathing in the sweet, clean talc scent of her, every last shred of common sense demanding that he back away. She should have at least tried to dart past him. Instead, she stayed, foolish girl, her expression filled with wounded pride.

"Why are you laughing? Is it inconceivable that someone could be carried away because of me?" Her voice quavered. "Well, perhaps it is. But that is what he said, and I'll thank you not to laugh at it. Or him. Or me." Her mouth, her gorgeous, lush, ripe mouth, trembled.

God. She didn't know. She didn't have a clue. He shouldn't take advantage. He mustn't. But even as he thought this, he clasped her shoulders, his head dipped down, and he muttered, "Carried away? *That* was carried away? Oh, no. *I'll* show you 'carried away.' "

He swooped down before she could react, covering her mouth with his. Pure sensual pleasure burned through his veins. Her lips... Lord, her lips were pleasure, her mouth a feast. He heard her sigh, a little exultant, inarticulate exclamation of wonder, a womanly sound of surprised gratification.

It shook him, how deeply that sound affected him. His body seemed a tuning fork, vibrating with the reception of that sweet, pleasured sound. He drank it from her lips, telling himself to go slow, to move gently, but ardor rolled through him, setting its own tempo. His hands slipped down her arms and wrapped around her waist.

She was small, delicate as china and just as refined. But resilient. Like a willow wand, green and supple and feminine. So beautifully accommodating. He pulled her nearer, felt her slight resistance and the second she yielded.

He stroked up her back. She moved and her shoulder blades lifted like wings beneath his palm. His other hand smoothed a trail along the inward curve of her waist. She didn't stop him. She didn't back away. She stood with her head thrown back, accepting his kisses. Not yet involved. Not yet a partner. Like a beggar or a goddess, accepting alms or homage. He couldn't tell. He doubted she could.

His mouth opened over hers, burnishing her lips with tender, velvety strokes. Back and forth. His lips caressed, clung. Pressed deeper. The blood surged through his body, quickening him.

He counted to ten, letting his mouth play over hers, certain he could control this. He could keep his head. He *would* keep his head. He was a man who stood fast in any situation. But there'd never been *her* before. Never been anything like her, or the demands made by her sweetly relinquished mouth or her slowly awakening desire.

His hands glided up her sides, stopping just beneath the first soft swells of her breasts. She arched. Just an increment. Just a degree. Just enough to shift her breasts against his fingers.

He tore his mouth away, snatched his hands away from the temptation, and wrapped them around her upper arms. He looked down into her upturned face. Her lips were voluptuous and rosy, the seam between them a darkly sexual provocation.

"Is that carried away?" Evie asked in a bemused voice.

"No." His response was harsh, unlike any tone she'd heard him use.

She nodded, accepting his words as a well-deserved reproof. It had been a stupid question. Twenty-five years old and she didn't know anything, so untutored in the . . . the amorous arts that she didn't even know what to do with her hands when a man kissed her. They hung from her shoulders like the weights on a grandfather clock, while the rest of her body canted toward his, wanting to be absorbed by him.

His face was set in a hard, unreadable mask. Anger? Yes. She tilted her head, her thoughts swimming futilely against a riptide of impulses. Why was he angry? She'd never seen Justin angry. Annoyed. Irritated. But not angry.

His beautiful blue-green eyes were shuttered, his mouth drawn into a taut line. *Why* did she have to be so ignorant?

He flicked open her collar. Somehow it had come unbuttoned. His thumb slipped under the lace and settled over the pulse at the base of her throat, while his fingers curled around her neck beneath the thick, uncoiling mass of hair. He tipped her head back, reading her giddy pulse with the pad of his thumb.

Never had she felt so womanly, yet at the same time been so maddeningly aware of her inadequacies as a woman.

"You were right," she said, striving for an objective tone and succeeding only in sounding breathy. His thumb swirled in fire-inducing circles against her breastbone. Her lashes fluttered like a captive butterfly's wings against the insides of her lenses. "He wasn't carried away."

He made an inarticulate sound and suddenly he was pulling her to him, her breasts flattening against his chest, his fingers knotting into the thick coil of hair. His mouth descended on hers, crushing her lips.

And now, *now* her hands found their way. With a soft cry, she flung her arms around his neck. Her lips parted, not a small, tentative opening, but fully, wanting something more . . . something— *Ah! Yes! That!*

His tongue dipped inside, stroking the sleek lining

of her cheeks, finding her own tongue. Every chord within her responded. *Caviar.*

"Evie," he whispered.

The soft, wet sounds of this naughty, lush, open-mouthed kissing filled her ears. His arm hooked around her waist and she arched back, obliging him to follow her, the movement forcing her hips against his.

With a curse, Justin tore his mouth from Evelyn's. He heard his breath drawn sharply between his teeth and shuddered with agonized sensitivity. He pushed his erection against her; he was hard, so damn hard. She sighed, as laxly as a pampered cat, as wantonly as coquette.

A smile curved her lower lip. Innocent, carnal, unknowing, completely aware. He wanted to sink his teeth into that plush lower lip. He wanted more. He wanted to see the soft, rounded breasts he felt. He wanted to lick her, undress her, play with her. To be inside of her.

"More."

He shifted her, holding her balanced against his forearm as his free hand slipped beneath her blouse and his fingertips played along her collarbone as though it were a woodwind instrument. Her whole body sang. Her breath caught in a promise of abandonment, her legs trembled at the challenge of holding her upright.

He dipped his head and grazed his teeth along the elegant column of her throat. Another button undone. Another. One more and he'd exposed a softly flushed breast, as finely veined as the rarest marble but buoyant, ripe.

His lips followed his fingers as he pushed the ugly wool away. His fingers brushed across her nipple and felt it clench beneath her chemise into a tight, ready pearl. His mouth passed across the thin cotton, a moist heated kiss of breath.

A thin cry seeped from her throat. Her back arched further, offering her breast. He laid his tongue against the thin cotton and she jerked, her breath hitched in a sound of amazement. He stopped and let his tongue rest against the hard nub, shivered with this terrible exercise in restraint.

"Justin!"

She furrowed her fingers though his hair, pulling him down, wanting his mouth on her. There! Where it was most wicked of all! She couldn't breathe, couldn't speak. Words caught in her throat, turned into gasps and pants.

Speak? She couldn't even bear her own weight. He simply moved her body, at turns limp and agitated, restless and lax, opening her to pleasure after pleasure. Then, abruptly, the warm, wet kisses were gone.

She opened her eyes as he opened the tiny seed buttons on her chemise, his tanned hand extravagantly masculine against its whiteness. His gaze was intent on the body he worked so hard to reveal....

*Her* body. Her small, scrawny, underformed body.

A thread of panic infiltrated her haze of sexual bliss. She found his wrist and clasped it, stopping him from undressing her. He met her gaze, his intent expression first questioning, then accepting. He nodded.

She'd been right to panic. He'd come to his senses. A man like him would expect more. More experience.

More polish. More woman. Something inside of her, something that had felt like wings expanding, cringed, curling back into a tight little chrysalis.

"Yes, you're right. Of course," he muttered, twitching her blouse back into place. "You must think me a bounder of the worst sort. Forgive me."

He lifted her to her feet, stepping back and turning away from her. He was breathing heavily. "Can you forgive me? Can you ever feel safe with me again? No. Of course not. What an asinine question."

He paced back and forth over the uneven cobbled floor, his shadow stalking the dingy, mold-covered far wall.

"If I promise never again to touch you . . . ?" he said. "I would leave, I swear I would, but—I wish I could explain—"

"I understand," she said. She sounded so reasonable, so calm, when inside she was shattering.

He stopped, looked at her. "You do?"

"Of course. You told me you'd reformed."

His face furrowed into a look of frenzied bewilderment. "What has that to do with this?"

She tried to button her dress, but her fingers were numb. At least her voice was under her command. "Well. I expect—I mean, you *did* get carried away."

"God." His smile was acrimonious. "I guess you could say that. But that's no excuse."

"Not an excuse, no. But an explanation. I mean, I expect it's rather being like an opium addict, isn't it?"

He stood rock still.

"Being a womanizer, I mean," she elucidated.

"What are you talking about?"

"Your reformation. And you have reformed. I quite believe you. In fact, I suspect that you've been reformed for a long time. I mean, all the evidence up until now proves it. Until these past few minutes, that is."

She was becoming increasingly aware that while her tone might be under her control, the words themselves were not. But she couldn't seem to stop. "I mean, you don't lose a propensity like that through lack of use, do you?" she went on idiotically. "It must be like riding a bicycle. Get a woman into your arms and all the old magic returns and it *is* magic. I *quite* see now why you were successful. I do," she said sincerely. He swam in her vision and she blinked rapidly.

"Are you out of your mind?" he asked.

"No. I don't think so," she replied honestly. "I was just trying to reassure you that I know I don't have anything to fear from you and that this . . . episode is an isolated incident, and you won't—" God, she was going to cry! She bit her lip hard, blinking like a blind bat in a beam of light. "—won't ever happen—" Where were her damn glasses? They must have slipped off during their . . . She felt naked without them. Ah! There. On the floor. She picked them up and put them on. Immediately she felt better. Safer. "Won't ever happen again!"

Why was he scowling like that?

"And just *how* do you know this?" he ground out. Her own nature, combative and proud, rose from the ashes of humiliation and answered his belligerent pose.

"Well," she said stiffly, "I expect that sex is like a

drug." She ignored his growl. "And as with a drug addict, *any* chance to enjoy the old vice would be hard to resist. Especially after a long abstinence."

" '*Any* chance'? Even you?" he asked coldly.

She blanched, but went doggedly on, driven to prove her point. "Well. Yes. Even me."

He stalked forward. She withstood the temptation to scuttle back. He looked as if he wanted to hit something. This last half-hour had been a series of revelations. First she'd seen him grow angry, not only once, but twice, and now she saw him look violent.

She held her ground. He stopped a yard from her. His hands clenched and unclenched at his side. "*That* is a pile of bullshit!"

She gasped.

He grabbed her arms, lifting her off her feet and pulling her close. "I was carried away because I want you. *You.* Evelyn Cummings Whyte. I want to make love to you. I want to feel you beneath me, every svelte, delicate inch of you. I want *you* naked beneath my hand, my mouth, my flesh. I want to taste you, have you, *own* you!"

He shouldn't be saying these things to her! The blood boiled to the surface of her skin, burning her with embarrassment, but more, with a fever of longing.

She believed him. Her amazement turned into a sudden, dazzling sense of her own power. He wanted her. Enough to "get carried away."

For the first time in her life, Evie felt completely, ravishingly female. And for the first time in her life, she did not weigh her response, she simply gave in to it. Purposefully, she lifted her hands and spread them against his chest. His heartbeat thundered through her palms as her fingers rode his heaving chest. *She'd* done that.

She looked up into his face, delighted with herself. She studied him from beneath the spiky fringe of her lashes. "Do you?"

"Do I what?"

"Want me?"

His hands dropped from her side; he stepped back. His face grew still. "Are you taunting me, Evie?" he asked in a careful voice.

"No," she replied at once. "I'm trying to tempt you. I want you to kiss me. And those other things."

"The hell you do!" The words burst from him. He didn't make a move, he just stood there, his stance wide, his hands at his sides like a boxer waiting for the first blow.

Her gaze slid down his face, to his torso, to his trousers. His fly tented out. With a start, she realized by what. He was . . . enlarged. His gaze followed hers.

"Yes," he finally replied to her question. "I want you. But that's rather obvious."

"Very obvious." She knew she should be horribly self-conscious, that she should be fainting with mortification, and she was: deep inside, she *was* abashed and self-conscious and uncomfortable. And if he showed the least amusement, she would sink right through the floor.

But he didn't. He looked as shaken as she felt. Even his sarcasm had been delivered in an unsteady voice. The idea fascinated her.

She slid one foot forward. "Then," she said hesitantly, her eyes never leaving his face, "can we do those things again?"

"No."

"Please?"

"God." He struggled.

"Is that still a no?"

He lost.

He snatched her up, crushing her in his embrace, his mouth descending upon hers in uncontrolled hunger, his tongue plunging inside her mouth, feasting on the taste of her. He growled deep in his throat, sexual imperative compelling him to ignore the demands made by a fast-vanishing conscience.

Precocious learner that she was, this time she was not content to simply accept his passion. This time, foolish girl, she must participate. It would be her undoing. Or his. She returned his ardent kisses, her head lifted, her mouth open, her tongue meeting his and making its own sweet exploration.

"Evelyn," he panted, breaking away. "Evie. You don't know. You don't understand—"

"Yes. No. I don't know." She sounded dazed and single-minded. "Want me. Show me. Please."

"Yes. Oh. Yes."

She yanked at his shirtfront, undoing some buttons, sending others skittering across the cobbles. Her hand slid beneath his open shirt. He froze at her touch, his kiss ending, his lips still clinging lightly to hers, his harsh breath sluicing over her mouth as he closed his eyes and soaked up the heady, eviscerating sensation.

"Justin!" she whispered against his lips.

His forehead fell against hers, his body unwillingly relaxed. She undid him, unraveled him. With the brush of her fingers across his heart, she swept away a lifetime of careful autonomy. She scared the hell out of him.

Because for her, he couldn't say what he wouldn't do.

The realization brought his head snapping up. He jerked her to her feet. He couldn't stay with her. Couldn't look at her, all sweetly tousled. Couldn't even begin to explain. He wouldn't make it past the first sentence before he had her in his arms again. And he didn't know what would stop him if he began kissing her again.

"Tell me to stop," he asked her.

"I don't want you to stop."

He made a strangled sound, raising his eyes to heaven. "*Yes*. You *do*."

She shook her head at once, certain, honest to a fault. Manipulative, prickly, funny, touching, smart, and most of all, abysmally ignorant, because she'd made it clear she wouldn't stop him. Which left all matters of self-control up to him.

"Bloody hell!" He pushed her away and bolted for the stairs, taking them two at a time. At the top, he grabbed the handle and pushed. Nothing happened.

He shoved. The door stayed stubbornly shut. Frustration, both sexual and otherwise, combined within him. He rammed his shoulder against the door. It held.

"Bloody, bloody hell!" he shouted.

"Justin?"

He looked over his shoulder and found her halfway up the stairs, holding the lantern. Its light shimmered on her face, playing with the satin texture of her skin, burnishing the gleaming coils of her hair and the ripe swell of her lips. He banged his forehead against the door.

"Justin? Are you all right?"

"Yes!" *No!* "Stay there. We're locked in."

"Perhaps I could—"

"No!"

"I say, this is all wrong." There was something odd about her voice.... She was giggling! "I mean, as the unsullied maiden, aren't I supposed to be the one pounding on the door?"

"Go away!" He was at the end of his rope. He'd no more reserves, nothing left with which to resist her. If he looked into her merry, wicked eyes, he'd be lost. He could barely keep away from her as it was. He stood no chance against her in her current winsome, wicked mood. With a strangled oath, he pounded against the heavy oak door. "Let us out! Let us the hell—!"

The door suddenly swung out, the bright light blinding him. He squinted. Figures stood in a cluster outside the cellar door: a pair of women in driving bonnets, a stranger wearing a pair of goggles, several workmen straining to peer over his shoulder, and Beverly looking even more stoic than usual. Only Merry seemed pertly interested.

He heard Evelyn coming up the stairs behind him.

All his protective instincts came surging to the fore, protective instincts he didn't even know he owned. He stepped between Evelyn and the gaping crowd.

"Who the bloody hell are you?" he demanded, ramming his shirttails into his trousers.

The closest woman's thin, aristocratic nostrils quivered. "Mrs. Edith Vandervoort."

"Who?" he repeated irritably. He was dusty, overwrought, underused, and in an altogether vile temper.

"I'm the bride."

# Chapter 16

MERRY SAW BEVERLY FURTIVELY SLIP SOMEthing into his coat pocket. Something, she assumed, being the key to the wine cellar.

Just like a man, she thought, about as subtle as a sledgehammer. But she had to admit it seemed to have gotten results. Mr. Powell had come out of that cellar missing half a dozen buttons, and Evelyn looked frankly blowsy. Her collar was buttoned, her eyes were bright as stars, and pink colored her cheeks.

Merry gave Beverly a conspiratorial thumbs-up, to which he responded by shutting his eyes and shuddering.

"Mrs. Vandervoort, we didn't expect you!" Evelyn said.

"Your hair is coming down," was the only reply

Mrs. Vandervoort made as she handed her gloves to the silent, veiled woman beside her.

With a little start, Evelyn grabbed a swatch of loosened hair and jabbed pins into it. "The door jammed and we were locked in," she explained.

"I see," Mrs. Vandervoort replied with a lingering look at Justin Powell. His answer to her questioning gaze was to glare, an attitude so unlike that of the easygoing scapegrace Merry had come to know that she found herself studying him more closely.

His shoulders were set forward like a street fighter's, half shielding Evelyn. He looked very ill-tempered. Really, he looked quite delectable.

"Mrs. Vandervoort," Evelyn stammered out, "may I present Justin Powell, the owner of North Cross Abbey?"

Mrs. Vandervoort inclined her head. "How do you do?"

"Fine, I hope," Mr. Powell muttered and then, subtly but undeniably, his expression smoothed to bland affability. Now, that was interesting, thought Merry.

"Mr. Powell," Evelyn continued, thoroughly flustered, "my client, Mrs. Edith Vandervoort."

"Pleased to meet you," Justin said. "You'll forgive how we look?" He smiled charmingly, yet Merry could not help but feel there was an underlying warning in his good-natured question.

"After all," he continued, "we were down in that miserable hole hunting up an acceptable quaff for your wedding toast. Found it, too. Where's the wine, Evie? Ah, there it is."

Mutely, Evelyn thrust two dust-covered bottles at Mrs. Vandervoort. Justin nodded like a fond tutor whose student has produced the correct answer at orals.

Mrs. Vandervoort glanced at the labels. "Very nice."

Justin adopted an expression of profound regret. "Can't begin to express my sorrow that my grandsire was such a rotter to your grandmum. 'Spect a wedding will lay the old girl's ghost, though, eh?"

Though Merry had no idea what he was talking about, Mrs. Vandervoort obviously did. Her gaze shot toward Evelyn, who fidgeted guiltily.

"How kind of you, Mr. Powell," Mrs. Vandervoort said. "But regardless of my sentimental desire to be married here, I believe the past is best left in the past. I'm sure you agree."

She didn't wait for his concurrence before continuing, "Would you be so kind as to have one of your men help with my secretary, Quail? He is outside. He was taken ill some days ago and has been unable to leave his sickbed. But he insisted on accompanying me, and now is unable to walk without assistance."

Evelyn looked around and spied Beverly trying to sneak out the back way. "Beverly! Go help Mrs. Vandervoort's man into the house."

"I fly. Ma'am." Bev crooked his finger, gesturing for the chauffeur—the fellow in goggles—to follow him, and retreated.

"Now," Mrs. Vandervoort continued, "as I originally informed you, I have brought my staff: Hector, my chauffeur; Quail, my secretary; and Grace Angelina Rose, my maid." She motioned toward the big, silent woman.

"I expect the guests to arrive within the next day or two, followed by my fiancé." She paused. "Will that prove a problem, Lady Evelyn?" As she spoke she looked around the hall, taking in the newly plastered walls, the freshly waxed floorboards, and the sparkling silver on the sideboard. Her gaze neither approved nor condemned; it weighed and evaluated.

When she turned it on Evelyn, Merry had the uncomfortable sensation that her small friend, too, had been weighed, evaluated, and judged... as a woman who'd just emerged from a man's embrace. Her gaze moved to Justin, who looked every bit the part of the self-satisfied libertine.

He'd crossed his arms, making no attempt to hide the fact that several shirt buttons were missing. His blue-green eyes were hooded, his smile disarming.

"*Do* you foresee any problems?" Mrs. Vandervoort asked Evelyn again, this time looking pointedly at Justin. It didn't take a scholar to figure out that the American lady was really asking whether Evelyn could control herself—and Justin Powell—until after Mrs. Vandervoort had left. A violent blush spread over Evelyn's entire body.

"No, no problem at all," Merry interjected while Evelyn struggled to find her voice. "Lady Evelyn has exhausted herself in preparing for your wedding festivities. Why, look at the poor thing! She's a mess!"

Thankfully, the front door opened at this moment,

sparing Merry the necessity of providing further explanations. Beverly and Mrs. Vandervoort's chauffeur, Hector, entered supporting a slight, youngish-looking man.

The poor creature was in terrible condition. Blond and of middling height, he slumped between the men, breathing hoarsely through his mouth. His skin was an unhealthy pasty color, glistening with sweat, and his shirt collar was wilted with perspiration.

"Heavens!" Evelyn cried in alarm. "Merry, have Buck go to town and telegram for a doctor."

Merry started forward at once, but the man raised a hand, forestalling her. "Thank you, but . . ." He swallowed painfully. "Please don't."

"Oh, my," Mrs. Vandervoort murmured to Evelyn. "He is much worse than when I left him a short while ago. Perhaps you ought to send for someone."

The sick man shook his head. "There's nothing they could do," he haltingly said. "It's malaria, ma'am. I have the medicine in my valise. Please. I just need rest."

Mrs. Vandervoort's mouth pinched with distress. "Please. Help him."

"Of course," Evelyn said, leading the way down the hall. "Merry, please show Mrs. Vandervoort and, er, Grace Angelina Rose to their rooms. Beverly, this way."

Evelyn ushered Mrs. Vandervoort's secretary to his room, and would have stayed to see him comfortable except that the poor man's embarrassment was so acute, and his desire for solitude so obvious, that she deemed it the better course to simply withdraw, with a promise to look in on him later.

She hurried back to the front hall, hoping to repair the abominable impression she and the helpful Merry had made on Mrs. Vandervoort. The hall was empty. Even Justin had vanished.

At once her mind provided a plethora of suppositions and conjectures, fears and frets—none of them having to do with Mrs. Vandervoort.

What was he thinking? Was he even now packing, congratulating himself on a near escape? She supposed she shouldn't have giggled, but the absurdity of the situation had suddenly overwhelmed her, and he really had been pounding on the door like a man possessed. Or a man terrified... Of what? Her? Could he be as interested in her as she was in him?

The thought hit her like a physical blow, disorienting her.

A few minutes later Merry came sauntering down the hall and found her still standing there. The ladies, she said, were resting before dinner, and Buck had transported Mrs. Vandervoort's crates to her room. "And most unhappy she looked that they'd preceded her here, too."

"And Mr. Powell?" Evelyn asked casually.

"Went off as soon as you did. Should I find him?"

"No, no," Evelyn answered hurriedly. "I just, ah, I just wondered where he'd gone." Gads.

Merry nodded. "I should find him. You obviously want to talk to him—"

"No!" She cast about for something to explain her

sudden interest in Justin's whereabouts. "The fact is that Mr. Powell isn't supposed to be here at all." That was good. And true, too. "He promised to make himself scarce once Mrs. Vandervoort had arrived." She stopped in sudden realization and looked helplessly at Merry. "You don't think he's really *left,* do you?!"

Merry snorted as if the idea were daft.

"Not that it's any of my business, mind you," Evelyn said, much heartened by Merry's snort. "But it would make things more difficult if he left now. It's such an old house. So many little quirks and things only he would know about. Why, that door is a perfect example!"

"Door?"

Evelyn nodded. "To the wine cellar. Who'd have guessed that the drat thing could lock by itself. Is anything wrong, Merry? You look odd."

"Nothing is wrong, Evelyn. I was just pondering the oddness of old houses and old butlers."

Evelyn frowned. "I'm not sure what one has to do with the other."

"It's an old French saying."

"Oh!" Evelyn said, enlightened. She strode by Merry. "Well. I'll be off then. Carry on doing whatever you're doing."

"That would be Buck."

Evelyn jolted to a stop. *"What?"*

Merry's expression was bland. "I am doing his uniform for the wedding. The poor man can't drive the wedding carriage in homespun."

Evelyn blushed. Clearly, her mind had taken to dwelling in the gutter.

Merry reached out and patted her on the cheek. "*Réveille-toi, ma belle dormeuse,*" she said fondly before chugging off down the hall, presumably in search of Buck.

Evelyn hurried in the opposite direction, the need to sort her thoughts driving her to the solitude of her room. She closed and locked the door behind her, then threw herself on the middle of the bed.

She could still feel his hand, hear his voice, taste him. It was an example of her newborn depravity that she hadn't even cared much that Mrs. Vandervoort had almost caught them being, well, depraved. He'd kissed her and she'd liked it. And *he'd* liked doing it. She didn't have a single, solitary doubt about that.

She had always been very careful where men were concerned. From the time of her coming-out, she'd watched every nuance of a man's reaction to her. She'd been quick to spy the subtlest signs of feigned interest, so that she could be the first to disengage her attention. It wasn't that she'd never been smitten; she'd simply never allowed herself to believe anything could come of it.

Oh, without doubt she *could* have caught a husband. After all, her grandfather was a duke. But she didn't want to *catch* a husband. Because, as much as she was a realist about her looks, she was equally realistic about the good qualities that she did own. She was proud of her accomplishments, and she would not marry a man who didn't appreciate them, too.

And what becomes of a proud *golem*? It lives alone and dies.

She shook her head, denying a desent into distasteful self-pity. She was smart, capable, useful, needed. Aunt Agatha needed her. Her family needed her. Mrs. Vandervoort needed her.

And now she was wanted, too. By Justin Powell.

The muscles in her shoulders relaxed. Her heart submerged itself in unaccustomed bliss. The feeling of euphoria was indescribable, a warm bath of contentment washing through her, a shimmering river of happiness suffusing her not only emotionally but physically.

Everything was *perfect*. The wedding preparations couldn't be going any more smoothly. Every one of her ideas had come to magnificent fruition. North Cross Abbey had been dug out from a century of neglect, and under her watchful eye had been reborn into, well, not precisely splendor, but certainly quaintness. But best of all, Justin Powell had been carried away by his attraction to her!

How could her life be any better?

The specter of the old Evelyn Cummings Whyte, the Evelyn Cummings Whyte of that morning, tapped nervously at her contentment, willing to point out a few possibilities and urging an analysis of the facts. Why *would* he want her? How long would he want her? What then? What next?

She refused to listen, closing her mind to that poor creature's urgent protests. She rolled over onto her back and dragged the pillow to her chest, hugging it.

She didn't want to die alone without ever knowing just what "carried away" ultimately led to. Not that she believed for a second that Justin Powell would marry her! The idea was ludicrous. But he *did* want her.

She rolled over, her eyelids slipping shut in languid repletion, replaying every second, every touch, every look and caress. She wanted him, too. And she was going to have him. But how? She opened her eyes. She was going to need some expert advice.

With that thought, she hopped to her feet and strode to another bedchamber farther down the hallway. She knocked. The door swung open a second later, and when Merry saw who stood there, her ingenuous face broke into a wide, knowing smile.

She took Evelyn's hand and pulled her inside saying, "Come in, *ma petite*. I have been expecting you."

# Chapter 17

JUSTIN STRODE DOWN THE HALL WEARING an irritable expression, looking into the rooms he passed as he went by. For the past six days—ever since Mrs. Vandervoort had found them in the wine cellar—he hadn't caught more than a few glimpses of Evie. True, he hadn't gone out of his way to look for her, but he'd been waiting, anticipating the arrival of the diabolical device while he charged Beverly with the task of watching her.

Justin had purposefully stayed away from the manor, taking his meals in town while he tried to ferret out news of any recent arrivals—besides Mrs. Vandervoort's guests, whom he'd adroitly avoided. His questions about anyone sporting a bruised face led to naught. As far as he could tell, no one had scraped their knuckles in the whole bloody town. Soon, the bruises would fade and be useless as a means of identifying his assailant.

Thwarted in town, he'd spent the next few days on the forest roads around Henley Wells trusting Beverly to keep an eye out for the "device." At least he'd been doing what he was supposed to have been doing. And if in the course of doing it he hadn't seen Evie—and thus hadn't been tempted by Evie—didn't he have a good reason?

What was he supposed to *do* with all these immensely distracting feelings? They were grossly inconvenient. He'd never been a particularly randy chap, yet just the thought of Evie in his arms, pliant and sweetly lax and . . . *There,* that's all it took. A simple moment of recollection and he was primed and ready.

*Not* the best way to conduct a covert operation.

And it angered him that at the ripe age of thirty-two, after what anyone would account several lifetimes' worth of adventures and dangers, he'd been overwhelmed by a pint-sized, black-haired hoyden masquerading as a dowd in a stiff wool dress.

And now she wasn't even anywhere around. Where the bloody hell was she?

He popped his head through the door to one of the rooms she'd overturned just as easily and thoroughly as she had his life. A trio of strangers stood by the windows, teacups in their hands. Blast. More of the Vandervoort woman's friends. They'd been arriving in dribs and drabs for the last few days, well groomed, well dressed, well heeled. They regarded him with interested smiles. He wasn't interested back. He wanted to know where Evie was.

"Mr. Powell, isn't it?" one of the men asked.

"Yes," Justin answered shortly, and after peering around to see if Evie was hiding in some corner somewhere, he left.

Poor Evie. *She* probably was hiding from him, now that he thought of it. If he was rattled by their last encounter, she must be shaken to her very core. Slipping out of side doors, jumping at the sound of a male voice . . .

Suddenly, it seemed essential that he find her and reassure her. And if part of him was aware of the absurdity of this abrupt decision, after dodging her for days, well, *everything* about his behavior lately was absurd. The knowledge didn't provide him with any comfort.

A knock on the front door attracted his notice, and he moved toward it, distracted by the thought of a miserable Evie ducking him. He pulled the door open. Ernst Blumfield stood outside dressed in dinner clothes with his hat in his hand. Blast.

"I have been invited to dine with Lady Evelyn," he announced with a shade of conceit. "And, of course, the delightful Mrs. Vandervoort. If you would be so kind—?"

"Don't know anything about it." Justin let the door go. It shut with a satisfying click. Since when had Blumfield become so cozy with Evie that he thought himself invited to dinner? And how had he contrived to meet "the delightful" Mrs. Vandervoort? Clearly, matters had become muddled while he'd been assiduously pursuing Her Majesty's enemies. Humph.

Midway down the hall, a door opened. A pair of

trousered legs crowned with a mountain of white froufrou began waddling down the hall.

"Beverly!" Justin called out, striding to meet him.

The mountain ceased moving and turned. "Sir."

"What the blazes are you doing?"

A short pause. "Pretending to be a blancmange? Sir?"

"Did *she* set you up to this?"

"Yes, if by 'she' you are referring to Mistress Persistence, She of Myriad Wants and Needs, Her Most—"

"And just who gave you leave to neglect your duties to me and our other," Justin groped around for an appropriately discreet word, "*commitments*?"

"You did. Sir," the blancmange answered. "You told me to stay close to Her."

"Blast you, Beverly. Where is she?"

"The last time I was the happy recipient of one of her honeyed requests, she was in the east courtyard. Wielding a sledgehammer."

"How long ago was this?"

"This afternoon, sir."

"Any idea where she might be now?"

"Mrs. Vandervoort often insists that she join her and her guests for the evening meal."

"She does?" Justin felt his indignation rising. "That seems a bit autocratic, doesn't it?"

"I think Lady Evelyn enjoys it. Not that I'm paying such close attention, you understand. But she's hardly one to mask her feelings."

"No, she isn't, is she?" Justin said softly before clearing his throat. "Well, then I 'spect that's all right."

The mountain of white froufrou shifted. "Will there be anything else, sir? Lady Evelyn required that I bring these to Mlle. Molière, after which I am to check Quail—"

"Quail?"

"Mrs. Vandervoort's secretary. The fellow with malaria."

"Oh, yes," Justin said, a trifle guilty at having forgotten a sick guest in his home. "Bad luck, that. How's the poor chap faring?"

"I believe he is on the mend, sir. His fevers come less frequently. But he is wary of leaving his room lest he collapse again. He has a great deal of pride, unlike some others who shall go nameless."

Justin smiled amiably, not having really attended Beverly's answer. "Very good. I suspect I should go see if Evie would like a friendly face about, what with all these strangers here."

The tower of white rustled and a hand dug a small, dark tunnel through the silk and ribbons. A single, morose eyeball glowered at him from the shadowed depths. "Like *that,* sir?"

Justin scowled. "What do you mean?"

"It's dinnertime, sir."

"So?"

The ribbons about the tunneled hole quivered with the exhalation of a heartfelt sigh. "Mrs. Vandervoort and her guests generally dress for dinner."

"I *am* dressed," Justin huffed.

"Respectably. Sir."

"Pah!"

"If you return to your room, you will find your black coat is ironed and there are new collars in your drawer. And if you need assistance—?"

"I don't," Justin said.

"As you say, sir," Beverly replied doubtfully, the single eye fixed on Justin's head. "But perhaps you wouldn't object to my making merry with a pair of scissors?"

"I would indeed object. There's nothing wrong with my hair." With that, he left Beverly and hurried to his room.

Ten minutes later he emerged, settling his jacket more comfortably about his shoulders and yanking the collar into alignment. He headed directly for the great hall as the most likely place to dine. When he arrived, he found he barely recognized the deserted room. It took only a few seconds to realize why. Evie had transformed the place.

From an echoing, drafty vestibule, she'd created a high lofty bower, a romantic fantasy reminiscent of Avalon and Camelot, knights and ladies, and eternal springs. Garlands of white silk flowers fell in graceful swags from the vaulted ceiling high overhead. Atop the beams she'd set hundreds of white candles of varying height and thickness, some half and even three-quarters spent, wading in thick tallow pools of their own luminous wax, creating pearly stalactites dripping from the beams.

Set in the new plaster covering the ceiling were diamond-shaped mirrors. When the candles were lit and the French doors flung wide, the currents of warm air would flutter the garlands and make the candles dance, and the mirrors above would throw back the light a thousand times over. It would be breathtaking.

He wandered into the center of the room and noticed the gleaming glass doors that gave out to the once damp and musty little courtyard. He released a slow appreciative whistle. Whatever she'd paid, Mrs. Vandervoort had gotten the best of the bargain.

The courtyard, too, had been altered nearly beyond recognition. Somewhere, Evelyn had found workmen to dredge and enlarge the mud hole, transforming it into a lovely goldfish pond. Giant white lilies lifted waxy fragrant heads above the smooth, mirrored surface. A charming white footbridge spanned its width, leading to a series of platforms of differing levels and varying sizes, giving the impression of a craggy, magical dell. Each platform blended artfully into the next by means of huge banks of flowers and cunningly fashioned papier-mâché boulders.

How she'd managed, he could not guess, just as he could not guess at the engineering and carpentry skill that allowed the entire thing. And he'd tell her as soon as he saw her. He'd read her need for approval years ago, when she'd sat swinging her spindly legs on her parents' kitchen table. Her legs were no longer spindly, but the desire to please, the need to prove herself, was intense as ever.

He left and went to the back room where his grandfather had once had his meals served. Laughter filtered through the heavy oak door; the sound of voices, muffled and indistinct, masculine and feminine, followed. He pushed it open.

Inside, twenty people sat around a long oval table. They were an elegant crew. Pomade polished the carefully groomed heads of gentlemen wearing coats so dark they ate the light, and whose high, starched collars were so crisp they dented their smoothly shaven jaws. Unconsciously, Justin ran a thumb along his own jaw. Perhaps he should have shaved.

If the men reminded Justin of urbane Thoroughbreds, the women did even more so. Diamonds winked from their ears and shimmered round their throats. Form-fitting velvet encased their long equine torsos, and spotless white gloves sheathed their slender arms from fingertip to elbow.

They hadn't spied him yet, and with an unusual prick of self-consciousness, Justin raked his hair back from his temples, looking about for Evie's dark gray gown. It took him a moment to realize there were no gray gowns, dark or otherwise. Nor any dark, tightly braided coiffures. Nor high-necked gowns of any sort at all. In fact, from where he stood, he could see eight ladies' faces, and none of them was Evie's. He also noticed five ladies' backs, all practically naked.

Clearly, Beverly had been wrong. Evie was not amongst the Vandervoort dinner party. Either that or she had developed a headache. . . .

While he'd been searching for Evelyn, the diners had slowly become aware of him. Conversation grew hushed. The gentleman and ladies seated opposite where he stood looked at him askance, while those with their backs to him turned to see who had interrupted their party.

Only one lithe female form remained facing forward, a lady sheathed in deep ruby-colored velvet, the flawless expanse of her alabaster shoulders a foil for the dark tendrils spilling from a low, loose knot of hair.

Then she, too, swiveled at the waist. For a heartbeat they stared at one another. Then her mouth cocked up at the corners in a smile of casual, offhand welcome.

"Oh. 'Allo, Justin," said Evie.

# *Chapter 18*

"AH, MR. POWELL." MRS. VANDERVOORT SWEPT her hand toward a seat at the opposite end of the table from Evelyn. "Won't you join us?"

Justin didn't answer. He stood in the doorway, gorgeous in dinner jacket, collar, and cuffs that, given their slightly twisted appearance, Evelyn suspected he'd donned without Beverly's aid.

Her heartbeat thumped into a frenzied rhythm. She tried valiantly to retard it. She had orders to be friendly, bright, and flirtatious, but under no circumstance to let on that she cared for him. She schooled her expression to bland friendliness, knowing that if he looked closely, he'd see how much she'd missed him.

She mustn't let that happen. But she was having the hardest time remembering why. Oh, yes. Merry.

Merry was an expert. After all, hadn't Merry foretold the abrupt manner in which Justin would emerge from seclusion, as well as how, the moment he saw her, he'd become mute?

She should congratulate herself on her newly acquired sophistication. Four days ago she'd have been uncomfortable with her uncovered figure and new coiffure. Not until she'd seen Mrs. Vandervoort's expression of cool approbation and the undisguised admiration of the gentlemen had she accepted that she didn't look bizarre.

*I am not naked. I am as covered up as any lady at this table. Ruby velvet looks nice on me. My shoulders are not bony. My skin is unblemished.* She silently recited the litany Merry had given her, wishing she believed it more.

If only she'd had enough courage to really study her image in the mirror. But she hadn't dared more than a few glances at the polished surface Merry kept thrusting in front of her. Old habits die hard, and it had been the habit of a decade to avoid looking in a mirror.

*Be suave, Evelyn.* Only it would be easier to be suave without Justin staring at her so disconcertingly. He hadn't moved in minutes. He wasn't smiling, and the rapt adoration Merry had foretold looked more like wary scrutiny.

"Justin?" she said with a calmness she was far from feeling. "Do you anticipate joining us soon, or should we expect you after the cheese course?"

Her dinner companion, a portly Dutchman named Dekker, hid a smile. In answer, Justin paced to the vacant seat originally assigned Ernst, who was unaccountably absent. He sat down, snapped open his napkin, and settled it across his lap. He met her eye. "Where are your spectacles?"

Evelyn's cheeks grew warm, but with a masterful display of composure she kept from reaching up to adjust phantom lenses. Even if the last days had taught her that they were unnecessary, she still missed them.

"I... I misplaced them." Her skin grew even warmer at the lie, but she couldn't very well blurt out that she didn't need them and possibly hadn't *ever* needed them. She'd look like an idiot!

"Hm," Justin said, frowning, and Evelyn regarded him with surprise. On this score, too, Merry had been correct.

The Justin Powell sitting down the table from her was both familiar and alien. *Her* Justin, the Justin she'd spent the past four weeks with, was given to saying whatever came to his mind, was indifferent to social niceties, and was unimpressed by titles.

Well, this Justin was certainly all of that, but *her* Justin had been all of that *and* comfortable as warm toast and tea. This Justin looked hard and cold as adamant.

"You have a lovely place here, Signor Powell," the slender Italian gentleman, Signor Coladarci, said.

"Thank you," Justin clipped out. He suddenly lifted his spoon and gestured. "Nasty bruise on your jaw, there. Hope you didn't hurt yourself too badly."

Signor Coladarci flushed. "It is not a bruise, but a birthmark."

"Oh," Justin said with every appearance of disappointment. He dipped his spoon into the vichyssoise.

"Lady Evelyn tells us you are an avid ornithologist, Mr. Powell," the lady to Justin's right said.

"That's right," Justin said and went back to his soup.

The Dutchman cleared his throat. "I am something of an enthusiast myself, Herr Powell."

"Are you?" Justin asked disinterestedly.

"Indeed, yes. But I cannot claim your preeminence."

"Oh?" Justin murmured as he chased a bit onion around his bowl. "And what preeminence might that be?"

"Sir," the Dutchman demurred, "you are modest, indeed, if you have had the honor of identifying an entirely new species without—how do you say?—blowing your own horn."

"Oh, that. Yes." He settled back in his chair and adopted a look of complacent satisfaction. "Well, to be perfectly frank, *she* discovered *me*. Flew into my window."

"No!"

Justin lifted a hand. "True. Flew straight in. Of course, I could see she was unique as soon as I laid eyes on her, and once I heard her odd, insistent little call, I confess, I was besotted."

"Fascinating!" the Dutchman said. "Lady Evelyn could not recall the name of your discovery. What is it?"

For a second, Justin simply sat still. He frowned,

reached for the goblet of water by his plate, took a gulp, and suddenly smiled. "Why, *Bubo Formosa Plurimus*." He glanced at Evelyn. "*Minor*."

"Ah! A new *Bubo*, eh? Though, I say, I am amazed she flew into your window in broad daylight. I thought the entire genus nocturnal."

"Oh, my first encounter with her was nocturnal," Justin said, clearly in charity with the Dutchman.

"Forgive me. My Latin is quite rusty," the Italian gentleman's wife said in her heavily accented voice, "but is not *formosus* the word for beauty?"

"Just so," said the Dutchman.

"And *plurimus* is?"

"A crashing bore to everyone else at the table, I'm afraid," Justin said, taking the signora's hand and dropping a kiss on it. She giggled. Evelyn felt something uncharitable.

"You indulge me, signora," Justin went on. "Pretending to be interested in a pair of miscreants like Herr . . ." He looked inquiringly at the Dutchman.

"Dekker, sir," the Dutchman said happily, clearly not averse to being denoted—probably for the first time in his life—as a miscreant.

"Herr Dekker and me."

"You are gracious, Mr. Powell," Mrs. Vandervoort said. "As well as modest."

Modesty not being one of the qualities Evelyn would have ascribed to Justin, she kept her mouth closed and eyed him closely. He was relaxing into his role now, companionable and pleasing.

For a minute Evelyn didn't realize the importance of her observation. Then it dawned on her. Justin *was* playing a role. Why, he was slipping into it as she watched. He smiled blandly, flirted without any real compunction, and drawled in the most irritating public school fashion.

"—must give all the credit to Lady Evelyn." At the sound of her name, Evelyn started. Mrs. Vandervoort was smiling at her.

"She designed and supervised everything and I must say, it is marvelous."

Evelyn lowered her eyelids and feigned modesty. "Feigned" because it *was* marvelous. She'd bullied and prodded, threatened, begged, and beguiled every silk flower, every piece of fretwork, every plastered boulder into existence. "Thank you."

"I can hardly wait to see it!" breathed Signora Coladarci.

"You will have to wait for the wedding," Mrs. Vandervoort replied. "Only two more days."

She turned to Evelyn. "I cannot believe how much you have accomplished, you and the talented Mme. Molière. All is ready, is it not? Now if only the shipment containing my future mother-in-law's wedding canopy arrives."

Evelyn smiled, delighted at being able to bring more good news. "I think it has."

Mrs. Vandervoort, who'd been about to take a sip of wine, set her glass down instead. "Oh?"

"Yes. A crate arrived just before we came in to dinner.

Justin's head snapped up. "Silsby brought it up from the station?"

She shook her head. "No. It came all the way from London by private van and was delivered directly to the back door. I was in the garden when it arrived."

"No one was with you?" It was an odd question, made even odder by the scowl Justin wore.

"Beverly. He came out at once and signed for it."

"Ah." The frown melted from Justin's face.

"And I must say, Mr. Powell," Evelyn added severely, "Beverly's behavior bordered on the impertinent when I ordered it taken to my rooms."

In fact, Beverly's behavior had far overstepped impertinence. He'd actually tried to wrestle the crate away from the van driver, muttering on about how he was sure it was Mr. Powell's taxidermy equipment—which wasn't likely, unless Justin planned on stuffing an elephant. The crate was heavy.

"Your rooms?" said Mrs. Vandervoort. Once more, Justin was frowning.

"Yes." Evelyn dimpled. "As you wished it as a surprise for Sir Cuthbert, I thought it best. Besides, Merry can work on it in my room in case the satin needs repair."

"Well, I'll have to come and see, won't I?" Mrs. Vandervoort said smoothly. "Wise of you to hide it from Bunny. He's insatiably curious."

"You are a wonder, Edith," an older gentleman said. "How do you manage to be so serene with your wedding so close and your secretary ill and abed and your maid, too, pleading sick?"

Grace Angelina Rose was ill? The tall, rawboned woman had seemed the picture of health when Evelyn saw her yesterday, even though it would be hard to discern pallor under the layer of thick makeup she wore.

"Is there anything I can do for her?" she asked.

"You are, as always, thoughtful, Lady Evelyn," Mrs. Vandervoort said, "but Grace Angelina suffers from migraine on occasion. It's nothing a day's rest won't cure. However, I do confess to feeling my secretary's loss."

"I believe he is better," Evelyn said cautiously. "He may be able to resume his job in the next day or so."

With Merry engaged in a flurry of last-minute detail work, and Beverly having kittens about the condition of the silverware, it had been left to Evelyn to see Quail that morning. He'd been out, probably testing his strength by taking a short walk, but the oily imprint she'd glimpsed on his pillow told her he wouldn't be resuming his duties anytime soon. He was still sweating profusely.

"He mustn't push himself," Mrs. Vandervoort was saying, and then, as if finding conversation about the health of one's servant slightly vulgar, she turned her attention to her other guests.

Signor Coladarci began telling Evelyn about the palazzos of Rome. Though he was interesting, and his gaze clearly admiring, Evelyn could not help being conscious of Justin lounging idly at the far end of the table, making little attempt to converse with the ladies on either side of him. Another five minutes had passed when suddenly Justin leaned over the table, looked down its length directly at her, and said, "Evie. I say, Evie!"

She ignored him. Unfortunately, her dinner companion didn't. "I think Signor Powell would like to speak to you," he said quietly.

With an exasperated sigh, Evelyn leaned over her fish plate and glared down the table at Justin. "What?"

"Ah, there you are, thought you'd frozen solid in that dress and couldn't move."

She began to sputter but he went blithely on. "Forgot to mention," he said, "but old Blumfield was scratching at the door, looking to be fed. I told him I didn't know anything about any dinner."

"Good heavens, Justin!" Evelyn exclaimed, aghast. "Why ever did you tell him that?"

"Because it was the truth," Justin said innocently. "He might still be hanging about the door kicking stones if you've a mind to let him in. It wasn't *that* long ago."

The others at the table traded fascinated looks, making Evelyn acutely self-conscious. She picked up the bell and rang it fiercely. A second later, Beverly appeared at the door. "She desires?"

"Please, go at once and see if Mr. Blumfield is outside—" She noted his peculiar smile and rose to her feet, exasperated, embarrassed, and annoyed. "No, never mind. I'll go myself."

She'd already made a spectacle of herself—or, rather, Justin had a made a spectacle of her. But she would deal with him later. As she would deal with Merry.

Good intentions aside, the Frenchwoman shouldn't have filled her head with all sorts of absurd ideas about her womanliness and Justin's interest, and how she'd need only to crook her little finger to have him fall to his knees. It was all . . . pipe dreams!

"If you would all excuse me?" She swept down the

length of the table and left in a rustle of taffeta petticoats.

A few minutes later, Justin Powell touched his hand to his forehead, pleaded a headache (while winking brazenly beneath his palm at the Italian signora who, sensing an affair of the heart brewing, sighed with pleasure), and rose to saunter from the room.

"Ernst, can you forgive me? I am sure Mr. Powell—"

"I know exactly what Mr. Powell was doing. Such matters know no international boundaries, my dear," Ernst said, smiling gently. He took her hand and held it between his two. "In his situation, I would do the same."

She had run out the front door just as Ernst had been taking his leave of one of the gardeners. Dear Ernst. He must always take the time to politely, and at length, inquire after his fellow man. From there she'd persuaded him to follow her back into the front hall. But he had resisted actually coming in to dine. He had something he needed to say to her.

How to get across to this dear, naive man that his suspicions regarding Justin were completely unfounded? Her head had cleared. The preceding days were like a child's dream, all wishful thinking and dress-up.

"Ernst, please. You are mistaken. Mr. Powell's oversight had nothing to do with any personal feelings either toward you or me."

Ernst *tch*ed, shaking his head. "You are honest, so you think others are. It is, sadly, not so. Mr. Powell is not as impartial as he would appear."

Evelyn ceased trying to argue. Surely she, who'd lived with Justin for over a month, knew him better than this dear gentleman. Justin had hidden propensities? The notion was absurd. Why, Justin was an open book. A big, uninterested open book. He hadn't even noticed the "new" Evelyn.

Even Ernst didn't seem to notice her transformation—or if he did, he apparently didn't think it worth commenting on. Perhaps he thought she looked silly. Perhaps *Justin* thought she looked silly!

"It's the gown, isn't it?" she asked anxiously.

He blinked. "The . . . ah, gown?"

"It's not my style, is it? Looks bizarre on me. Rather like a chicken got up in ostrich plumes, aren't I?"

He gazed at her helplessly. "Ostrich? Chicken? I don't understand. Your gown is most . . ." He faltered to a halt, his answer unfortunately quite clear.

"Incongruous?" she supplied.

"Well," he said, "unexpected." He smiled in what she was sure he felt was a heartening manner. "I like the gray dress. It is like you. The real you."

"The real me."

"Yes." He nodded vigorously. "Simple. Unadorned. Honest and hardworking."

She returned his smile as well as she could, but apparently not well enough, for poor Ernst's expression turned into one of misery. "I have spoken poorly! Forgive me!" he cried. "I only meant that, my *dear* Lady Evelyn, you have always seemed so easy with who and what you are, so disdainful of artifice and superfluities."

"I actually rather like superfluities, if by that you mean geegaws and furbelows. I just don't think they look right on m—on certain women."

"Right?" As he tested the word and frowned in frustration over his failure to grasp the subtleties of the language, Evelyn became conscious of the unpleasant position she had put Ernst in.

She smiled. "No matter. It's just a dress, correct?"

"Right!" Ernst said with relief. "And you mustn't fret over your appearance. You always look," he hunted for the term and found it with a delighted smile, "just so."

*Just so.* She gave a mental wince. Better than "passable," she supposed. Perhaps "just so" was the highest praise she could expect. When had she become so greedy for a man's praise? No, not a man's praise. Justin's.

"I hadn't dared to assume, but your confiding in me gives me courage to say those things which a gentleman usually only says to a lady after many months' association. At least, it is so in my country, but here things are different. Things go so fast. I feel if I do not seize the moment, the moment will pass me by and I will regret it."

He fixed her with an earnest, soulful stare.

From thoughts of Justin, Evelyn's attention snapped back fully to Ernst. *Uh-oh.* She knew what was coming.

For an instant, a frantic voice within her squealed for her to take what he was about to offer, knowing it was born of true affection and deep regard and honest appreciation. And wasn't appreciation the one thing she'd always insisted she would have from a husband?

A half year ago she might have heeded that voice. Three months ago, she would have said she owed it to herself to joyfully accept Ernst's imminent proposal. A month ago, she would have made him a good wife, even three weeks ago.

But not today.

The knowledge filled her with melancholy, because whatever else had become of her, she wasn't the same woman she'd been before she'd come to North Cross Abbey. Yet her feelings for Justin, and the suspicion that they were just as futile, gave her empathy for Ernst.

She turned her hands in his and clasped them warmly. "My *dear* Ernst," she said. "When I came to North Cross Abbey, I never expected to meet someone who shared so many of the same interests as I. Someone with whom I felt immediately comfortable."

"It is the same for me!" he said eagerly, and would have continued except that she squeezed his hands, gently silencing him.

"How very happy I shall be when I return to London, knowing that our *friendship* has meant as much to you as to me. And how happily I shall look forward to that time when we might renew our acquaintance. Perhaps in your country. I would love to see it. Someday." She spoke softly, her voice light but sober.

He understood. The tips of his ears grew crimson. But he was a gentleman; he would never impose upon her feelings she clearly didn't reciprocate.

"And I would love to show it to you. It is most beautiful," he finally managed. "There. It is settled. Someday you must visit us there."

"I'd like that," Evelyn said. "Now then," she laughed a little, trying to make the situation easier, "the fish course is a lost cause I am afraid, but we should be in time for the main—"

"No. No, thank you, but I am remembering something at the cottage that needs my immediate attention." Ernst shook his head. Gentleman though he might be, he was not yet able to play dinner companion to a lady he'd hoped to make so much more. "I will take a . . . rain check?"

"Yes. Rain check."

"Good. My English improves, does it not?" he asked, struggling for a casualness his pink complexion belied.

"Wonderfully," she answered sincerely. He stood a second longer, simply looking at her, and then he moved past her, opening the front door. He turned. "I will see you later, Lady Evelyn."

"Evelyn."

"Ah, yes," he said. "But *he* calls you Evie, doesn't he?" And with that enigmatic query he left, quietly shutting the door behind him.

For a long minute she stood still, before finally wandering morosely back toward the dining room. She was halfway there when she realized she didn't feel up to putting on the required pleasant façade.

Nor did she much feel like meeting Justin's taunting gaze.

Instead, she turned toward her room.

*Dear God, let it be the bloody wedding canopy and not Bernard's diabolical machine,* Justin thought, racing toward Evie's bedroom. Of all the damnable pieces of misfortune!

And Evie! He reached her door and snapped open the penknife with a flick of his wrist, ramming the thin blade into the lock and jostling it angrily. Evie *would* have to take possession of it in full view of any patch of grass that could hide interested eyes. God, if the man who'd attacked him in the library thought Evie was part of this . . .

Damn! He had to get the bloody thing out of her room if, indeed, it was Bernard's expected shipment. And if it was nothing more than an antique canopy? Then somehow he had to make sure that everyone in the abbey knew it, lest some ambitious little spy leap to the conclusion that Evelyn was the shipment's alternate recipient. In other words, another spy. Justin would do just about anything to make sure no one made that mistake. Anything.

The door swung open and he slipped inside. She'd left the crate in the center of the room, a box four feet high and four feet long. A quick survey of the room told Justin that the windows hadn't been tampered with and the crate hadn't been opened.

He found a pair of heavy shears lying on a

makeshift table and slid the blades under one corner, pushing down. With barely a groan, the lid at once popped off. He peered into the dark interior. Inside was another, smaller, ominously unadorned crate stenciled over in several languages: Caution. So, there it was: the Diabolical Machine.

He stood deliberating his next move. Whoever had been watching for this shipment would know now where it was and its approximate size and possibly weight and, most importantly, who had taken possession of it. Under normal circumstances—well, as normal as circumstances could be in the espionage game—he would not *think* of tampering with that interior crate. God knew what sort of damage he might do to a delicate instrument by unpacking it.

But someone was after this crate. Weighing the options, Justin decided that the only reasonable course would be to repack the device into a different container, of a different size and configuration, as carefully as he could.

It was his job to see it ended its journey in Bernard's scientist's hands, and he would. He'd repack the damn thing, get it out of here to somewhere more secure, and telegram to Bernard to send his boys down here for it posthaste. He only needed to keep it safe for a few days more. But he would need to repack it before Evie finished dinner.

He rammed the shears beneath the interior box's lid. As soon as this was over, he was done. Quits. And if he was very lucky, Evie would never know anything about his current occupation. Instead, she would blissfully think that he'd been an aimless, purposeless dilettante whom her good example had reformed to dutiful functionality.

Evie would adore reforming him. The thought made him smile. The lid of the inside box had begun to splinter when he heard the bedroom door opening. Quickly he dropped the shears and turned.

Evelyn stood framed in the doorway, her hair a shimmering cascade of black curls, her bare white shoulders polished to an alabaster sheen.

"And just what," she asked coldly, "do you think you're doing in here?"

# *Chapter 19*

"I . . . I CAME TO APOLOGIZE."

Evie regarded Justin with flat disbelief. Apparently, she had some opinion regarding his capacity for contrition and his apology had exceeded it. Not very flattering.

He cast about for another excuse for his presence, coming around to block her view of the crate. He didn't think she realized what he'd been doing. He would tell her the truth if he could, if it were his to tell, but it wasn't.

"Couldn't catch up to old Blumfield?" he finally blurted out.

She stiffened. All the smooth expanse of skin exposed by that dress turned a delicate pink. "I didn't have to 'catch up with' him," she said. "He hadn't left."

"What?" Justin hooted derisively. "Still mooncalving around, was he?"

Her beautiful dark eyes narrowed. Why should she now be willing to sacrifice her eyesight to vanity? Besides, there was no reason on God's green earth anyone but he need know their true color was deep, clear amber. Like gold-filigreed onyx or tiger's-eyes. Only, he suddenly realized, these tiger's-eyes were awash in tears.

He stretched out his hand, the Diabolical Machine, Bernard, his duty, his honor, his *role*, all forgotten in the horrifying realization that he'd made Evie cry.

"Evie," he said. "Forgive me. Please, don't cry."

"I'm not crying." She blinked fiercely. "Why would I cry? Simply because a known womanizer—"

"Dear God, not that again."

"A known womanizer," she repeated with fierce emphasis, "should find another man's liking for, or *choice* of, a certain woman pathetic, doesn't make it so."

"You misunderstand me..." he began—then her words sank in. *Another man's "choice"?* "What do you mean, 'choice'?"

"You know, Justin," Evelyn set her hands on her hips and they disappeared into the voluminous velvet skirts, "not every man is at the mercy of his baser instincts."

She forged on, determined to make him feel as shallow and superficial as he'd made her feel unwanted and unattractive. "Some men find a lively, inquisitive mind appealing." Drat her voice for trembling! "And extreme competence more attractive than, than," she glanced at the meager bosom Merry had so ruthlessly cinched up in order to give the allusion of bounty, "being buxom!"

"Evie—"

"Some men don't need a pretty picture to kiss or a—"

He seized her arm, snatching her close and saying, "He *kissed* you? Again?"

She tossed her head. "Is that so inconceivable? That someone should want to kiss me? *You* did."

She threw the accusation at him like a slur, as if she thought that by accusing him of wanting to kiss her she could somehow shame him.... As if...

And then, finally, he understood.

He could scarce believe it. She *couldn't* not know. She couldn't fail to see.... With a sense of awed disbelief he clasped her wrist and wheeled, searching for a... Ah! There! Small and inconspicuous and all but hidden.

He pulled her to the mirror in the corner of her bedchamber, tossing aside the clothes that hung over the top of it. He dragged Evelyn in front of him.

"What are you—?"

"Hush," he said, clasping her by the shoulders and spinning her around to face the mirror. She glanced quickly at it and away, as one would something vaguely offensive and subtly threatening.

"What the devil are you doing?" she asked angrily when he refused to let her turn away, keeping her pinned with her back against him, her shoulder blades pressed into his chest.

"Look."

"I don't want to play these games, Justin," she said irritably. But, he noted, her reflected gaze kept dancing back to her image.

"Look," he insisted.

She glared up at him for an instant, meeting the challenge in his blue-green eyes and then, because she was brave, because she did not have anything to be ashamed of, because a woman who had proven her worth in as many areas as she had more than simple good looks to recommend her, she stared defiantly into the mirror.

He stood over and behind her, watching her gaze at her reflected image. She stood like a soldier at attention, every muscle taut, every chord of her vibrating self-mastery. And nothing else. No slow, dawning comprehension. Nothing.

"Enough yet?" she finally croaked and lifted her dark eyes to meet his. "Satisfied?"

She was near tears again. He could hear them in her voice. But this time they didn't ignite a fire of self-loathing; they stunned him in an altogether different manner.

"What do you see?" he asked softly. She was such a small woman. One forgot, because nothing except her size was diminutive. He bent his head near her ear, took one stolen breath of her fragrance, and whispered, "Come, Evie. Tell me. What do you see?"

He felt a little shiver course through her. For a second, he thought she'd refuse to answer, but then he heard her say defiantly. "A woman who looks like a girl."

"A youthful-looking woman," he paraphrased her words. "What else?"

"Little."

"Petite."

This time he'd startled her. Her brows flew together in disapproval. Of him, of his words, or of the fact that he'd dared correct her—she was an opinionated woman, his Evie—he wasn't sure.

"Skinny," she stated emphatically.

"Delicate," he whispered, his lips brushing her earlobe. He barely heard her sigh, but hear it he did. His head dipped lower, his mouth skated up the nape of her neck, nibbled the downy hairs there.

"Bony. Sinewy." She sounded breathless and confused.

He *felt* breathless and confused. His head swam with her fragrance. "Lithe. Svelte."

She shivered. His hand slipped from her shoulder to her hair, tunneling up through the soft cloud of curls. Pins scattered. Her hair came down, uncoiling in springy dark spirals.

"Black, wooly hair."

"Perfect," he murmured. "Perfect ebony ringlets."

"Ringlets?" she questioned so softly that he had to strain to hear.

"Aye. Such as the queen of night would envy."

Her breath caught. Her eyelids fluttered and fell shut. A little line of anguish appeared between her brows. He laughed against her creamy white skin and felt her stiffen.

Poor Evie. So confused, so unsure of what to believe when he was just struggling to keep things under control. Each passing second, it grew more difficult. She was so pliant, so yielding. So trusting and so damnably appealingly in distress.

It would be so easy to be a knight in shining armor here. To slay her dragons and ride off into the sunset. Except that sunset would give way to another day, when saving the bloody, blasted world would demand his allegiance.

He kneaded the nape of her neck and her body relaxed. Her shoulders rolled back against his chest. He could feel her heartbeat racing.

Yet even as she responded to his touch, he knew she devoured his words even more greedily. She drank every bit of praise with equal parts trepidation and eagerness, like a bacchant convert at her first orgy, willing to be seduced, fearful of the consequences.

"You think me . . . attractive?"

He heard the price that soft query cost her pride, and for the life of him could not think of a sufficient answer. So, instead, he pulled her roughly against him, making her aware in no uncertain terms of the extent of his attraction.

She felt him, hard and long and excitingly, disturbingly male, pressed against her hip, heard his breath rough against her neck, and opened her eyes, slowly, unwilling to release the magic of these minutes. Her gaze crept up the reflected ruby velvet skirts to where Justin's big, tanned hand spread flat across her stomach, pinning her against him.

His face nestled in the curve of her throat, his brown hair brushed the tops of her breasts. She trembled. His mouth pressed lightly to the pulse at the bottom of her throat, as though reading her heart's fluttering. "I want you," he murmured against her flesh. "I desire you. You know I do."

She drew a shaky breath, never wanting this to end and, conversely, wanting it to end sooner, that they might continue with all the things Merry had told her about, things wicked and enticing and disturbing.

She should push him away and hope that convention would persuade this preeminently unconventional man into marriage before she dared a physical relationship. But she'd always balked at the notion of a man having to be persuaded into marrying her; she'd too much pride. And she *wouldn't* lose this opportunity to *make love,* to know what it was to be a woman, not a maid. She didn't want to spend a lifetime wondering what could have been. She wouldn't.

She was twenty-five. If it wasn't Justin, she didn't want it to be anyone else.

She'd been so absorbed in her thoughts that she hadn't noticed him lift his face until she saw him regarding her in the mirror. "Do you see it yet?"

"See what?"

"How absolutely ravishing you are?"

At the sound of Justin's voice, Beverly stopped, his knuckles inches from knocking on the door. He'd come here fully expecting to find the room empty and his access to the crate unimpeded. He'd loitered in the hall until Lady Evelyn went down for dinner, and had been just about to enter and relieve her of the crate when one of the guests had seen and hailed him. He'd had no choice but to see what he wanted.

He hoped nothing had happened to the crate in the interim. But it had been only a short while....

The sound of Justin's voice caught him off guard, and then he realized that *she* was with him, too. He froze, more from surprise than from any real desire to eavesdrop.

He'd never heard that tone in Justin's voice, one of wonderment and reverence and something more, something hotter and more elemental. It caused him to blush, and he was still blushing when he heard an unmistakable and unwelcome French-accented voice hail him.

"Listening at doors, Mr. Beverly?"

He turned, hoping that a simple, speaking glower would chastise if not completely quiet her. She was standing at the end of the hall, her head tilted to the side, her puff of red hair squatting atop her head like a turban. She'd didn't look in the least chastised. She looked saucy.

She sashayed her way to his side and thumped on his chest with one stubby finger before waggling it under his nose. "What are you doing here?" she asked in an amused whisper. "Standing outside Miss Evelyn's room red as the beet and... Ah!" Her whisper turned into a gasp as she heard Justin's muffled voice.

Beverly grabbed her plump arm and hauled her some distance down the hall, only releasing her when he was certain they could not be overheard.

"He— She— They—" Merry stuttered.

"Oh, for heaven's sake," he interrupted in disgust. "You are always going to such pains to let every male in the vicinity know that you are an experienced woman, and here you are sputtering like the greenest girl."

"How dare you question my sophistication?" She drew herself up, the picture of outraged womanhood. He couldn't help smiling. How many women would see a jaded past as being something worth defending?

"Then stop acting like a peahen. Mr. Powell is the last of his line and, coming from another line that's been serving his mother's family for three generations, I tell you quite sincerely that it is a line worth perpetuating."

Her eyes rolled toward the ceiling. "*Oui, oui,* the line is worth keeping. What of it?"

"He has chosen her. Which I approve. They suit."

She narrowed her eyes, puckering her mouth. "Ah . . . and they are . . . suiting, right now? Then your plot has worked?"

"There was never any plot, per se," he said indignantly, "merely the removal of obstacles and the provision of opportunity."

"Excellent!" she cackled. "*I* approve, too! As will her mama— Oh! *Mon Dieu*!" Her face fell. She bit her lip. "Her mother may not be so . . . sophisticated as we. I was told to encourage her interest, not procure her for him."

"I believe things are now well beyond even your ability to affect."

With sudden continental fatalism, she lifted both shoulders. "*Mais oui*. You are correct. Now," she tucked her arm through his, "tell me. What more can I do to help our lovebirds?"

With a slight pinching of his nostrils, Beverly disentangled himself from the female's grip. It would never do to let her know that for one fell instant, he'd felt a little tickle of something—rather like static from wool. She would mistake it for something else. Instead, he said, "You can leave."

And with that suggestion, he took his own advice and marched proudly away.

Thoughtfully, Merry watched the little butler stalk down the hall. He wasn't at all her type. He was too old, he was too stiff, and he hated women. She turned in the opposite direction and began walking toward the kitchen, Evelyn and Justin Powell having slipped to the back of her mind.

While she and Buck Newton had had a good time, there wasn't, well, any *challenge* left in seducing Buck, partially because she strongly suspected the reason he was called "Buck." Any reasonably attractive—no, honesty compelled her to amend—any reasonably *willing* woman could do the same.

But Beverly—now *that* would be a challenge!

# *Chapter 20*

EVELYN LOOKED INTO THE MIRROR FOR A long, silent moment. "Yes," she whispered. "Yes. I see."

And she did. But not in her reflection. She saw it in his eyes. Whatever else she knew, or believed, for this night she had no doubt that in Justin Powell's eyes she was, indeed, a fountain of loveliness.

"Yes," he whispered. "Beautiful."

She pirouetted slowly, his hand still lightly on her waist, and encircled his neck with her arms. Everything she knew about herself had collapsed and been rebuilt in the space of a few minutes. The grace of confidence flowed in her movements and glistened in the darkening awareness of her eye.

She robbed him of speech. His glibness had finally run out, replaced by want, simple visceral need so acute it nearly brought him to his knees. Silently, he cupped her face between his hands, her hair tumbling like silk over their backs. He bent and grazed her mouth lightly with his. She was warm, her fragrance rising with her body's temperature, powdery, elusively sweet, feminine, and provocative.

His loins ached, his arms trembled with his restraint. Want and need weren't any excuse. She was acting on an impulse, a pull of attraction, on her gratitude to him for telling her what was manifestly clear, that she was beautiful.

But even as he thought these things, he was lifting her, shifting her toward her bed, nearing his perdition. His paradise. He wavered on the cusp of doing the unthinkable, seducing a young, unmarried, innocent woman. But then she raised herself on tiptoe and pulled his head down to hers. She pressed her lips beneath his ear and whispered in a ragged voice, "And I want you."

Her words ground his scruples to dust and blew them away. Desire coursed like a liquid inferno through his veins and muscles. Seducer? Seduced. The line was blurred. He sank to his knees, his arms tight around her upper thighs, and pressed his lips to the soft swelling curve under her breast, damping the silky velvet nap with his tongue. He heard her inhale, and made one last stab at honor.

"Tell me to stop," he said hoarsely. "I can. I will. But *you* need to say it. I'm a strong man, Evie, but you undo me. I'm ashamed of how weak I am, how much I would give to have you beneath me, to feel myself buried in you."

He hoped the crudeness of his words, the images

he evoked—images that sent his breath laboring, that thickened his blood—would frighten her. Or entice her. He clasped her hips and pulled her sharply against him, throwing her off balance, so that she needed to catch herself from falling by clutching his shoulders.

"Last chance, Evie. Tell me to go." He closed his eyes, yearning.

"No." The word came at once, quavering but certain.

He looked up and met her darkling gaze. His hands slipped around to her back. Fingertips trained to a cracksman's sensitivity found and within minutes dispatched the dozens of seed pearl buttons. The ribbons on her corset took less time and then, in a fluid movement, he rose, pushing the gown from her shoulders. It dropped in a deep crimson pool about her feet as he peeled the embroidered corset away and threw it to the side.

His body was so hot and tense it felt alien, too hard, too unyielding. He would scare her. So he moved warily, skimming his fingertips along her jaw, through her hair, down her throat, and over her shoulders. He skated a caress along her slight ribcage to the elegant dip of her waist and the gentle flare of her hip. Then, with the backs of his fingers, he followed the swell of her buttocks beneath the taffeta confection of a petticoat to a narrow ribbon that came loose with a single tug. The petticoats followed the dress down, mounding around her pretty calves.

All she wore was a revealing chemise, a pair of lacy drawers with silk ribbons at the calves, a pair of stockings, and—dear God—she still wore shoes. She followed his gaze and, as if aware of the incongruity of them, stepped out of the kid slippers, losing two inches of height in the process.

Abruptly, he felt too big, menacing. He would hurt her. Especially as she was a virgin and he was in all ways a big man. And as he stood, wrestling with the issue, she reached out, and clasped his shirt's placket.

"It seems only fair." She tugged at the buttons.

In amazed gratitude, he shrugged out of his coat and dropped it, tore open his dress shirt, and flung it after. Then he stood, waiting. Except for the tacit knowledge that he could physically do whatever needed to be done, he'd never thought much about his body. But now he suddenly wondered what he saw in her wide-eyed gaze. Approval? Fear? Was he too big? Too ungainly?

He waited, counting an eternity of heartbeats while she simply looked at him. He prayed for her to touch him, and as if in answer to his silent entreaty, her hand rose, suspended an inch from his flesh. The anticipation would kill him.

"Careful," he advised hoarsely

"I don't want to be careful."

"Why do you have to be so damned argumentat—ah!" She touched him. Her fingers played across his chest with winsome lightness, twining gingerly in the dark whorls of hair. She looked up at him, a little breathless, a little exultant, divinely female. "You like it when I touch you. You liked it in the wine cellar. You like it now."

*"Like?"* He took a step nearer, and she retreated

before whatever she read in his eyes, at last yielding to common sense. Too late.

"Evie," he said in a low, harsh voice. "I'd commit hideous crimes for your touch."

"You shouldn't say things like that," she murmured, reaching automatically for her collar and discovering instead her nakedness. A blush flooded her delicate skin. He could see the color blooming, even under the sheer silk of her undergarments.

"Why not?" He took another step forward; she countered with another step back. Her thighs bumped into the bed.

"It sounds wicked."

"It is. Blasphemous. Excessive. True."

She turned her head away, the color deepening in her cheeks, and he knew that she was searching for words to stop him, to tell him that she'd changed her mind. He couldn't allow that.

He swept her into his arms and toppled her back onto the bed, following her down, kissing her deeply, his tongue delving into her warm, moist mouth. A demanding growl vibrated through him. In answer, Evelyn opened her mouth wider, wantonly, hungrily, completely forgetting her former reluctance.

Suddenly, he pushed himself up on his forearms, breaking their kiss. She stared up at him, braced above her on trembling arms, the glorious, muscular planes of his chest glinting in the gaslight, the sound of his breath a rushing locomotive.

He shifted, nudging her thighs apart with his knee, and rolled his hips into the resultant opening. He did so purposefully, intently watching her, gauging her response to the manner in which he deliberately fit that hard ridge between her legs. He rocked against her, and little channels of heat trickled out from the point of contact, enticing and agitating.

He rocked against her again, more insistently this time, bumping erotically against her most tender part. Trickling heat became a torrent of molten desire. And he knew it. His watchful and intent eyes grew triumphant. Again, he thrust against her mons. Pleasure careened there, pooling, spreading. Her thoughts diffused; her senses telescoped.

Her hands slipped to his shoulders, her fingers pressing deeply into his skin. She lifted herself, clinging to him, sweeping her tongue along his lower lip. He turned his face, catching her mouth fully opened, and licked her tongue, nipping her lips, dazing her with his passion.

Excitement skittered along her skin, thrummed in her body, pulsing, there, against the hard length of him. When he rocked against her this time, she raised her hips, meeting his advance, her legs opening wider, inviting more.

"Evie. God in heaven." He tumbled down atop her, his body heavy and dense and excitingly, solidly masculine. Then he wrapped his arms around her and rolled with her so that she lay atop him, her legs sprawled shamelessly on either side of his hips, her hands splayed against his hard, flat belly as she tried to push herself up.

He wouldn't let her. He'd twined a handful of her hair around his fist, pulling her down, plying her face and throat and bosom with wet, lingering kisses, while with his other hand he dug into the silk layers still separating them, his knuckles rubbing against her as he jerked the sheer, moist fabric away and . . . and . . .

Dear heaven! He was naked. There! And so was she! She could feel the silky, heated ridge glide against her, a blunt polished knob part her swollen folds. With a sound like pain, Justin fell back, letting go of her hair. He seized her hips tightly and then, slowly, began pushing *into* her.

Evelyn knew—Merry had told her, others had whispered—but nothing could have prepared her for this . . . filling. He stretched her, entering her, *hurting* her!

Sensual pleasure was forgotten. Instinctively, she tried to pull away, pushing herself upright on his belly, her knees digging into the soft mattress on either side of his hips and in doing so inadvertently seating him deeper inside.

"Mother of mercy!" The words burst from his lips. His eyes closed tightly as if he were expending profound effort. His throat corded with veins. He caught her by her shoulders, pulling her down, flattening her against him.

"Wait. Still! Please, Evie, for both our sakes, stay still. Just a moment. *Please.*" Tremors raced down the length of his body, yet his lips moved tenderly against her temple. Gently, he began to rub her back. "Trust me."

She did trust him. Bit by bit, she relaxed, and quickly, the pain ebbed. The tension drained from her under his soothing ministrations, her body draped over his solid form, molding to him. Slowly, little flickers of sensuality prickled back to life under his long, soothing caresses.

His hands moved down her spine, her hips, and over her buttocks with nerve-shattering deliberation. Then they started back up again, each circuit bringing her body back to panting involvement, each moment turning the alien feel of his possession from discomfort to something erotic.

His free hand slipped between them, cupping her breast. He began playing with her through the chemise, plucking gently at her nipple. She raised herself on her arms without even being aware she did so, so that he could touch her more easily. Casually, he unknotted the chemise's ribbon and the silk fell open.

He lifted his head, and slowly, deliberately licked her breast. She jerked back. She should feel hot with shame. Except that she liked it. Liked it when he lifted her breast in his hand and opened his mouth over her nipple and suckled her. It was indescribable.

He moved his head, tasting her other breast, and she pushed herself further upright, offering herself more fully to him.

This time there was no pain, just a harrowing sort of pleasure.

Justin felt the tension return to her body. The wet velvet glove of her body tightened, her back arched slightly. He clasped her hip and rolled her beneath him, surging into her, moving now with an ancient rhythm. His eyes closed as he lost himself in escalating desire. Each thrust intensified the nearly unbearable pleasure. Each thrust tested his self-control.

And she clung to him, hot and damp from his mouth, a faint sheen glistening over her, tight around him like rough, oiled silk. She cried out as his body broke the laws he'd imposed on it, finding a new, deeper rhythm, a fiercer sort of coupling.

Her inky hair spilled across the white linen, her breast pink with abrasions left by his beard and mouth, her eyes shut, her throat arched in abandonment. He'd never seen so erotic a sight.

Her body opened to him. For him. He thrust into her with primitive passion, holding her head still as he did so, bruising her lips with a kiss. Abruptly, her body clenched around him, her inner shudder closing around him like a fist. Every muscle in her body grew taut, stretched on the razor's edge of pleasure. She cried out once, a long rising song of climax achieved, of sated pleasure.

It toppled him. Destroyed him. Ended all hopes of a dry withdrawal. He crushed her to him, burying himself deep within her, and his own orgasm spun out like molten heat, spiraling into a single deepening vortex before exploding.

Justin slipped his leg into his trousers and stood at the side of the bed. He buttoned his fly and looked around for his shirt, crossing the room to where he'd flung it earlier. He retrieved it from the floor and shrugged into it, only then allowing himself to glance at Evie, sprawled across the bed in exhausted repletion.

He turned away, his thoughts bound by the knowledge of his deception and how she would react. His entire life he'd tried unsuccessfully to imagine loving a woman so much that she became crucial to his happiness. To feel such indiscriminate emotion had not only seemed foreign but frankly doubtful. And now?

Now, he couldn't imagine not loving her. He couldn't imagine being without her. He suspected that if she walked out of his life tomorrow, he would spend his lifetime listening for her light tread, straining to hear her calm, no-nonsense speeches unexpectedly dissolve into irresistible laughter. What would his life be without her, now that he'd begun to imagine what it might be with her?

He didn't want to know.

Fear constricted about his chest, its pressure unfamiliar. Only the light chime of the mantel clock broke his immobility. With a sound of exasperation, he finished buttoning his shirt and thrust the ends into his trousers. Before he considered the future, he first needed to finish with the past. He needed to complete Bernard's assignment with every constraint observed, silently, anonymously, as were all a spy's jobs. *Then* he would offer Bernard his resignation, his service record unimpeachable.

Hell, he thought with wry humor, there might even be a knighthood in it. He wondered if Evie might like that, and decided that she wouldn't give a fig for a title. But he would like to bring her something more than an ornithologist's notebook and a pocketful of suspect talents. In a way, it was too bad they would go to waste, but he couldn't ask that of her. He couldn't imagine Evie waiting without knowing where he was or what he was doing or when he would return.

He wanted Evie to be his wife. He waited for some taint of apprehension to poison his pleasure. There was none. He only felt a heightening urgency, a fervent sense of anticipation.

With that, he moved toward the crate, intending to liberate the Diabolical Machine before anyone else came looking for it. The gaslights in the room still glowed in their sconces and outside he could just hear the first predawn bird song as he slipped his pocket knife under the inside box's wooden lid. He'd done most of the loosening earlier; all it wanted was a good tug and— A glint of something wedged between the two crates caught his eye. He reached down and grasped a smooth metal something. It took a few hard jerks, but finally he pulled it up. It was a small metal jimmy used to open crates.

He stared at the jimmy. Someone had been here before him. Someone had already opened the outer crate and knew what it contained. But whoever had done so hadn't opened the inner box, probably for the same reasons he had been loath to; in doing so the contents might be damaged. The ramifications made his mouth grow dry.

He pushed and the interior lid came free in his hands.

He stared into the dark recesses of the crate.

He was still staring when he heard Evie move.

Evelyn rolled over. Muscles she'd never used, hadn't even known she'd owned, twitched in protest. She scowled, irritated that something so perfect should have any penalty attached to it. But, of course, there *were* penalties.

*No*. She would not think like that. She had no regrets. None. It had been simply, profoundly wonderful. And it felt good. Right. Oh, wicked, too, there was no denying that. But wicked in a lovely way. Wicked like angels dancing.

She stretched her arm out and it fell into a shallow indentation, still warm from Justin's body. Anxiety pricked her. Was he gone? Crept from her room as he'd crept from Mrs. Underhill's so many years ago?

Her eyelids flew open. Immediately, she saw him, already dressed and standing beside the crate that had been delivered from London. She relaxed, even though her pulse accelerated at the sight of his unruly hair curling on the nape of his neck, the way his shoulders stretched his shirt, the dark color of his tanned forearms against its bleached whiteness, because—of course—he'd rolled the sleeves up.

As if he felt her gaze, he straightened and turned. The dim frost of gray dawn touched his features. At the sight of them, the smile she'd meant to greet him with wavered. His eyes were dark, his lips tightly compressed.

"Evelyn."

*Not Evie.*

"Evelyn," he repeated, "you must get up. We have to talk."

She heard in his grim voice the ashes of her dreams. She twined herself in the sheet, acutely conscious of her nakedness beneath the soft Egyptian cotton, and clutched it closed at her throat.

He came to her, his gaze unwavering, his brow lowered, his entire aspect alien to everything she knew about him, thought she knew of him. And that, the idea that she'd shared something so remarkable, so altering, with someone so altered, alarmed her most of all.

She was not a child. She had always been careful to be honest with herself so that the realities that ambushed others never caught her by surprise. Realities such as the fact that mirrors reflected what was there; realities such as the fact that a man's past foretold his future; realities such as the fact that a womanizer seduces women.

Justin looked down at her. "I need you to listen, Evelyn," he said intently. "I need you to understand."

She nodded, not trusting her voice.

"That crate," he jerked his chin toward the wooden box without looking away from her, "I've been waiting for that crate."

Whatever she'd expected, it hadn't been this. She twitched sideways, staring at the wooden box behind him in bewilderment. The lid was off and lying tilted against its side. "I don't understand."

"I was meant to take possession of the crate. But you got to it first."

"What?"

"The crate!" he repeated, the fierceness in his tone making her shrink back. He noted it and clenched his teeth.

"I'm a spy, Evelyn," he said.

She froze, stunned.

"I work for the British government," he went on tersely. "My assignment was to take possession of a certain item—a certain very important invention—that one of our men had stolen from an unfriendly source and shipped here."

*"What?"*

He reached out and pulled her up into his arms. "Quiet!"

His heart thundered in his chest, and she realized that in spite of his cold voice, he was struggling to control powerful emotions.

"I'd been *told* that we weren't the only government interested in the shipment. More, I was informed that the country from which it had been . . . liberated had its own agents scouring the ports, desperate for its retrieval.

"As a means of keeping it secret and obscuring its location, the men for whom I work asked me to devise a plan. Some way we could get this thing into the country to be inspected by one of our scientists. But it had to be somewhere safe. Somewhere the 'original owners' wouldn't think to look. A place where we could slip this scientist in without raising a brow."

"Then?" she prompted.

"Then, I was to destroy the prototype."

She felt a slow trickle of dread course down her spine. Incidents and scenes, snatches of conversation, chance glimpsed expressions that she'd placed no meaning in at the time—all of them now took on a whole new significance. She pulled free of his arms.

"Beverly's part of it," she said.

"Yes."

"And," she looked into his eyes, "I'm part of it, too."

He didn't deny it. He didn't make any effort to justify it. He'd used her and Mrs. Vandervoort's wedding to conduct what was in reality nothing but a theft.

He nodded wearily, as though he'd read her mind. "My superior wanted me to find some way of receiving the crate where it wouldn't be expected. Then you came along with your wedding plans and renovation schemes, all of them entailing shipment upon shipment of goods." He met her eye squarely, without apology. "It was too good an opportunity to let pass."

"You mean exploit," she said.

"Yes," he answered. "If it makes it any more palatable, you weren't supposed to know anything about it."

"It doesn't."

He almost smiled. His gaze flickered briefly away from her, and a muscle leapt at the corner of his jaw. The implicit pain nearly caused her to reach out. She didn't. It could be a ploy. Another bit of fakery.

"Nothing I did was supposed to have interfered with your plans or the wedding. It was supposed to be a simple drop-and-catch."

"Drop-and-catch?" she echoed, masking her sense of betrayal behind a cool, disaffected interest.

"I was supposed to collect the damn thing. No one anticipated that anyone would find it here. At least, that's what I was told."

"But why didn't the government just have a troop waiting for it on the dock? Why the subterfuge?" She wasn't even sure why she asked; she could barely stand to look him in the eye. But the inner nattering, the never-satisfied gluttony for knowledge that ruled her life, refused to shut up.

This time his laugh held a tincture of honest amusement. "Because, dear, honest Evie, it's supposedly a *stolen* device. Openly stealing another country's inventions tends to evolve into sticky political problems. Not only with the country from which we steal, but with our own public. We Brits dearly love to think ourselves above that sort of thing."

"Oh. So you were trying to sneak it into the country," she said flatly.

"Yes," he answered. "Only someone leaked information about its arrival." His expression darkened. Not in rage but in something more considered, more focused.

"Remember the night you fell asleep in the sitting room and heard me in the library?" he asked. "That was him. The man they set me up for."

"*What*?"

"Unfortunately, I didn't catch the blighter," he said, ignoring her stunned query. "He got away before I got a look at his face.

"But I did manage to land a blow to his face, and

have spent the days since looking for a fellow sporting a bruise. No joy, I'm afraid, and by this time the bruise is likely to have faded."

"What did you mean 'the man they'd set you up for'?" she insisted.

"Look." He pointed to the open crate.

With ill grace, she obeyed and peered in. Inside was another smaller box and in that . . . nothing.

# Chapter 21

JUSTIN COULD SEE THE WHEELS SPINNING smoothly behind Evelyn's puckered brow. Ramifications and implications, she was probably tallying them up faster than he had. She astonished him. Most women he knew would have been raging at him, and rightfully so. From the very beginning he'd used her, coldly and without compunction, and then, when she'd been most vulnerable, he'd taken her virginity. But she was considering his words.

He felt only disgust for his sudden virtuous recognition of his sins. Why the hell couldn't he have been so clear-sighted five hours ago? Because five hours ago she'd been in his arms, filling every fiber of his being with pleasure.

"You've been set up." The chill flatness of her tone

abruptly returned him to the present. "By your own superiors."

Bright, canny little owlet. "That's what I think."

"But why? Why didn't they just tell you, warn you so that you could help?"

His smile was humorless. "You don't tell the bait it's bait, darling. It starts to act like bait, and the caliber of man they're after would sniff that out in no time. Because that's what this is really all about. That's the only thing that makes sense. This empty box and I have been used as bait to ferret out an enemy agent. That's why Bernard didn't tell me. Added to which," his smile faded to a cold grimace. "Bernard knew I would never have exposed you to danger of that sort."

"What about danger of *this* sort?" she asked, flushing hotly.

"There wasn't supposed to be *any* danger," he said grimly, a tic jumping in his cheek. "No one was supposed to give a bloody damn about you. Even if an agent did manage to find out about the shipment and did come looking for it, he would be a thief, not an assassin, and—" He stopped. Closed his eyes. His jaw clenched and he took a deep breath.

"Don't you think I know what I've done with my little setup? The danger I've put you in? Do you think I don't know how unforgivable that is? I do."

She lifted her chin. "I love irony, don't you? Your superiors used you as you used me. How novel it must be for you to be on the other end of that equation."

He no longer felt obligated to maintain dutiful

silence. To keep her safe—and he *would* keep her safe—she would need to know everything. Nothing else mattered now.

"Believe it or not, Evie, I have always comported myself honorably. At least as honorably as the situation allowed."

"I'm sure that is no end of comfort to those you've used. I know I feel immeasurably better. Poor Mr. Underhill must be in paroxysms of patriotic joy," she said in a cold, bright voice, "knowing he was cuckolded by a man who was as honorable as he could be, *given the situation.*"

He flushed hotly and, remorse not being an emotion he wore easily, anger flared at her condemnation. Especially since he didn't have any idea what she was talking about. "Mr. Who? What the devil is that supposed to mean?"

Her eyes widened first in disbelief, then flashed with hurt. "Are there so many that you cannot remember the names of the men whose wives you..." She couldn't finish. "Tell me, how does one convince oneself of one's honor under those circumstances? Do you snap off a smart salute and whisper, 'For God and country' before hopping into their beds?"

She blinked rapidly and dashed the back of her hand against her eyes.

He stared at her in disbelief. He was a spy, not a rutting debauchee. She should *know* that, by God!

"And," she sniffed loudly, "in case you're curious, Mr. Underhill is the husband of the lady whose bedroom I caught you sneaking out of ten years ago."

He'd had enough. His amusement at her misperception of him as a "wolf" had long since ceased to be humorous.

"I never touched Mrs. Underhill," he said. "You've built an entire fantasy around a misconstrued episode from your childhood, and pinned me with a reputation I have in no way earned or deserved.

"Mrs. Underhill acted as a courier for highly classified information. I went to her room to receive it. And that is all, and that is the truth," he said.

Her dark eyes narrowed. "Seeing how the truth seems to have had little to do with who and what you are, I am supposed to blithely accept your word?" she asked.

Damn. She had him there. He *had* made a career out of lies. He stood flexing his hands at his side, knowing that anything he said would only further damn him. So, he said nothing.

Haughtily, she flipped the end of her sheet over her shoulder. It was ridiculous that a woman could look so absurd and so desirable at the same time. "I would like you to go now."

"No."

Her mouth gaped and snapped shut. "*Pardon me*?"

"I can't go yet. Not until something has been done about this. You still don't understand, Evie. There's more. The external crate had already been opened by the time I got here. By the man my superiors are trying to catch. He's in the house, maybe as a guest, maybe as a servant. And he knows you have the crate."

Something in his tone alerted her to the gravity of the situation. She forced herself to ignore her anger and pain and listen, because she was suddenly frightened and, whether she liked it or not, she instinctively knew Justin would do whatever he could—which she'd begun to suspect was considerable—to protect her.

"Think, Evie," Justin began. "This spy. He's very good. He's extremely cautious. My superiors would have been very careful about just what sort of rumors and hints they provided him regarding my identity."

"Why would he care to identify you? I don't understand. What makes you such irresistible bait?"

"Aside from the rewards certain governments have offered for my identity? The cachet of exposing me."

"You're that important? That good?" she said, regarding him closely, seeing him in a new light.

"Yes. And being as good as my opponent must be, the hints my superiors planted would have had to be very subtle hints, or this agent would suspect something. Do you understand yet?"

"No."

"Evie, he couldn't be certain that I am the man he's hunting, so he's been watching me. But, Evie," he said, "*you* took possession of the crate."

At last she understood. "But it was a mistake. Surely this man, whoever he is, he'd have to take into account that it's only reasonable for me to accept deliveries."

"Maybe once, Evie. But not twice. This is the second time you've taken possession of crates without addresses. But most damning and irrefutable, you *did* take possession of the crate he thinks contains the device."

She felt light-headed, her thoughts shredding on a

slow rising panic. "But he doesn't want *me*! He wants the crate!"

"He wants both the device and the spy he thinks you are." He regarded her with something akin to pity.

"Don't look at me that way," she said frantically. "I'm sure I'd be a picture of nonchalance, too, if I were a spy! But I'm not!"

His stance grew rigid. "I assure you, I am not in the least indifferent to the situation. You are the most intelligent and resourceful woman I know. Rather than castigating me, won't you use your considerable gifts to help me find a way out of this conundrum?"

He was also in peril, she realized, and the knowledge eradicated her rising terror. He'd appealed to who she was and what she was: competent, ingenuous, and persevering. She could not refuse him.

She took a deep breath. "Right. We can't just leave the crate and the empty inner box renailed shut. We have to assume he knows we're in here with it and if he came in he would open the inner box, find it empty, and assume it was a red herring and that we'd simply already removed the thing from it."

She paced away from him, her thoughts whirling. "We must find out who he is. But how?"

"We have to make some reasoned assumptions," Justin said. "The first being that since he knew where the crates Blumfield brought were stored, and has somehow apparently discerned that none of the shipments delivered until today has contained anything other than supplies for the wedding and guests, our spy has access to the house, or someone working in the house who acts as his eyes and ears."

She dropped to the bed, staring. Someone in the house? One of the servants?

"Whoever he is, he is definitely keeping a close watch on the abbey," he said. "Tomorrow is the wedding. He'll expect you to try to move it then, when there are lots of comings and goings. It's the logical time to do so."

"You have a plan," she said.

"Yes. We won't disappoint him. I'll sneak out with a wagon during the wedding celebration tomorrow. Hopefully, what with trying to keep an eye on you, it will take him a while to realize I've lit out and it will take him some time to catch up to me. When he does, he'll find me towing a crate full of bricks."

"But won't he . . ." Her face lightened with understanding. "Ah! He'll think *you* were a diversionary tactic and that another person drove off with the real contents. Me?"

"No!" he thundered. Good God, the woman was a menace to herself! "*Beverly* will drive out in the opposite direction."

For a second, he thought she was actually going to argue with him, but then she sighed. "Yes, I have prior commitments. Mrs. Vandervoort, you know," she explained to him, as though he was going to question her about why she wasn't willing to be a decoy. He was torn between wanting to shake her and kiss her.

"It's an excellent plan," she allowed, looking greatly relieved. He didn't tell her that in all likelihood the man who rode after him would also be trying to kill him.

If the Agency had set up such an elaborate plan to

expose this person, he must be a very important, strategically placed spy. Someone who would stop at nothing to maintain his secret identity, certainly not murder. And if Evie thought about it long enough, she'd realize that. So, he had to keep her thinking about other things.

"Of course," he said, "we might find aid in another quarter."

"Oh? Oh! Of course, why didn't I realize it earlier?" she crowed. "If you and the crate are bait, *then who is supposed to spring the trap?*"

"Exactly," Justin said. "This wouldn't have been set up if they weren't going to have someone here to take care of this agent once he'd revealed himself. But I don't know who. Someone good. Maybe even better than me."

"You don't have any idea?" she asked, relaxing and crossing her legs under her.

"No," he said.

Apparently they had navigated beyond animosity to a sort of détente, he thought dryly. At least, *she* had. What he was feeling couldn't be defined as anything so tepid. Guilt and desire raged within him. The way the brightening morning light washed her smooth skin heated his blood; the thought of how careless he'd been with her chilled it.

"Hm," she mused, tapping her fingertip against her bottom lip. "Is there any way to find out?"

"I would suggest that my superiors don't want me to find out, or they would have already informed me. But if our unknown compatriot discovers our spy's identity, we might reasonably expect him to act."

He was having a hard time keeping his mind on the matter at hand. Evie had canted sideways, leaning on her elbow, thinking.

"I should leave," he said.

She glanced up at him. "What about the crate?"

"Best thing would be to hide it in plain sight. I'll replace the lids, and then we'll ring for Beverly to come and take this down to—"

"—to the conservatory!" Evie piped in. "It's where all the wedding gifts that have been arriving are being stored. We can even post a couple of men in there under the guise of not wanting to test the moral fortitude of the workers too far."

"Excellent." Justin regarded her approvingly. "Our unknown assailant is too concerned with maintaining his anonymity to risk going for it there."

"He is?" She sounded disappointed, and that unnerved him. He'd fallen in love with an danger addict. With a shudder, he replaced the lid on the inner box and banged it down with a paperweight before quickly doing the same to the outer crate. He'd best leave before she found some other way to inveigle herself into this mess.

He picked up his jacket and headed for the door.

"Are you sure I can't do something?"

"Yes!" He yanked the door open.

And came face-to-face with Evie's mother.

"Lady Broughton!" Justin said.

Evie, in the process of rising to go after him, froze.

"My dear lady, when did you arrive? Your daughter

didn't mention you were one of the guests. How charming!" Justin said in profoundly amazed tones; Evelyn was struck by how easily he'd transformed from focused spy to affable rattlebrain.

Hard on the heels of her grudging admiration came a sweep of gratitude. He was buying her time. He'd firmly planted himself in the doorway, his hand on the knob, holding it halfway closed.

She rolled from the bed, tossed the sheets back, and scooped up last night's abandoned garments before diving behind the dressing screen. She dropped the clothes and grabbed her chemise, slipping it on over her head, straining to hear what was being said.

"Evelyn didn't know I'd been invited," she heard her mother say. "Mrs. Vandervoort thought it would be a nice surprise for her. Where *is* my daughter?"

"Evie?" she heard Justin ask. She wriggled the petticoat up over her hips. "Oh, in the room."

Evelyn peeked over the top of the screen as she scrambled into a shirtwaist. Justin had leaned his shoulder nonchalantly against the door, still obscuring Francesca's view, settling in as if for a cozy chat.

Gads, he did it well! One would think he was either utterly innocent or that he had more brass than any man alive. She alone knew that the latter was closest to the truth.

"Poor lambkins," he lowered his voice, "I think she's nodded off. Hate to wake her. She's been up all night seeing to last-minute details about the wedding. You'll be proud of her, Lady Broughton, when you see the wonders she's worked."

"I am always been proud of my daughter," Lady

Broughton said calmly, but with a stiffness that Evelyn barely recognized.

Furiously, Evelyn looked about for the blue serge skirt she'd worn— Ah! There! She pounced on it and snapped it open, stepping into it and wrenching it over her hips.

"And well you should be, ma'am," Justin said gravely. "She's an extraordinary woman."

Evelyn dragged her hair back from her face, twisting it savagely into a knot and securing it with a comb.

"Hm," Francesca said slowly. "I understand why Evelyn might be burning the midnight oil, Mr. Powell, but I confess to being surprised at finding you here."

The question was implicit. Evelyn held her breath.

"Oh. Well, I was out bird-watching. Good night for birding. Bright moon, no wind."

"I'd forgotten you were an expert ornithologist," Evelyn's mother said consideringly.

She saw Justin shrug, the muscles in his shoulders bunching with oiled grace. "Not an *expert,* per se."

"Didn't Evie say you'd discovered a species?"

"Ah, yes. *Bubo Formosa Plurimus.*" He paused as he always did at this point and added, *"Minor."*

Francesca was silent a long moment. "You know, it's been years since I was at the convent school, but I was always a dab hand with languages. Now, correct me if I'm wrong, but doesn't that translate into something like 'Most Beautiful Owl'?" she asked. She paused—as Justin had—and added, "'Small'?"

"Ah, mostly." He sounded distinctly uncomfortable.

"Or maybe," Francesca murmured in an absorbed

tone, "it would be better translated as 'Most Beautiful Little Owl,' or even better, 'Most Beautiful Owlet.' "

*Owlet?* But he was always calling her . . . Her hands froze, arrested in the act of buttoning the skirt.

Why, he'd never discovered a bird. He'd been speaking about *her*. Hadn't he said something to Herr Dekker about the bird flying into his window? He'd been making fun of her!

The bounder! Doubtless, he thought himself fabulously clever. Well, as soon as she—

"But I'm keeping you from explaining what exactly you are doing here in my daughter's room while she sleeps."

All thoughts of Justin's duplicity vanished. Evelyn waited, her heart hammering in her chest.

"Oh, that." His voice was all cheery ease again. "Only been here since sunrise. I was coming back from the woods when I saw Evie's light on and her moving about inside. So, I decided to come say 'allo. We've become great friends, your daughter and I."

"Really. How 'great'?"

Evelyn choked at her mother's flat tone, but Justin was made of better—or was that worse?—stuff. She could almost see his expression, perfectly oblivious to her mother's implied accusation.

"Oh, very great," Justin enthused. She would never trust that candid tone again. "She's a pip."

She stabbed another pin into her hair. There. She was as ready as she was ever going to be. She only hoped she was half as good at dissemblance as Justin. She took her place on the chaise, tucked her bare feet under her, laid her head on the arm, and called out in what she hoped was a sleepy voice, "Who's a pip?"

She noted the slight tensing of Justin's broad shoulders, and then he was flinging the door wide, stepping back, and allowing her mother to sweep into the room. Justin turned to face Evelyn, beaming with bonhomie.

She pushed herself to a sitting position. "Mother? Mother! What are you doing here!" she cried, pushing to her feet and racing across the room to meet her mother halfway. Her mother enfolded her in a fond embrace. Only after she felt her mother's arm wrap around her did Evelyn realize how much she wanted her here, her guidance and counsel.

Amazing. Why, ever since Verity's coming-out, she'd been the one family members came to to organize things, manage things, and find solutions. But now, suddenly, she wanted her mother.

Evelyn's eyes stung and she clung more tightly.

"Why, Evelyn dear!" her mother exclaimed. "Are you all right?"

This was stupid. Evelyn pushed herself away and smiled brightly. "Yes," she said, "yes, of course! It's just that I didn't expect to see you, and when I did, I realized how much I missed you!"

"You missed me?" Francesca asked, wide-eyed. "Well, I missed you, too," she said, sounding a little giddy. Hadn't she ever told her mother she missed her? How strange.

Evelyn took her hand and led her to the chair beside her desk. "Sit down and tell me why you are here and so early—and where is Father?"

Francesca laughed. "At home in bed, I should imagine. He couldn't come. I arrived just a short while ago and couldn't resist coming to see you at once. Happily, you were already awake, or mostly so, or so Mr. Powell was kind enough to inform me. He guarded your slumber quite vigilantly."

Francesca looked over her shoulder at Justin, who stood by the doorway smiling benevolently. The ass.

She returned her attention to Evelyn. "Remember when Mrs. Vandervoort and I met at your aunt Agatha's offices? Well, chance led us to meet again a few days later. One thing led to another and we've become friends.

"When she invited us to the abbey for her wedding celebration, I was most pleased to accept."

Evelyn squeezed her mother's hand. "I'm so glad you did."

"I was to arrive last night, but a train derailed—no, no! You mustn't look like that. It was a freight train, nothing lost but a good deal of coal. Still, we were forced to wait while they cleared the tracks."

"How tiresome for you," Evelyn exclaimed.

"Not at all. It happened that there were other wedding guests on the train: Lord and Lady Dalton, the Gould-Hedgeses, and Lord Stow. Between the lot of us we made quite a lively party. Played charades all night," she finished.

From the corner of her eye, Evelyn saw Justin's fatuous smile fade. Something her mother had said had surprised him.

"I'm glad you didn't find it too distressing."

"Not at all." Francesca leaned over and kissed

Evelyn's cheek and in doing so dislodged a pile of correspondence from the corner of the desk. Letters and envelopes fluttered to the ground.

"Oh, bother! Now look what I've done!" she exclaimed, bending over to retrieve the fallen pile. She scooped up one after another letter, pausing at the third and frowning. With a cluck of her tongue, she rifled through the letters she held. She studied them with a furrowed brow. "Well, that's odd," she said.

"What's odd, Lady Broughton?" Evelyn looked up to find Justin standing near. She hadn't even heard him come over. His expression was mild.

"These letters from Agatha," she replied. "They can't be from her."

"What do you mean?" Once again, it was Justin who spoke.

"They can't be," Francesca insisted, shaking her head in bewilderment. "Either these are forged, or the ones *I've* been receiving from her are."

"Why would you say that?" Evelyn asked.

"Because these are posted from all sorts of foreign destinations, whereas the letters we've received were written from one place, the same location in France."

Evelyn felt Justin's tension.

"That doesn't make any sense. Why would someone pretend to be Agatha writing to you from foreign countries?" her mother murmured. She looked up, laughing a little at the absurdity of it. "Ah, well. I suppose we'll just have to wait until Agatha returns and ask her."

Evelyn didn't feel amused and, judging from the

dangerous glint in Justin's eyes, neither did he. A horrifying explanation for the letters had occurred to her, and as her thoughts raced back over the last months—and all the letters supposedly from foreign countries written in an unfamiliar hand, the vaguely labeled crates delivered—the suspicion grew into a conviction.

Justin had not been the only person "set up."

She met his gaze. His expression was cautionary. He thought the same thing. But how was she involved? What role could she possibly play?

As an alternate bait? Another red herring?

Suddenly the bedroom door flew open. Merry stood in the door, panting for breath, her hand at her chest. "*Vite! Vite*! Your mother is here! *Mon Dieu!* You have to get rid of..." Her voice trailed off as her gaze fell on Francesca. Lady Broughton had swiveled slowly in her chair at Merry's dramatic entrance and was regarding the puffing maid with a faintly inimical gaze.

"Why, hello, Merry," she said smoothly. "So nice to see you. I trust you are well?"

Merry's head bobbed up and down, her eyes bulging as if she were regarding some dangerous beast instead of Evelyn's sweet mother.

"Good," said Francesca. "Pray, don't let me keep you from speaking. What fascinating thing were you encouraging my daughter to 'get rid of'?"

"Ah.... This mess!" Merry grinned with gargoyle brightness. "Yes! *Il un scandale!*" She *tch*ed in disgust.

"Ah!" Justin said, drawing Evelyn's attention. "I hear the sound of a work crew being assembled and that means it is time for me to bid you ladies adieu."

"Must you?" Evelyn couldn't control the tincture of panic that escaped into her voice and tried to hide it with a bright smile.

Her mother glanced at her, surprised she'd been so forward. Evelyn didn't care. She wanted to know what he thought, what she should do. She wasn't a spy! She was a wedding planner! This was his area of expertise, not hers!

"Yes. I'm sure you want to conduct your reunion in privacy. But I *promise* I'll be back later to help you drag all these what-nots to their appointed place. And I'll send Beverly for that other thing," he said. "Pleasure to see you again, Lady Broughton. Miss Molière."

And before Evelyn could protest further, he bowed and made his escape.

As Justin closed the bedroom door behind him, his face became transformed. He strode past a housemaid who took one look at him and scurried out of his way, linens clutched to her chest.

At the end of the long hall, Beverly appeared, panting. "Sir!" he called. "Sir! Stow is here."

"I know," Justin answered without breaking stride. How the devil had Beverly known to look for him here? And he could have sworn that Merry had come expressly to warn Evie to get *him* out of her bedroom before Lady Broughton arrived. It was an interesting thread to follow and, had not other matters been far more pressing, one he would have.

"What room has Stow been assigned?"

"The third down from yours. But he's in the dining

room now, taking an early breakfast with the other guests who've just arrived." He swung around as Justin strode past him and trotted after him. "Where are you going?"

"To see Bernard," Justin answered grimly. "I'll need to talk to you immediately after. Meet me in my room in forty-five minutes."

"Yes, sir, but—"

"Forty-five minutes," Justin repeated and, forcing a congenial smile, pushed open the door to the dining hall.

"There you are!" He paused at the threshold and gazed about in feigned delight. "You are Mrs. Vandervoort's latest arriving guests, are you not? Jolly good. No, no, madame, pray don't halt your breakfast on my account. I'm just the owner of the place, what?"

He smiled engagingly at the stout brunette who, along with her two male companions, looked up at his entrance, fork half-raised to her open mouth.

The two gentlemen rose. "Pleased to meet you. . . ." The taller gentleman hesitated, clearly embarrassed that he did not know the name of the man who was, in whatever roundabout way, his host.

"Powell. Justin Powell. Likewise, Mr. . . . ?" he trailed off invitingly.

"Sir Bernard Stow. And these are my companions, Tom and Ida Gould-Hedges."

"Charmed," Justin said before turning back to Bernard. "This is good luck. I was actually looking for you, sir."

"Me?" Bernard didn't do it nearly as well as Justin did. His gaze clearly held a warning.

"Yes, you, sir. There's some confusion over which bags are yours. They have the lot spread out in the back hall and the poor maid is in tears, not wanting to make a mistake. She's never served such exalted guests, poor creature. I'm sure you understand."

"Of course," piped in the brunette lady, her round face kind.

"Would you mind popping down the hall and clearing the matter up? Won't take but a minute."

"Er, yes, I suppose." Bernard crumpled his napkin with rather more force than necessary and dashed it next to his plate before excusing himself. Wordlessly, he exited into the hall. With one last smile at the Gould-Hedgeses, Justin followed, closing the door firmly behind him.

He did not look at Bernard. He didn't trust himself. Not yet. Instead, he moved past him, and heard his superior fall into step behind him, hastening to catch up. Only after he'd led Bernard into a small niche off of the front sitting room did he swing to face him.

"You had better have a bloody good reason for this, Justin," Bernard said in a flat voice.

"Oh, I do," Justin muttered, and unleashed a right hook straight at Bernard's jaw.

# Chapter 22

JUSTIN WASN'T SUICIDAL. WHETHER OR NOT he liked it, he was an officer in the army, and Bernard was the man from whom he took his orders. At the very last instant, he pulled his punch. The blow, which would have felled a man much larger than Bernard, flew by his face, grazing his cheek.

Still, Justin could not deny his satisfaction when Bernard jerked back seconds too late to have avoided the blow—if Justin's intent had been to hit him—and realized it. Sweat broke out on his forehead and his hand shook as he took a handkerchief from his coat pocket and mopped his face.

"What the hell do you think you're doing?" he demanded in a hoarse whisper. "Have you lost you mind, man?"

"No. But I begin to think I work for a madman,"

Justin said with controlled fury. "That was just a demonstration, Bernard."

"Are you threatening me?" Bernard asked in amazement.

"Yes," Justin answered. "Oh, yes."

"I won't stand here and listen to this. I'm your—"

"You're *nothing* right now, Bernard. Nothing to me except a source of information."

The coldness in Justin's eyes caused Bernard to start. Until that moment he'd never realized just how dangerous a man worked for him. *Had* worked for him. Because he would certainly have Justin's rank for this outrage, once the present situation was cleaned up.

Right now, however, Bernard needed Justin, and Bernard was the ultimate pragmatist—even more so than Justin. Except that Justin apparently wasn't as pragmatic as Bernard had assumed, which begged the question: What had changed him?

"I assume you've discovered the crate is empty."

"Yes."

"That was the one thing I feared." Bernard shrugged, delving into a pocket for his silver cigarette case. Casually, he selected an American blend and tapped it on the lid, his thoughts racing, picking through and discarding different options. He would pace as close to the truth as he dared, and see just how much his one-time prize pupil had hypothesized.

For a second, his face reflected his regret. It was criminal, really, this waste of Justin's talents.

"We used you to find an agent. Not just any agent, but an extraordinary one, and extraordinarily dangerous." He watched Justin's face carefully. "But I see you've already surmised as much. He's been working for years. Always in the shadows, always a step ahead. We know virtually nothing about him other than that he's always at the center of international intrigue, passing out vital information to the highest bidder."

"Including us?"

Bernard should have seen that coming. "Occasionally," he admitted.

"And that's the reason you want to find him," Justin said thoughtfully. "You don't want to take him into custody. You want to identify him. Because then you can feed him whatever information you want."

"Bravo. You were ever a cunning lad." Bernard lit the cigarette and took a puff.

Justin wasn't interested in praise. His thoughts were running down different avenues. "That's why all the blinds and double blinds. You set me to guard an empty crate because you knew I'd keep it out of his hands or die in the effort. For as soon as your spy realized he'd been gulled, he'd fade back into the woodwork.

"You had to keep me between him and the crate so he'd keep trying to get at it and you'd have more opportunities to identify him. I suppose I should be flattered by your faith in me."

Bernard wisely refrained from speaking.

"Do you realize he thinks Evelyn is *me*? He found the crate in her room and broke into it. Unfortunately I must have chased him off when I arrived."

Bernard cursed the miniscule hesitation in his breathing. But Justin had heard it. His smile was venal. "Why did you set her up? Oh, yes. I know you set her up. I know about the letters you sent her from every hotbed of political intrigue. Anyone watching the incoming posts would be fascinated by those postmarks, wouldn't they? I was. But how did you keep—" He broke off and sneered delicately.

"You simply diverted any real posts from her aunt, didn't you? I won't even ask how. For you, I should imagine tampering with the post would be a relatively easy matter. But why, Bernard? Why her? *Why* set her up?"

Carefully, Bernard knocked the ash from his cigarette and wet his lips. "Simple, really. The man we are after stands very close to discovering the most importantly positioned agent we have ever had. He may not even know it. The only reason we do is because the information that he passes on, and which we have intercepted, is almost identical to the information our agent sends us."

"What has this to do with Lady Evelyn?"

"She fits the criteria. She moves in the same circles, has access and entrée similar to our agent. She wouldn't stand up under close, intense scrutiny, but as a short-lived red herring she is perfect. Besides, every piece of bait we angle makes it more likely we discover the spy."

There was a tense watchfulness about Justin that Bernard disliked.

"You gave me the idea, you know."

"Did I?" Justin asked mildly.

"Yes. When we met on the Thames and you told me about her aunt being off on her honeymoon. I knew her family had diplomatic connections, and immediately thought how advantageous it would be to have someone think that Miss Cummings Whyte was, in fact, receiving messages from international sources."

"Someone being your spy," Justin said. "You might have told her what you were doing, the situation in which you were placing her."

"Impossible. She might have refused, and that was a chance I wasn't going to take. No. This time her work for us was gratis. Of course, in the future she'll be fully apprised of all aspects of a situation."

"There'll be no future!" Before Bernard could react, Justin's hand shot out, stopping just short of touching him. With a shiver, Justin rammed his hand into his pocket. The effort it cost him showed in his face.

"You can't seriously be willing to involve an innocent young woman in your machinations, Bernard," he ground out.

Uncomfortably, Bernard fidgeted with his cigarette in order to hide his trepidation.

"Why not? She's invaluable as a way to dispense erroneous information," he said. "She seems a game sort of lass; she might welcome it as a bit of patriotic adventuring." He paused, his gaze meeting Justin's. "You did."

"Damn you, you wouldn't play on her susceptibilities that way!"

Bernard blinked in hurt surprise. "She can always say no. But why should she? Think of how perfect she is! She has access to all the right people. Not only is she the Duke of Lally's granddaughter, she's in and out of the houses of some of the most prominent members in government—every household that has a daughter of marriageable age, that is."

"She can't because it's dangerous," Justin said in carefully measured tones.

"Not at all. We wouldn't actually have her do anything. Simply pop in here and there, keeping people interested in her activities so they wouldn't be looking at others'. Occasionally receive an odd letter. That's about the sum of it."

"As long as she stays in England. But what if she decides she'd like to travel abroad, and what if someone decides her true value is as a hostage?"

Bernard pulled deeply on his cigarette and blew the smoke in a thin stream. "You're being melodramatic. What are the chances of that happening?" He snorted. "How often have *you* been taken hostage?"

"Never. But I've been detained a number of times. Besides, that's not the point."

"Oh? And what is?" Bernard asked irritably. He disliked the path this conversation had taken.

"The point is, Bernard," Justin said, gently taking the half-burnt cigarette from Bernard's hand and dropping it to the flagstone floor, "that that chance isn't going to be taken."

He ground the cigarette slowly and thoroughly under his boot heel.

Bernard felt the animosity rolling off Justin like cold from a glacier. Involuntarily, he recoiled, then checked himself. It would never do for a subordinate to think he had the upper hand. Nothing was more dangerous than a rogue spy. Justin knew that. Just as he knew that rogue spies were dealt with in the age-old manner of all rogue animals: They were destroyed. He must be very involved with Lady Evelyn, if he was willing to intimate threats.

"Be very careful, Justin," he cautioned.

"I would offer the same advice," Justin replied, holding Bernard's gaze. They stood regarding one another a long minute before Bernard sighed, a saddened middle-aged professor disappointed in a star pupil. "We'll do what we deem best, Justin. You know that."

" 'We'?" Justin pounced on the pronoun.

"I co-opted the royal prerogative. I meant me." He reached for his cigarette case again and thought better of it.

"So you're here to discover this agent, eh?"

Bernard lifted his hands palms up and lowered his eyes modestly. "Who better? I would have been here when the blighter broke into Lady Evelyn's room, except that thanks to the train derailment, the damn crate we sent arrived before I did."

"How did you manage an invitation?"

Bernard was being questioned and he resented it. But he still had affection for Justin. He still would like to save his life.

"Bunny Cuthbert and I have sat on several committees together. It wasn't too hard to flatter an invitation from him. The poor bloke hasn't any family, you know, only that fool dog. In fact, he was rather pathetically pleased to think he could add a name to the guest list."

"I see."

Once more Bernard heaved a heartfelt sigh. "I'll

tell you what, Justin. Play the game to its end and then we'll see what's what. This is too important to muck up now, just because you've developed a tendresse for a pert speck of womanhood."

Justin didn't reply.

"That's the best I'll offer, Justin."

With an unreadable expression, Justin drew himself up. "Then I suppose I'd best take it." He hesitated, a bitter curl to his lips. "I suppose there never was a Diabolical Machine?"

"Like what? An internal combustion engine?" Bernard gave a humorless snort. "Don't be absurd."

At the door to her bedroom, Evelyn smiled and kissed her mother's cheek. Behind her, Merry bustled about the room, muttering French imprecations and studiously avoiding Lady Broughton's eye.

"You're sure you are all right?" her mother asked, her brow pleated.

"I'm fine. Just a little tired. But there's still so much to do and only one more day to do it. But after that, I may not wake for a month."

"You must be tired if you could fall asleep right in front of Mr. Powell."

Evelyn prayed the still murky early morning light hid any betraying color in her cheeks. "Yes."

Francesca looked toward Merry. "Merry, dear, I was wondering if you would be so kind as to stop by my room later. I'm not sure the dress I brought for the wedding fits as well as it should."

"As soon as time allows, Lady Broughton," Merry nodded vigorously, "but you can see how it is." She gestured around the cluttered room.

A housemaid appeared at the door, her arms filled with fresh bed linen. "Should I come back later, ma'am?"

"No, no," Evelyn said, happy for an excuse to send her mother off. The maid dropped a curtsey and bustled toward the bed.

Francesca, thwarted at every turn in her attempts to secure a private interview with either her daughter or the woman she'd sent to "chaperon" her, finally gave way, kissing Evelyn on the forehead and murmuring, "Later, then, dear," before retreating.

As soon as she left, Evelyn closed her eyes and pressed her fingers into her temples. Her head throbbed, filled with so many conflicting emotions that no single thought could complete itself.

In the space of twelve hours she had taken a lover and been betrayed by him; she'd learned that she was at the center of international intrigue and that she'd been placed there by a man she thought was a womanizer but who was nothing of the sort. She felt abused, used, cherished, and pleasured.

She despised him. She loved him. She mistrusted him. She had complete faith in him. "Ah!"

As disconcerting as it was, however, the one notion that kept popping up through the maelstrom of emotions and fears and uncertainties was the bald, impatient thought, *I don't have time for this.*

She'd contracted with Mrs. Vandervoort to produce a beautiful wedding reception. Her aunt's livelihood depended on her. Mrs. Vandervoort depended on her. And she needed, more than ever before, to prove herself. To redeem herself.

Let Justin deal with spies. He could do his job, and she? She would do hers.

"All right, Merry," she said, steeling her back and her resolve. "First things first. Is the bunting for the head table done?"

"Yes," Merry answered.

"Mrs. Vandervoort's dress?"

"*Mais oui*. For days now."

"The silk flowers for the table arrangements?"

"I completed them all last night."

"Good. As soon as I have breakfast, I'll make sure the workmen have finished. Then we'll hang the bunting. The cook promises the cake will be completed this afternoon." She thought hard, her mind picking through a seemingly interminable list of details to see if she'd missed anything. "Do the waiters know their duties?"

"Oh, yes. All arrived and most professional."

"Good." Evelyn relaxed, but then immediately tensed again. She'd thought she had everything in hand the last few times she'd planned wedding receptions, too. "And everyone is well? None of the staff has come down with measles or anything?" she asked suspiciously.

Merry laughed. "No, no, Evelyn. The only one who is sick is Mr. Quail with his malaria."

"Poor Mr. Quail." Evelyn sighed. "What a pity he is too ill to attend his employer's wedding."

The maid, who was busily snapping a clean sheet

over the bed, made a rude sound. Merry scowled at her.

"You have something to say?" Merry demanded haughtily, clearly intending to terrify the little maid into respectful silence.

But the maid was the product of an egalitarian rural society. No French dressmaker was going to act *her* better. "Only that Mr. Quail ain't *that* sick," she answered calmly, tucking the ends of the sheet beneath the mattress.

"Oh?" Merry asked mockingly. "And how would you know this? Unless of course you are secretly a physician only pretending to be a small little mouse housemaid."

The maid ignored her, addressing Evelyn instead. "Don't need to be a physician to know that a fellow who's bringing ladies into his room ain't feelin' that terrible. Goldbricking if you ask me. And 'as been right from the beginning."

"What?" Merry burst out. "How do you know this? Have you seen these ladies?"

The maid straightened, pleased to be the center of attention. "Didn't have to. I'm the one as does his bedclothes, and every time I go in to change his sheets, I'm washing makeup off his pillowcases. Don't take a genius to put two and two together, right, miss?"

"No," Evelyn breathed, her eyes wide. "No. It doesn't."

Justin paced his room, raking his hair back with both hands. He had to do something. He had to make sure

Evelyn was safe, not only for the present but in the future, too. He had to get her out of this quagmire he'd inadvertently landed her in.

He was still pacing when he heard a light knock on his door. Bernard again? Or perhaps Beverly, with some information. He jerked the door open.

Evelyn stood in the hall, her eyes enormous in her small angular face.

"What is it?" he demanded urgently.

"I know who the spy is."

# *Chapter 23*

EVELYN MOVED DOWN THE LINE OF MALE servers in a last-minute check before the bride, the groom, and their guests arrived from the wedding. Each one stood at attention, eyes fixed straight ahead, gloved hands clasped lightly behind their backs.

"Very good," she said to Beverly, who, with the pride of a mother hen presenting her first brood, sniffed at the faint praise and nodded at the head-waiter, dismissing the staff to await the arrival of the guests.

Evelyn walked down the hall to the great room, a critical eye scanning the pristine swan-shaped napkin beside each china place setting, the drape of satin bunting, the sheen of silver, the sparkle of crystal. Banks of imported flowers, silvery blue hydrangeas and creamy wax gardenias, fey delicate larkspurs and blowsy white peonies, filled every nook and cranny of the artificially constructed faerie glen. Overhead, the last taper had been lit, and the mirror-sprinkled ceiling shimmered with a thousand reflected lights, while in the pool outside, the lighted wax lotus blossoms floated serenely beneath the bridge.

On the opposite bank, across the bridge, the workmen had built a shallow niche of faux rock; in it stood a three-foot-tall slab of rose-colored quartz, the cost of which had been enormous. The effect achieved, however, was well worth the expense, for it appeared as if champagne sprang magically from its top—an effect cunningly achieved by means of a glass tube inserted through its center.

Not content with one chef d 'oeuvre, however, Evelyn had arranged for two to grace the Cuthbert-Vandervoort wedding celebration. On its own silk-draped table sat a huge, intricately arranged basket of flowers. Only when one drew near could one see that it was, in fact, a wedding cake, the flowers works of art in marzipan, each petal sparkling with colored sugars.

It was perfect.

No one, not even her aunt, could have done better. Now all that remained was to catch a spy.

It was a bold plan, but when Justin had explained all they needed to achieve, Evelyn had realized there was no reasonable alternative. They had only one trump card to play: the fact that Quail didn't know he'd been unmasked.

So, they would move first. And they had a plan. Successful spying, Evelyn was learning, left as little to chance as possible. In fact, spying sounded like the sort of job only very competent, capable, and clear-sighted individuals would be good at. Grudgingly, her respect for Justin had resurfaced.

Unfortunately, her role in the plan would be small, but very important. Best of all, Justin promised that their plan would not in any way effect the Cuthbert-Vandervoort celebration. No one at the party would ever know that an international incident was being narrowly averted in the rooms next door.

Evelyn pulled her small gold watch from the pocket hidden in her skirts and checked the time. The orchestra situated in the great room began warming up. Resolutely, she approached the conductor.

"Lady Evelyn?"

She inclined her head. "You understand that when the bride and groom arrive, you are to immediately begin a rousing rendition of 'The Star-Spangled Banner'?"

"Yes, ma'am."

"A most particularly robust version, you understand. We want to make the new Lady Cuthbert feel welcome."

"Indeed, yes." The small man nodded enthusiastically. "We will put great spirit into it."

"Excellent." The sound of voices coming down the hall brought her round. Beverly was bowing to the first arriving guests with an ostentation that bordered on the satiric. Beside him, Merry bobbed up and down, smiling with gamine delight—

Merry?! Who'd invited her? Good God, that's all

she needed, Merry shadowing her footsteps. With a gracious tilt of her head and a nod at the new arrivals, she approached the butler.

"Thank you, yes, I am. You're too kind," she demurred to a woman who asked if she was the lady responsible for the gorgeous rooms. Evelyn lowered her eyes modestly as the woman drifted by, and then seized Beverly's arm.

"Keep Merry with you!" she whispered.

"Must I?" Beverly asked, his expression hounded. She didn't have time to indulge him in his little dislikes.

"Yes!" She turned to greet a trio of people she'd dined with a few nights ago. "Oh, do you like it? I am so pleased!" They moved on.

"And how am I to achieve this?" Beverly asked.

"I don't care! Just do it!" she said, and with a brilliant smile flowed by him and out into the hall. A queue had gathered at the front door—just as they were supposed to, because the door next to it led into the library where the decoy crate stood, safe only as long as a crowd of people protected it.

A second later a ripple of excitement spread through the crowd and they parted to admit the bride and groom. Mrs. Vandervoort—now Lady Cuthbert—swept in, regal in Merry's magnificent blue organdy gown, her blond hair piled atop her head. Behind her, clearing his throat and beaming, came Lord Cuthbert, his stocky figure trussed most pleasingly into his cutaway, his blunt, unremarkable features pink with delight as he moved awkwardly to his new bride's side.

Lady Cuthbert greeted well-wishers while asking her guests to join them, an invitation to which Evelyn added her voice. Within minutes, the greater part of the crowd had entered the great room, leaving only a few stragglers hastening behind.

Evelyn took a deep breath and looked into the mirror hanging in the hall, carefully appraising her image. Her dress was made of lilac and dark green jacquard, the off-the-shoulder neckline piped in green velvet. From where the dress fit her hips, the skirts fell in graceful folds to the floor, the crisp rustle of lilac taffeta skirts whispering over sequined shoes.

Merry had dressed Evelyn's hair up and wound a choker of pearls around her throat. Covering her hands were the finest kid gloves. Yes, she looked stylish. Maybe even elegant. But did she look *formidable*?

It was too late to do anything about it now. She must now rely on her not inconsiderable acting skills. Besides, in her own milieu, she *was* formidable. She must remember that.

From the open doors at the end of the hall, she heard the orchestra strike tentative notes. It was time.

She moved decisively down the hall and into the wing holding the bedchambers. At Quail's door, her courage began to falter. The hand that gripped the knob was slick with perspiration.

But then she thought of Justin. He was only a few feet away behind the next door, waiting. She could feel his eyes on her, the door must be ajar. She barely kept from looking over her shoulder, not because she feared witnesses, but because she did not want Justin to see she was afraid. For then he would call off their plan and they would be no better off than before, perhaps a good deal worse.

She knocked lightly and thought she heard from within the room the sound of hasty footsteps and the creak of a mattress. "Mr. Quail?"

He did not answer. He had to.

She knocked more loudly. "I say, Mr. Quail, are you all right? The maid said she thought she heard the sound of falling from within your room!"

Another short silence, then a man's voice, hoarse and feeble—apparently Justin was not the only one good at his job. "Lady Evelyn? I'm in bed. I am fine except I feel so . . . weak. Please, don't—"

But she already had. She turned the key in the door and pushed it open. The room was as it had been on her last visit, steeped in darkness, the curtains drawn, a single jet light glowing faintly on the far wall. Quail shivered beneath a pile of blankets, tossing his head fretfully, his hands clutching the sheets. His eyes were partially closed, but Evelyn would have sworn he tracked her every move.

"You are too kind, Lady Evelyn. But please, is that not music I hear?"

Evelyn turned toward the door she'd purposely left slightly ajar. "Yes."

"Then you must go at once. Mrs. Vandervoort will expect you. I will go back to sleep."

"Yes." Damn. She ought to be able to come up with some bit of dialogue better than that, but the machinery of her mind seemed to have become clogged. Outside the room, even from this distance, she suddenly heard the thundering first chords of "The Star-Spangled Banner." Time slowed to a crawl.

*He could kill me.*

She felt her feet carry her to the bed, saw Quail's eyes flicker with surprise, heard her own voice mutter something vague, and felt her lips stretch over her teeth in a rictuslike smile. She bent down. He recoiled as she laid her fingers against his cheek, the caring nursemaid testing his temperature.

He was cool. His makeup was slick... *Two, three, four. Now!*

Time catapulted forward again. She jerked upright, scrambling, backing toward the door, shouting above the din of the music, "Powell! It's Quail! It's Quail!"

It all happened so fast that for a second Quail froze, barely comprehending what was happening, that in an instant, she'd not only recognized that it was makeup on her fingertips but had figured out his identity and was screaming for backup.

He had no time to wonder at the rapidity of unfolding events. Not if he was to save himself. The paralysis that gripped him vanished. He leapt from the bed as Evelyn dashed into the hall, racing after her, intent on silencing her. But Justin Powell was already in the hall, coming at him fast, his unbuttoned dinner jacket flapping behind him.

There was no time. No time to nab the machine, no time to dress, no time to grab his notebook or his wallet, no time to do anything more than seize the small dark woman by the shoulders and hurl her at Justin Powell. He didn't pause to watch the consequences of his act, he turned and sprinted down the hall, hearing a sharp curse and the *uff!* of colliding bodies. Good!

Anger and frustration nearly choked him as he swung toward the main section of the house heading for the front door, hearing Powell's footsteps pounding after him. He'd been found out. Exposed. All the years of careful—and lucrative—work destroyed with the touch of *that* woman's hand.

But at least if he'd been exposed, he had the savage satisfaction of knowing he would return the favor. They'd long suspected Powell's role, but no one had foreseen the Whyte woman's involvement. Oh, yes. They'd known there was another secret agent somewhere amongst the English aristocracy. The subtle clues were everywhere, thwarting their best-laid plans. Well, he may have lost the device but at least he'd unmasked *her*!

And yes, he'd have to retire from the game now, but at least he'd render Lady Evelyn Whyte useless to England's covert operation committee. That is, if he got out alive to make his report.

Quail turned the corner of the hall leading to the main corridor and saw the front door. He raced toward it, tearing off the nightshirt he'd worn over his clothes, his stocking feet slipping on the bare floorboards.

Ten more feet. A carriage or horse was certain to be without! He reached for the handle but before he could turn it the door swung out and a thick flange of guests crowded through, chatting and laughing as they hurried in, late for the reception.

He couldn't believe his foul luck! He skittered to a

stop and turned, cursing. He dashed back down the hall, passing the corridor leading to the bedroom just as Powell emerged, with the Whyte woman trailing behind.

There was only one place in the abbey where a man who didn't want to get caught could go.

Quail headed straight for the wedding party.

"He's going the wrong way!" Evelyn shouted, picking up her heavy skirts and bolting after Quail. She dashed past Justin, who started after her, only to lend verisimilitude to the encounter. The plan hadn't been to actually *catch* Quail, only make him think they wanted to catch him. Then, after a narrow escape, Quail would tell his employers he had unmasked the identity of a hitherto unsuspected master spy, Evelyn Cummings Whyte. The real master spy, whoever he was, would remain safely anonymous.

Because everyone now ostensibly knew who everyone was, everyone's effectiveness as spies would be neutralized and everyone would be safe. As an identified "spy" Evelyn would be assumed to be retired; Justin himself *would* retire, and so, too, would Quail. All's well that ends well....

Justin suddenly realized that for the few moments he'd been cogitating, his owlet was pursuing their escaping spy as if the hounds of hell were on her heels.

He could hear her ululating cry, "Not my wedding!" reverberating up the corridor. At the pace she was closing the distance between her and the secretary, if Justin didn't do something to stop her, she was actually going to catch Quail. And that would be disastrous.

Justin sprinted in pursuit, arriving in the great hall just as Quail headed toward the French doors leading to the courtyard. Madly, the spy scrambled through the knots of dining tables and chairs, knocking over several, sending china, crystal, and silver crashing to the ground. The diners leapt to their feet, backing away from the madman, their mouths forming "o's" of shock.

Behind Quail came Evelyn. For one second, she stopped at the entrance to the solarium. Her hair fell in a witchy black cloud about her white shoulders, and her eyes grew huge as she looked around at the destruction: shattered crystal, overturned tables, the floor covered in smashed food and soggy puddles of wine, the terrified guests. Then, like knife points, her gaze turned toward Quail and she wailed, "YOU BASTARD, YOU RUINED MY WEDDING!"

Clutching her skirts in one hand, with the other she snatched a silver butter knife from a table and sprang after Quail, her gaze fixed with cross-hair intensity on his back. She came after him in a straight line, kicking over pots of flowers and ferns, clambering over upended chairs as she followed him into the courtyard with its pond, bridge, and fake glen.

"Stop him! STOP HIM!"

A few of the male guests valiantly put themselves in Quail's path, but he simply bowled over them, using them as a means to hinder her progress. It only made her angrier. Justin could have sworn he heard her growling, and now it occurred to him that he ought to at least *appear* to be making some sort of attempt to come to Evie's aid, or the whole mess would be revealed as the staged production it was, or would have been had not some of the key players forgotten their roles.

Blast!

He vaulted over a table and sped along the far wall, heading toward the open end of the courtyard, hoping that Quail would see where he was going and realize that only one man stood between him and freedom.

Quail did see. Unfortunately, he saw an extremely large, fit, and athletic-looking man wearing a *very* grim expression that he could not possibly know wasn't directed at him but at the virago chasing him. So, rather than head toward Justin, Quail abruptly switched directions, scrambling back over the fake rocks.

He was close to panicking. He flung about, looking for an escape route, and saw none. The damn guests were not milling like they were supposed to; they were standing well back. Only his damn former employer stood beside the cake table on the far side of the stupid fishpond, staring at him as though he'd grown horns. Her new husband was nowhere in sight.

He looked back around. Powell blocked the open end, a crowd was forming on his side of the pond, and that black-haired *harpy* was coming at him like a demon from hell, wielding some sort of knife! He thought she was supposed to be a duke's granddaughter!

He didn't stop to think any more about the sorry pass modern aristocracy had come to. He climbed out on a fake crag and jumped, landing square in the middle of the fragile-looking bridge. Only it wasn't made to be leapt on.

With a huge crash, the structure collapsed beneath him. Only extraordinary skill allowed him to leap clear of the falling edifice and land safely on the far side of the pond.

Behind him the preternatural silence was broken by a long, eerie wail. He turned. *She* stood on the opposite bank, her face awful in its whiteness. He smiled.

It was not a good decision. She drew in a sharp breath, her eyes narrowed, and waded right into the fishpond, coming straight at him.

"Jesus!" He looked around for a weapon and spied the quartz champagne fountain. He grabbed it in both hands and launched it though the air. It landed short of her, achieving nothing but to give the witch a good soaking. She didn't even notice.

And now, Quail was beginning to fear not only capture, but for his very life. He had never seen such an expression on a lady's face before.

He looked around and spotted the bride. He could have kissed Lady Cuthbert in his relief. A hostage! He grabbed her wrist and dragged her to his side. "Stay back!" he ordered. *Finally,* something stopped the Whyte woman's inexorable approach.

On the other side of the room, Justin Powell had begun to slip along the wall. "You, too, Powell. Stop where you are or I shall be forced to hurt her!"

"You wouldn't dare," Evelyn muttered, taking another step in the pond.

"Are you sure?" Quail twisted Lady Cuthbert's arm. She winced.

Evelyn stopped, her head lowered, her eyes riveted on him in smoldering hatred. The knife flashed at her side and Quail seized on the inspiration, snatching up the cake knife and bringing it to the bride's throat.

"I am leaving here now. I am taking her with me. If anyone follows me, I shall slash her throat."

"No!" A choked cry rose from the doorway. Every head swung toward it. Lord Boniface Cuthbert stood quivering in the doorway, one hand clutched on the doorjamb, the other to his heart. A little dog stood at his feet, his hackles raised in alarm. "Please. Don't hurt her!"

"Then see that you all stay here!"

Finally, Quail thought, things were starting to fall into place. The witch looked paralyzed; Powell looked grim; Cuthbert, the silly toad, had clutched his fool dog to his chest; and Lady Cuthbert was staring at him in unfeigned horror.

Yes. He could work with this.

He dragged Lady Cuthbert after him, down the stupid papier-mâché glen and back in through the French doors. The guests inside cringed back, eyes wide with fear. He ignored them, pulling his hostage quickly after him. She did not say a word.

They'd just got to the point where the corridor branched off to the sleeping quarters when Quail heard a peculiar scrabbling sound. Frowning, he glanced over his shoulder just in time to see a brown-and-white-furred demon launch itself at his leg. With the tenacity born of a hundred generation of ratters, the terrier clamped down on Quail's calf.

With a howl, Quail released Lady Cuthbert and swooped down, slashing wildly at the dog. But the dog was a street-smart fighter. He twisted out of the way, his jaws still locked in the meat of Quail's leg. But smart as he was, he couldn't hope to avoid Quail's knife for long.

Luckily, he didn't have to. For as Quail bent down, Mrs. Vandervoort squealed—and later Quail would recount to his superiors that that was the most surprising point in the entire affair, that his composed, collected employer should *squeal* over a miserable cur's threatened life—and began pummeling him about the head and shoulders. Added to all of this, as Quail lifted his arms attempting to ward off her blows, Evelyn Cummings Whyte rounded the corner like Medea Enraged.

And she *still* had that damn butter knife.

It was time to cut his losses. With one last effort, Quail managed a savage kick that sent the terrier flying and, at the same time, walloped Lady Cuthbert across the face, knocking her to the ground. Then he fled down the hall, running as fast as he ever had or ever would run again.

He disappeared out the front door as Evelyn, still intent on the chase, raced past Lady Cuthbert. Only the low moan of distress behind her caused her to break her stride and turn back. She knelt down by Lady Cuthbert as Justin hurled into view.

"You reckless idiot!" he bellowed on seeing her. He

slowed to a stiff-limbed march. "You scared the *hell* out of me! What did you think you were doing?"

"Seeing to Lady Cuthbert." Evelyn twitched her skirts back, revealing Lady Cuthbert and the little terrier dancing excitedly around them.

From the end of the hall came another group of men, their anger rising as the full impact of the insult they and their friends had suffered sank in. They marched with determination, some already calling for horses, other trotting ahead.

Evelyn longed to go with them and chase down the blackguard like the rabid creature he was. He'd ruined it, all of it. Destroyed all her work, her every effort, the atonement she'd been about to make for all the disasters in the past, the proof that she could do well in the future.

"Where did he go?" one of the men asked Lady Cuthbert.

Justin had helped her to her feet and she stood swaying slightly, her face noble and brave. She raised her hand and pointed. "There . . . I . . . I think . . . Now, Mr. Powell, if you could take me to my room—"

From down the hall they heard a cry of relief as Lord Cuthbert arrived and, seeing his bride whole and unharmed, hobbled forward and tenderly enfolded her in his arms.

# Chapter 24

QUAIL GOT AWAY.

A group of outraged male guests went after him, but by the time the horses were saddled, Quail was long gone, never to be seen again. They returned shortly to the house, where the women and the men who'd stayed to protect them anxiously awaited news, and there discussed the matter at some length.

Lord Stow quickly dispelled their air of disappointment by pointing out that at least they had the satisfaction of having thwarted a burglary which had obviously been in the planning for a long time, and which would have, if successful, reaped an astronomical amount of jewelry. Others eagerly embraced the point of view.

Such a bold bastard! To have struck at a couple's

happiest and most vulnerable moments! Thank God, he'd been stopped in time.

And with the bride and groom more than willing to accept the patina of heroism that quickly was settling over the whole rather sordid affair, it was ultimately Francesca Whyte, Lady Broughton, who gaily suggested that since the party had transformed into a hunt ball of sorts, might it not be too, too whimsical if they were all to adjourn to the local pub? They could even take the orchestra with them. Besides, traditional manor weddings invariably ended up in the town square.

So, their collective spirits having been bolstered by the knowledge that they had faced down evil and emerged, if not precisely victorious, in no way bested, they drove off.

Quail himself, after his flight across East Sussex, hightailed it to Dover, where he caught a packet ship bound for the Netherlands; from there he made his way to secret places. When he finally made his appearance before those men who employed him, he was able to assuage their disappointment about his unmasking by offering them invaluable information.

He had incontrovertible proof not only that Justin Powell was a spy but that Evelyn Cummings Whyte was the mysterious and troublesome agent they'd suspected had been placed amongst the aristocracy. At their expressions of disbelief, he recounted all the pieces of evidence that pointed to her, ending with a dramatic narrative of his final hours at North Cross Abbey, her terrible aspect as she had realized she'd been unmasked, the maniacal single-mindedness with which she had pursued him in hopes of keeping his information from reaching her enemy's ears, the madness in her eyes when he'd last seen her.

No, he had no doubt at all that he had unearthed as dangerous and diabolical an agent as England had ever produced. And if he himself had to be exposed in the process, it was well worth the cost.

But that was days hence. Later on the day of the wedding, back at North Cross Abbey, while Quail was still hotfooting it over the countryside, Justin had just begun a brief but telling interview with Bernard.

"You always were a maverick, Powell," Bernard pronounced with heavy dissatisfaction. He looked up from behind the desk, where he was penning an encoded report about the affair. "Do you wonder now why we didn't advise you of our plans? As soon as you understood them, you changed them to suit your own purpose. Added to which you certainly didn't tell me what you and this . . . this chit were planning."

"No, sir," Justin said evenly. He stood at attention, his hands clasped lightly behind his back, his eyes forward. He was still too angry at the danger Evie had been put in to look at his superior without wanting to strike him.

"It would have been nice to know Quail was the enemy agent we sought *before* he ran amuck during the wedding. We might have managed to salvage something from an operation that has been in the making for nearly a year. Maybe the wedding cake?" he grated out sarcastically.

"Yes, sir." Justin could think of other responses,

but he didn't fancy serving a sentence for gross insubordination.

"Hm." The anger slowly ebbed from Bernard's heavy features. Curiosity warred with righteous indignation, and curiosity won—as it always would for men like Bernard. It was what made them good at their jobs. "How did you discover Quail was our man, anyway?"

Justin's own uncharacteristically rigid posture eased a bit. "Lady Evelyn discovered his identity, sir."

"Oh? How?"

"Quail arrived here sick, having conveniently developed a bout of malaria several days before his arrival. In fact, he had to be helped to his room and since then had stuck to his bed. Or so we thought.

"But yesterday a maid informed Lady Evelyn that each morning when she went to change Quail's linen she found makeup smears on the pillowcases. She thought it was because he was importing... company.

"I had just told Lady Evelyn that I was looking for a man with a bruise on his face, the man who had broken into the house last week and with whom I'd fought in the dark. I knew I'd hit him on the face, but not where."

Justin smiled. "Lady Evelyn did the math and came up with a few conclusions of her own, the first being that Quail, hearing of the arrival of a crate down here, popped himself in bed in London with a sudden recurrence of malaria—nice touch, that. Surprised I didn't think of it for myself. Frees a chap up for all sorts of naughtiness. Once ensconced, he could easily slip out of his room and travel the thirty-five miles here and back in one night. I suppose that you leaked the information about the unaddressed crates? Did you peel the labels off yourself?"

"No need to be sarcastic, Powell. As a matter of fact I did *not* send them. They were completely coincidental. As you well know, they belong to Mrs.—er, Lady Cuthbert. Why would I send them? I wasn't here to see who was interested in them. No. I had planned, as I told you, to be here by the time the crate I sent as bait had arrived."

Justin's eyes narrowed thoughtfully. "True. Then Quail must have had someone at the house or in town telegramming him about crate arrivals. Probably Silsby, the great greedy oaf. He wouldn't have realized that what he was doing was treasonous. He would have considered it an easy bit of cash for a harmless bit of information."

"All right." Bernard mentally put a check mark next to this fellow Silsby's name. Though Justin probably had it right, it would still have to be looked into. "I understand how you figured out Quail's identity, but now what I really want to know, what really piques my curiosity, is this: Why, knowing as you did that we wanted only to identify this man, did you take it upon yourself to expose him, thus rendering him useless to us? Do you know how *valuable* he would have been had he remained ignorant of our discovery of his identity? The misinformation we could have dispensed?"

"Do you know how *valuable* Lady Evelyn is to me?"

Justin countered at once, his hands finally releasing each other from behind his back. He leaned over the desk, bracing his hands on the edge, and met Bernard's gaze with glacial consideration. "You left me no choice. The only way to protect Evie, after all you did to suggest to Quail that she was a spy, was to confirm it."

"Because . . . ?"

Justin pushed himself upright and scoffed. "You know as well as I that once a master spy has been revealed, her usefulness ends. It will be assumed that she's retired, her career as a spy ended, and thus all interest in her soon evaporates."

"That's why you let Quail go. That's why you let Evelyn 'discover' him."

"Of course," Justin replied. "Evelyn *had* to be the one to reveal that his malaria was an act, because in doing so she could confirm in Quail's suspicious eyes that she was a member of England's espionage community. All she needed to do was yell to me that 'Quail is the one!'

"When Quail fled, it was with absolute assurance that he'd discovered England's premier female spy."

"And you had to let him go."

At this Justin laughed. "Yes. Bit of touch-and-go there. He was supposed to run out the front door; instead, he ran into the wedding reception." His expression grew contemplative. "I have never seen, nor hope to see again, a look of such violent animosity on a person's face as that worn by Lady Evelyn when Quail threw the champagne fountain into the fishpond." He shook his head, as though ridding himself of the image, and glanced down at Bernard, his expression growing chill again.

"You ought to be thanking me, Bernard. Certainly, you've lost my value as an agent—but that you would have lost anyway, once I realized what was what—and the conduit Quail might have provided is gone, but Lady Evelyn is safe, and that must count for something, even to you, and remember, we managed to keep your master spy's identity a secret."

Bernard pursed his lips and regarded Justin closely. An idea was beginning to form in his mind, probably ridiculous but perhaps . . . The truth was that Justin and his lady had done well, and while the ends weren't what Bernard had wanted, they had identified Quail before he realized how very close he stood to their agent. And that was the most important thing. That would have been disastrous.

One of Justin's brows rose with insouciant curiosity. "Don't suppose you'd care to tell me who the real master spy is?" He didn't really expect Bernard to answer.

But with his idea still fresh in his mind, Bernard did.

Twenty minutes later, Justin left the study and went in search of Evie.

He didn't find her, but he did find Lady Broughton. The look that lovely creature bent on him made his shirt collar seem suddenly tight.

"Mr. Powell."

"Lady Broughton."

"I would have a word with you, sir. Concerning my daughter."

"Any words concerning your daughter, ma'am, interest me. But right now, I'm afraid I must beg your pardon while I go and find your missing offspring." He tried to pass her. She stopped him with her hand on his sleeve.

"Why?"

"Why?" Blast! She was trying to force him to declare his intentions, and that he would not do. Because as certain as he was that the sun would rise in the east, he knew that if Evelyn ever found out that her mother had suggested in any manner, way, or form, by word, look, or inference, that they should marry, she would refuse him.

She was a suspicious owlet, was Evie. She would never accept as true that such an inspiration was his alone and not planted by another. And because she was a proud, mistrustful owlet, she would never marry a man she suspected might not be wholly in love with her.

Now the only trouble was how to convince her that he was.

But Lady Broughton was awaiting his answer so he gave her one that would allow him to slip away uncoerced.

"Because she owes me money," he said flatly. "And I want to make sure she realizes that simply because another one of her weddings went to hell doesn't mean she isn't liable for the agreed-upon sum."

Lady Broughton gasped at his vulgarity. Her hand dropped. "My daughter would never renege on an agreement!"

"Good," he said jovially, confident that any thoughts

of urging him to make a decent woman of her daughter had flown from Lady Broughton's head. "But one can't afford to take anything for granted. You'll excuse me?"

"I..." She looked flummoxed, and her beautiful eyes—though not so beautiful as Evie's—were wide and confused.

"Thank you." He didn't wait for her answer, but bowed and ducked past her.

He had an idea where Evie would be, and sure enough, as soon as he entered the disastrous scene of the wedding feast, he saw her. She was sitting on the edge of the fishpond, her feet in the water, splashing disconsolately at the gulls wading amongst the litter, gobbling bits of cake and the odd goldfish. On the one side of her head, her hair clung to her cheek and throat in black, oily-looking strands. The other side was still held up by jeweled pins.

Her gown was a horror. The velvet was drenched, clinging in wet folds to her hips, and the bodice sagged perilously close to revealing her small bosom. Worse, the dye had begun running and was staining those tender swells a distinct pea green.

And she'd been crying. The ridiculous black goop women sometimes wore had melted around her eyes, and black streaks blotted her cheeks. Her lower lip trembled and her shoulders, her beautiful, elegantly sparse shoulders, drooped.

And still he found her the most gorgeous, sweetly erotic thing he'd ever seen. He was either mad or in love. Possibly both.

He walked over and stood behind her. " 'Allo."

She looked up over her shoulder at him. Seeing who it was, she gave him a small, defeated smile that nearly broke his heart. She didn't even have any anger left for him, only weariness. And that, more than anything else, touched him.

"Oh. Hello, Justin," she said calmly. "Did we save the world, then?"

"Oh, yes," he said, and sat down beside her, facing the opposite direction, keeping his feet nicely dry. "World's all safe again. The bad'uns have fled, the secret crate remains secret, and my superior is tickled pink."

She nodded without looking at him. A pink marzipan rose floated by, only to be sucked below by some monstrous big carp with a sweet tooth.

"I spoke to him just a short while ago."

"Oh."

"Apparently, our assumptions about the situation were close."

"I know," she replied tonelessly. "Lady Cuthbert is England's master spy."

He started in surprise. "How did you know that?" he asked. "Quail never did, and he was her secretary. But he was close, close enough to make Bernard nervous and seek a likely alternative candidate." He looked at her angular little profile. She didn't appear to be listening. "You."

"Oh."

"But again," he once more asked, "how did you know?"

Finally she looked at him. "I didn't figure anything out by myself. I just saw things, remembered some things. Like how serendipitous it was that Mrs.

Vandervoort should insist her wedding take place here, at North Cross Abbey, which *you* owned. And how Beverly had once said that your grandfather's Indian chef only cooked curries, and Mrs. Vandervoort's grandmother obviously wasn't Indian. And then there was that last bit."

"Last bit?"

"When you all came charging out of the hall demanding to know which way Quail had gone."

"What of it?"

"She pointed in the wrong direction. And she kept trying to get her husband's dog to let Quail go. The only reason she would want Quail to escape with the erroneous information that I was a spy was because it protected her identity as the real spy. At least, that's what I reasoned."

Justin grinned, pleased that between the two of them they'd managed to get most of the truth out and in the open. It was a quite satisfying end to a mission.

But Evie wouldn't know that, not unless he told her. It might cheer her up to think that she'd accomplished that which even seasoned agents often failed to do.

"There are many chaps out there, working as agents, who never come close to understanding the big picture."

"Oh, why is that?" she asked more from rote politeness than through any real interest.

Her face truly was a sad little mess. He delved into his pocket for his handkerchief and wet the corner of it. Gently, he took her chin in his hand and began scrubbing the black tracks off her cheeks.

"There's a notion amongst the intelligence community—I know, I know, from what you've witnessed that must seem a strident oxymoron—anyway there's this notion that the less any one man knows of a situation, the less likely he is to affect it. But you—canny, bright," he searched around for a word that would please her, "*competent* Evie Whyte—have seen through the murk to the real issues, the real stakes."

"You did, too."

"And I'm jolly well congratulating myself on that matter, don't you disbelieve it. Circles within circles, darkness within shadows, enough intrigue to last a fellow a lifetime."

At this, she shot him an odd, unreadable look.

"But what I want to know, Evie, is why you aren't pleased? You take pride in your intellectual accomplishments—and well you should—but this doesn't seem to mean anything to you," he mused. He'd finished cleaning her cheeks but somehow neglected to stop stroking her cheek. Not that she appeared to notice.

"I'm sure to feel most self-satisfied in a while, but right now . . ." She sighed heavily and turned her head away. "Have you ever seen such a mess?"

He looked about at the collapsed tables, ruined cake, shattered china and crystal, and mired fishpond. "No."

She smiled at his honesty. At least she appreciated that. "No one will ever hire me to do their wedding now. Not anyone."

"I should think not."

At this her eyes grew brilliant under a renewed

assault of unshed tears. She lifted her small chin and bit at her lower lip but remained silent.

"Why should it matter so much?" he asked. "It's not as if you've cherished the idea of becoming a wedding planner from the cradle."

"I know." She sniffed. "It's just that . . . I tried so hard, Justin!" She turned, and suddenly she was in his arms, her face smashed against his white shirt, as he pressed his lips fervently to the crown of her head, the one spot on her person still silky and clean and sweetly fragrant.

"But, Justin . . . it wasn't my fault! I did everything right. It would have been a perfect wedding. Perfect and lovely and beautiful if it hadn't been for that horrible, wretched Quail!" She spat the last syllable.

He took a deep breath, and sent out a fervent prayer that he was about to say the right thing. "It wouldn't have been that perfect."

He felt her go absolutely still.

"What?" her muffled voice asked after a moment.

"It was all very pretty and everything but, Evie, it wasn't perfect."

She pushed away from him, her hands resting on his chest. "Exactly where did my wedding celebration fail to meet your expectations?" she asked stiffly.

"Oh, just, well, all these papier-mâché boulders, they seem a mite contrived, eh?"

One brow arched in an elegant inquisition so like her mother's it was startling.

"And the cake—so many flowers and so many different colors."

"It was meant to look festive."

"And in the right milieu doubtless it would have." *If that milieu happened to be a circus.*

"Did anything else fail to meet with your approval?" she asked.

"Oh, no," he hastened to reassure her. "The candles above, the mirrored ceiling, the floating candles, the rest was lovely. Though perhaps that big rock dripping champagne might have been replaced—"

At that she burst into tears. He tried to hold her, but she would have none of it. She twisted away from him and threw herself down on the fake bank of the fishpond, sobbing as if her heart would break.

And *he* would have none of that. Forcefully—if gently—he gathered her into his arms, scooping her up and settling her on his lap. She came with little resistance, finally flinging her arms about his neck and soaking his shirt with her tears. He let her cry for a few minutes. He doubted his Evie spent much time in tears.

"Evie, you're just not meant to be a wedding planner. For whatever reasons, circumstances seem to conspire against your every effort. *So what?*" He felt the hitch in her crying and pressed his point. "Why do you need to be a good wedding planner on top of everything else?"

"Because. Because Aunt Agatha is depending on me and I have *failed* her!"

"So?" he said reasonably.

She lifted her wet, tragic face and searched his eyes before burrowing her head back against his shirt. "Easy for you to say. You who look like you do."

And how was he supposed to take that?

"But for people like me, it is important," she went on in a muffled voice. "Because if you fail people they don't want you around. What benefit is a useless spinster? None. They are entirely superfluous."

Ah. There it was, then. He'd suspected. Now he knew. And he knew he had to be careful in the next few minutes, as careful as he'd ever been with any explosive, any sensitive document, or anyone's life. Because this was *his* life. She was his life, and the next few minutes would determine his future.

"Evie, my sweet Evie. Your aunt Agatha never asked you to take over her business. You told me so yourself; she eloped without leaving one word as to how the business should be conducted," he said. "My dear, she was not thinking about her business or her profits or her family or even you. She'll not blame you for not making a success of her enterprise, because she doesn't care. She's not concerned with anything but being in love."

"How can you know that?" she demanded, pushing back, her fists on his chest.

"Because I'm in love with you, Evie, and I have just had an object lesson in being in love and how it strips away all other considerations."

Her amazing eyes went round at his statement. Her mouth formed an *O* of amazement but then snapped shut.

"You are just saying that because of last night, because you feel obligated."

He could have shaken her, but that would mean

removing her and he wanted her touching him. He'd waited a lifetime for such intimacy. He wouldn't set it aside, not even to shake some sense into her.

"Well, yes. I do. I should. We slept together," he reminded her gently. "Of course that makes me obligated. But it makes you obligated, too."

"Aha!" she crowed in a voice whose triumph broke into a wretched sob.

"Aha, what?" he demanded, flummoxed.

"You want to marry me in order to satisfy your sense of honor."

He still didn't understand. She was looking at him as if he was some loathsome thing. What was so bloody wrong with honor?

"What's so bloody wrong with honor? I should think you would like the man who wishes to marry you to be honorable."

And now it was her turn to be frustrated. Of course she wanted him to be honorable. He was honorable. It was one of the things she loved about him. But she didn't want honor to be at the heart of his proposal. She wanted love to be.

But he *had* said he loved her. And he hadn't needed to say that, although he *would* say it if he thought it was the only way to persuade her to do the honorable thing, the right thing. Blast! Her thoughts were in a quandary!

"I just... I don't feel honorable toward you," she finally blurted out, suspecting she sounded like an ass, and certain she should be removing herself from his embrace. But the feeling of "rightness" she'd experienced in his arms had grown during this peculiar and infinitely wonderful interlude and she couldn't bestir herself.

"Don't you?" There was the flavor of laughter in his voice. "How do you feel, then?"

She wasn't going to be the first to make a declaration of love. Oh, yes, he already had. But for what purpose? Because it was the truth? Or because it was the way to achieve his goal? "Not honorable," she finally answered gruffly.

He tipped her head back. "Darling, wonderful, insecure, prideful Evie. I am not a green boy, and while my experience with the fairer sex is far more limited than you once thought, I am not, nor was I when I came to you, a virgin."

She blushed fiercely, and was amazed to see a dark answering bronze rise up his throat. "I am not the sort of man who gets carried away by sexual drives. And while I was and am and forever will be carried away by *you,* I could have—granted with no small discomfort and much unhappiness—walked out of your room well before we got to the point of no return."

She stared at him mutely, listening to his words and trying to hear the meaning behind them. He saw her confusion and once more rescued her.

"What I am trying to say, and doing a damn poor job of it, is that when I made love to you, the idea that I wanted to marry you was already fully formed and recognized and approved by every faculty I own: by body, mind, heart, and soul.

"But I erred, Evie. I admit it. I wanted you so much, so desperately, that I refused to tell you I loved you and then let you decide whether you could feel the same. So like a coward—and this hurts to admit because I detest cowards—I sought to bind you to me. That's why I made love to you without declaring my intention, hoping you'd be incurably conventional and then be obligated to marry me. I should have known better."

His mouth turned in a lopsided smile. "Can you forgive me?"

Her throat was tight and she felt tears rise in her eyes and she wanted so desperately to answer "yes!" and "yes!" and "yes!" But she had been a *golem* a long time and she had learned to mistrust men—and found that even though she wanted to believe Justin, even though her heart clamored in recognition of his veracity, her troubled mind would not allow it.

"*Why* do you love me?" she asked.

He looked at her. Her beautiful porcelain skin, her dark hooded eyes and tangle of silky coiling curls, the narrow feet, the slender arms and delicate collarbones, the thin wrists and blue-veined bosom. He looked around at the mess in which they sat and recalled her frantic confession, "What use is a functionless spinster?" and he had his answer.

"Because I am beautiful?" she threw the question out temptingly.

"Does it matter?"

"Maybe."

"Then, yes," he said simply. "You are beautiful. Your beauty undoes me and quickens me." She started to turn her head away but he caught her jaw lightly but implacably and forced her to meet his gaze, ardent and passionate. "I see you in a doorway, the curve of your cheek, the chance gesture of your hand, and I want to kiss you. I touch your skin and I grow hard with desire, I kiss your lips and I am consumed by need."

She felt the heat rise in her face, and her gaze lowered before the burning ardency in his. He lifted her chin again.

"But, Evie," he said, his tone potent, "should your features grow coarse, your skin wrinkle, and your body bend with age, I will *still* want you. You are pleasing to me in my heart; you quicken not only my blood but my soul; I desire to feel your embrace as much as to embrace you. The aesthetics of the heart, my darling, surpass the senses and make its own perfection."

She swallowed. His expression softened, his gaze candid and exposed. His touch was near reverent, and yet she trembled.

"Yes, I love you, Evie. You know I do."

And she did. He hadn't said a word about her wit, her intelligence, her abilities, or her competence, all the qualities she had spent her life honing and polishing so that she would have some boon to bring to a relationship—any relationship, whether with a friend, companion, or God-willing, lover.

No. He'd ignored all her wonderful attributes and spoken only about an ephemeral—and to her mind very suspect—beauty that he freely admitted he expected to fade. And yet, she'd never been so certain anyone spoke the truth as when he'd said, "I love you."

"There is only one question, really, isn't there, Evie?" he asked in a sure, quiet voice. "And that is, do you love me?"

She couldn't deny it. She didn't want to, and yet she was still afraid. She'd spent a lifetime protecting herself from potential pain, and now it stood shoulder to shoulder with a love she'd never dreamed possible. But that was probably always the way with true love, she thought with sudden clarity.

"Yes. Oh, yes. I love you. I think I've loved you since I was fifteen. Yes."

He hadn't been as confident as he'd sounded, because his eyes squeezed tightly together and his jaw pulsed in a hard little muscle. Then he was kissing her, raining kisses down upon her face, her cheeks, her eyes, and her mouth, and she was kissing him back as if there was nothing else in the world but him.

Only after a long, long time, after their kisses had finally grown less ardent and they more quietly confident, did she pull back and look long and lovingly into his face and say, "Do we really have to retire from spying?"

"Well, Mr. Beverly," Merry whispered from where she stood by the French doors leading into the courtyard, "a job well done, to my mind."

Beverly rolled his eyes and muttered a heavenly invocation against interfering women. Merry chuckled and turned to the little clutch of romantically inspired spectators who "happened" to be by the door just as Justin enfolded Evelyn in a passionate embrace.

"See, Lady Broughton? There was never any need to worry. I am most knowledgeable about the human heart, and I could see from the very first that this would be the end result. So alike. Both so..." She struggled to find the word.

"Peculiar?" Lady Broughton supplied.

"Yes," Merry agreed happily. "And oblivious. The only question is what two such naive, sweet, and guileless souls should do to make their way in this wicked, wicked world. A thief at the wedding! I worry for them, I do indeed. Someone is bound to take advantage."

"Oh, I shouldn't fret too much about those two," Lord Stow muttered enigmatically, and, with one last contemplative glance, he left.

## ABOUT THE AUTHOR

Connie Brockway is the author of *The Bridal Season,* the debut novel in the Bridal Season series. She is also the author of the McClairen's Isle trilogy, which includes the acclaimed novels *The Passionate One, The Reckless One,* and *The Ravishing One,* and four other historical romances: *My Dearest Enemy,* winner of the Romance Writers of America's prestigious RITA Award for Best Historical Romance, *All Through the Night, As You Desire,* and *A Dangerous Man.* She loves to hear from readers. Please write her at P.O. Box 828, Hopkins, MN 55343, or visit her website for excerpts and reviews of all her Dell books at www.conniebrockway.com.